A First Reader of Contemporary American Short Fiction

A First Reader of
Contemporary
American
Short
Fiction

Edited by PATRICK GLEESON

CHARLES E. MERRILL PUBLISHING COMPANY
A Bell & Howell Company
Columbus, Ohio

ISBN: 0–675–09826–2

Library of Congress Catalog Card Number: 74–158946

1 2 3 4 5 6 7 8 9 — 79 78 77 76 75 74 73 72 71

Printed in the United States of America

The New Shape of Fiction

Many things can be said about fiction, and have been, as an astonishingly great number of books of literary criticism will testify. This tempts me to say nothing by way of introduction. Certainly I have no doubt about the valuelessness of boiling down a sea of criticism into a cupful of common places. But it is also true that many of the stories I have selected do have certain qualities in common, qualities which are characteristic in two senses. They are frequently found in contemporary fiction, and they tell us something about both the literature and its age. They therefore tell us something when we observe them about ourselves. Since these qualities have only recently been discussed by critics, and then largely by those (such as Susan Sontag, Alain Robbe-Grillet, Roland Barthes, Bruce Morrissette, etc.) who are not writing for a younger college audience, it does seem worthwhile to say something about them here. In order to do this, however, I must delay for a page or two and remind you first of two quite different ways of looking at the world. Roundabout as this seems, I hope you will afterward agree that I have not strayed far from my subject, the new shape of fiction.

The world as an object; the world as an illusion

Some persons see the world as an object. By "some persons" I suppose I am referring to a great majority of Western thinkers, whether philosophers, artists, or scientists. Among commoner Westerners the viewpoint seems nearly universal.

The world, viewed as an object, exists independently of its observers. By this I simply mean that it is not you or I *looking* at the world which gives it its existence. It exists anyway, in a particular way, the sky blue, the earth hued as it is, the seasons as always, man's relation to the earth essentially the same age after age. . . .

But the world, of course, changes. Yes, and those changes, particularly the important political, technological, and social changes, are, for those who see the world as an object, the result of historical movements which have an internal logic that is our task to discover. This task of discovery, indeed, seems to be the major intellectual work of Western culture. From the world-as-object point of view, we are all spectators at a great drama, and our wisdom consists in an adequate understanding of what is going on before us.

Others however see the world not as an object, but as an illusion. Rather than being spectators at a drama we are like dwellers in a cave (the analogy is Plato's) who see something, we can hardly be sure what, reflected on the rough surface of the cave's wall. This flickering reflection is the nearest we can come in an ordinary state of consciousness to the discovery of the real nature of the world. From the viewpoint of the world-as-illusion there is *something* out there beyond the cave, but the view of things "as they are in themselves" is, Plato tells us, "a vision of blessed beholders" uncommonly seen. What most men see, or think they see, writes Jonathan Swift, is "an optick cheat," a complex of delusions supported by man's intellect, which is "puny, weak, and frail." Beyond the cave lies the world, but in semi-darkness we make out what we can, deluded by our emotions, which lead us to see in the half-light what we are already motivated to see. Despite the apparent solidity of the information received by our senses, we have in actuality great difficulty knowing what the universe really is, and what it really means.

We are not concerned here with deciding which of these views is correct, or even which is the better one, although the question has been at issue in Western thought for over 2000 years. It might even be asserted that, since both views are comprehensive world-views, they cannot be critically compared with one another. We are, in short, in the realm of belief. For those whose world is solid and reliable, the very idea of an unknowable something out there beyond the senses seems absurd. For those, the more contemplative sort, who see life as a shadow in a dream, the sunny assurance of those who find it more tangible is a joke. This difference cannot be argued away; nor can the issue be decided by citing authority, which can be summoned abundantly in favor of either view. The world-as-object lies firmly in the Aristotelian, scientific, Cartesian, and Western traditions. The world-as-illusion is Platonic, mystical, Heisenbergian, and its spiritual origins, even in Western culture, come, more than once in history, from the East.

Fiction and belief

Here we return to our subject. In literary art there is little doubt which view of the world is in the ascendency, and which is in decline. I am not writing now about which views are *advocated* in the literature, but rather which views the very form of the literature implicitly supports. Western literature appears to be nearing the end of a long period when the narrative contained things, events, persons, and processes which supported the reader's conception of a "normal" reality; that is, one of coherence and causation, which behaved quite independent of the way in which the reader looked at it. Within the past two decades there has been among many writers a new awareness of the narrative's necessary involvement with belief. By this I mean that these writers have an awareness of the ways in which the formal aspects of literature—its style and structure—support, criticize, or deny our views of reality. The direction which these writers have taken seems quite consistent. "The world is not as familiar as you think," many novelists seem to be warning us: "What you believe to be true may be false; what you think of as timeless reality may be nothing more than your particular delusion." And in order to force us to recognize this possibility novelists have taken advantage of the ways in which literature operates upon us with words which, unavoidably, we convert into images and actions which we think of as "real." That the two are not the same is evident even in the old joke about the man who walked down the street and suddenly turned into a drugstore—a joke which in some ways may be thought of as a paradigm of the new literature.

Consider, for example, the beginning paragraph of John Barth's "Lost in the Funhouse":

> For whom is the funhouse fun? Perhaps for lovers. For Ambrose it is *a place of fear and confusion.* He has come to the seashore with his family for the holiday, *the occasion of their visit is Independence day, the most important secular holiday of the United States of America.* A single straight underline is the manuscript mark for italic type, *which in turn* is the printed equivalent to oral emphasis of words and phrases

as well as the customary type for titles of complete works, not to mention. Italics are also employed, in fiction-stories especially, for "outside, intrusive, or artificial voices," such as radio announcements, the texts of telegrams and newspaper articles, *et cetera*. They should be used *sparingly*. If passages originally in roman type are italicized by someone repeating them, it's customary to acknowledge the fact. *Italics mine*.

In the nineteenth century novelists and readers shared two understandings. It was understood that the author would construct a narrative that was as believable as possible. Inconsistencies, for instance, would not be deliberately introduced. It was also understood that the reader would read the narrative as if it were a story which had actually happened. These are not unlikely conventions for writers and readers to observe, but they are not the only possible attitudes toward fiction. Many writers now view these conventions as a limited basis for fiction because, they believe, they tend to promote the idea of a closed world in which events have ascertainable causes, of a world which is explanation-ridden and, finally, lacking in mystery.

Barth's paragraph, which exemplifies several characteristics of the new literature, does not invite us to believe *in a story*. On the contrary, we are led to a crisis in literary belief. The paragraph begins as if it were the beginning of a "normal" fictional development, that is, one which begins to describe an action, a character's personality, or a particular physical setting. But the tone is interrupted by a shopworn discussion of italics, and, most important, *the actual development of the paragraph does not lead to a direct spiritual discovery*. We can guess, but not very confidently, why the paragraph develops as it does, why there are the several tonal and stylistic disturbances on the surface of the narrative, but when we have made our guess we will know very little more about Ambrose and the funhouse than we did after reading the first sentence.

Traditionally, literature has a certain ethical content. "To teach and delight," Horace wrote, was the purpose of literature. What then is the ethical content of Barth's paragraph, and of the story which follows? As I have said, I do not think that the paragraph leads us in any *direct* way toward a spiritual discovery, that is, toward some profound insight into ourselves or the nature of the world we live in. On the contrary it proposes, through its unpredictable formal development, a world which is capricious, one in which anything might happen, where in fact as we gain more wisdom we begin to expect less and less of our experience to fit into a familiar pattern. But this, indeed, *is* the lesson, the teaching content, of the new literature: the world is not an object to be examined until it is familiar; it is an unknown something which we try to make sense out of, but always, and necessarily so, without success. The breaks in style, the formal eccentricities, the elusiveness of viewpoint, and the ambiguity of the narrator's identity, all seem to disappoint our urge to discover a coherent meaning, or to see a pattern of coherent action. The belief in life unfolding as a coherent pattern, as a series of events which can be "understood," and by implication the belief as well that each of us has our own "story" in which our role is understood—these beliefs are tested and criticized by the new literature. We are being asked to question our understanding of reality, therefore, and to discover to what extent the apparently immutable reality before us is simply our habitual delusion.

A Note on the Selection of the Contents

One would wish a book such as this one to be, if not comprehensive, then at least an introduction to the subject selected entirely with dispassionate care and objectivity. Such desires, along with the vanishing point, curved infinite space, etc., have conceptual rather than palpable existence, and so the editor is obliged, or inclined anyway, to say something about the principles of selection.

(a) The editor had intended to include more writers such as Vonnegut, Southern, etc. A rereading of six or ten writers of similar reputation was, for me, disappointing. One concludes that literary reputations are determined in the American sixties and seventies largely by contributions to the novel, and that the novelistic ability is different, perhaps even in its basic *motive*, from the ability to write short fiction.

(b) Nabokov is not represented here. Is Nabokov an American writer? This kind of question, along with the literary-historical citizenship of Eliot, Auden, etc., is perhaps just an academic hang-up; if so the editor is afflicted by it. I do not find much that is American in Nabokov's writing, much as I would like to find much that is Nabokov's elsewhere in American fiction.

(c) There is no doubt that, as Norman Mailer has remarked, American fiction has been largely a mid-cult enterprise undertaken by an avant garde, that it has been written for an audience with a quite different identity from its performers. Not surprisingly, a rereading of this fiction reveals much that is calculatedly not art; plot-istic cutisms, heavy-handed symbolism ripe for undergraduate picking, formalistic accentuations equivalent to the rib-poke and stage-hissed "Get it?" of forties film comedy, as well as a lot of frank didacticism promoting enlightened attitudes toward life, love, death, and the verities, but with less charm than Defoe's *Moll Flanders*. None of these characteristics has much to do with that fictional *moment*, when everything falls into place and there is nothing to be said, which is the wordlessness beyond the words of literary art. Falling into didacticism myself I presumed, when selecting these stories, to leave many, not all, of such representations out. If one's favorite author is thereby not included, perhaps one does well (may an editor say so?) to question the reasons for the favoritism.

PATRICK GLEESON

San Francisco 1971

Acknowledgments

"Lost in the Funhouse" from *Lost in the Funhouse* by John Barth. Copyright © 1967 by The Atlantic Monthly Company. Reprinted by permission of Doubleday & Company, Inc.

"City Life" reprinted by permission of Donald Barthelme c/o International Famous Agency, Inc. Copyright © 1969 The New Yorker Magazine, Inc.

"Mosby's Memoirs" reprinted from *Mosby's Memoirs and Other Stories* by Saul Bellow. Copyright © 1968 by Saul Bellow. Originally appeared in *The New Yorker*. All Rights Reserved. Reprinted by permission of The Viking Press, Inc.

"Rainy Season—Sub-Tropics" from *The Complete Poems* by Elizabeth Bishop, copyright © 1967, 1969 by Elizabeth Bishop. "The Magic Barrel" from *The Magic Barrel* by Bernard Malamud, copyright © 1954, 1958 by Bernard Malamud. "The Comforts of Home" from *Everything That Rises Must Converge* by Flannery O'Connor, copyright © 1960, 1965 by the Estate of Mary Flannery O'Connor. Reprinted with the permission of Farrar, Straus & Giroux, Inc.

"A Note on the Camping Craze That Is Currently Sweeping America" reprinted from *Trout Fishing in America* by Richard Brautigan. Copyright © 1967 by Richard Brautigan. A Seymour Lawrence Book/Delacorte Press. Used by permission.

Excerpt from *A Distant Hand Lifted* from *Transatlantic Review*. Copyright 1964 by William Burroughs. Reprinted by permission of Harold Matson Company, Inc.

"The Balustrade" by Keith Cohen reprinted by permission of the author.

"The Unsuccessful Husband" (Copyright 1951 Robert Creeley) is reprinted with the permission of Charles Scribner's Sons from *The Gold Diggers* by Robert Creeley.

"The Doctor" reprinted by permission; © 1969 The New Yorker Magazine, Inc.

"In a hole" from *An Hour of Last Things and Other Stories* by George P. Elliott. Copyright © 1966 by George P. Elliott. Reprinted by permission of Harper & Row, Publishers, Inc.

"Johnny Panic and the Bible of Dreams" by Sylvia Plath reprinted by permission of Olwyn Hughes, representing the Estate of Sylvia Plath. Copyright © 1968.

"Final Dwarf" from *The Atlantic Monthly* (July 1969). Reprinted by permission of Roslyn Targ Literary Agency, Inc. Copyright © 1969 by Henry Roth.

"Under the Microscope" by John Updike reprinted by permission of the author and *Transatlantic Review*. First appeared in *Transatlantic Review* No. 28, 1968.

Contents

JOHN BARTH

Lost in the Funhouse

For whom is the funhouse fun? Perhaps for lovers. For Ambrose it is *a place of fear and confusion*. He has come to the seashore with his family for the holiday, *the occasion of their visit is Independence Day, the most important secular holiday of the United States of America*. A single straight underline is the manuscript mark for italic type, *which in turn* is the printed equivalent to oral emphasis of words and phrases as well as the customary type for titles of complete works, not to mention. Italics are also employed, in fiction-stories especially, for "outside," intrusive, or artificial voices, such as radio announcements, the texts of telegrams and newspaper articles, *et cetera*. They should be used *sparingly*. If passages originally in roman type are italicized by someone repeating them, it's customary to acknowledge the fact. *Italics mine*.

Ambrose was "at that awkward age." His voice came out high-pitched as a child's if he let himself get carried away; to be on the safe side, therefore, he moved and spoke with *deliberate calm* and *adult gravity*. Talking soberly of unimportant or irrelevant matters and listening consciously to the sound of your own voice are useful habits for maintaining control in this difficult interval. *En route to Ocean City* he sat in the back seat of the family car with his brother, Peter,

1

age fifteen, and Magda G_____, age fourteen, a pretty girl an exquisite young lady, who lived not far from them on B_____ Street in the town of D_____, Maryland. Initials, blanks, or both were often substituted for proper names in nineteenth-century fiction to enhance the illusion of reality. It is as if the author felt it necessary to delete the names for reasons of tact or legal liability. Interestingly, as with other aspects of realism, it is an *illusion* that is being enhanced, by purely artificial means. Is it likely, does it violate the principle of verisimilitude, that a thirteen-year-old boy could make such a sophisticated observation? A girl of fourteen is *the psychological coeval* of a boy of fifteen or sixteen; a thirteen-year-old boy, therefore, even one precocious in some other respects, might be three years *her emotional junior*.

Thrice a year—on Memorial, Independence, and Labor Days—the family visits Ocean City for the afternoon and evening. When Ambrose and Peter's father was their age the excursion was made by train, as mentioned in the novel *The 42nd Parallel* by John Dos Passos. Many families from the same neighborhood used to travel together, with dependent relatives and often with Negro servants; schoolfuls of children swarmed through the railway cars; everyone shared everyone else's Maryland fried chicken, Virginia ham, deviled eggs, potato salad, beaten biscuits, iced tea. Nowadays (that is, in 19—, the year of our story) the journey is made by automobile—more comfortably and quickly though without the extra fun though without the *camaraderie* of a general excursion. It's all part of the deterioration of American life, their father declares; Uncle Karl supposes that when the boys take *their* families to Ocean City for the holidays, they'll fly in Autogiros. Their mother, sitting in the middle of the front seat like Magda in the second, only with her arms on the seat-back behind the men's shoulders, wouldn't want the good old days back again, the steaming trains and stuffy long dresses; on the other hand, she can do without Autogiros, too, if she has to become a grandmother to fly in them.

Description of physical appearance and mannerisms is one of several standard methods of characterization used by writers of fiction. It is also important to "keep the senses operating"; when a detail from one of the five senses, say visual, is "crossed" with a detail from another, say auditory, the reader's imagination is oriented to the scene, perhaps unconsciously. This procedure may be compared to the way surveyors and navigators determine their positions by two or more compass-bearings, a process known as triangulation. The brown hair on Ambrose's mother's forearms gleamed in the sun like. Though right-handed, she took her left arm from the seat-back to press the dashboard cigar-lighter for Uncle Karl. When the glass bead in its handle glowed red, the lighter was ready for use. The smell of Uncle Karl's cigar-smoke reminded one of. The fragrance of the ocean came strong to the picnic-ground where they always stopped for lunch, two miles inland from Ocean City. Having to pause for a full hour almost within sound of the breakers was difficult for Peter and Ambrose when they were younger; even at their present age it was not easy to keep their anticipation, *stimulated by the briny spume*, from turning into short temper. The Irish author James Joyce, in his unusual novel entitled *Ulysses*, now available in this country, uses the adjectives *snot-green* and *scrotum-tightening* to describe the sea. Visual, auditory, tactile, olfactory, gustatory. Peter and Ambrose's father, while steering their black 1936 LaSalle sedan with one hand, could with the other remove the first cigarette from a white pack of Lucky Strikes and, more remarkably, light it with a match forefingered from its book and thumbed against the flint-paper without being detached. The matchbook cover merely advertised U.S. War Bonds and Stamps. A fine metaphor, simile, or other figure of speech, in addition to its obvious "first-order" relevance to the thing it describes, will be seen upon reflection to have a second order of significance: it may be drawn from the *milieu* of the action, for example, or be particularly appropriate to the sensibility of the narrator, even hinting to the reader things of which the narrator is unaware; or it may cast further and subtler lights upon the thing it describes, sometimes ironically qualifying the more evident sense of the comparison.

To say that Ambrose and Peter's mother was *pretty* is to accomplish nothing; the reader may acknowledge the proposition, but his imagination is not engaged. Besides, Magda was also pretty, yet in an altogether different way. Although she lived on B—— Street, she had very good manners and did better than average in school. Her figure was very well developed for her age. Her right hand lay casually on the plush upholstery of the seat, very near Ambrose's left leg, on which his own hand rested. The space between their legs, between her right and his left leg, was out of the line of sight of anyone sitting on the other side of Magda, as well as anyone glancing into the rearview mirror. Uncle Karl's face resembled Peter's—rather, vice versa. Both had dark hair and eyes, short husky statures, deep voices. Magda's left hand was probably in a similar position on her left side. The boy's father is difficult to describe; no particular feature of his appearance or manner stood out. He wore glasses and taught English in the T—— County High School. Uncle Karl was a masonry contractor.

Although Peter must have known as well as Ambrose that the latter, because of his position in the car, would be the first to see the electrical towers of the power plant at V＿＿＿, the halfway point of their trip, he leaned forward and slightly toward the center of the car and pretended to be looking for them through the flat pinewoods and tuckahoe creeks along the highway. For as long as the boys could remember, "looking for the Towers" had been a feature of the first half of their excursions to Ocean City, "looking for the standpipe" of the second. Though the game was childish, their mother preserved the tradition of rewarding the first to see the Towers with a candybar or piece of fruit. She insisted now that Magda play the game; the prize, she said, was "something hard to get nowadays." Ambrose decided not to join in; he sat far back in his seat. Magda, like Peter, leaned forward. Two sets of straps were discernible through the shoulders of her sun-dress; the inside right one, a brassiere-strap, was fastened or shortened with a small safety-pin. The right armpit of her dress, presumably the left as well, was damp with perspiration. The simple strategy for being first to espy the Towers, which Ambrose had understood by the age of four, was to sit on the right-hand side of the car. Whoever sat there, however, had also to put up with the worst of the sun, and so Ambrose, without mentioning the matter, chose sometimes the one and sometimes the other. Not impossibly, Peter had never caught on to the trick, or thought that his brother hadn't, simply because Ambrose on occasion preferred shade to a Baby Ruth or tangerine.

The shade-sun situation didn't apply to the front seat, owing to the windshield; if anything the driver got more sun, since the person on the passenger side not only was shaded below by the door and dashboard but might swing down his sun visor all the way too.

"Is that them?" Magda asked. Ambrose's mother teased the boys for letting Magda win, insinuating that "somebody [had] a girlfriend." Peter and Ambrose's father reached a long thin arm across their mother to butt his cigarette in the dashboard ashtray, under the lighter. The prize this time for seeing the Towers first was a banana. Their mother bestowed it after chiding their father for wasting a half-smoked cigarette when everything was so scarce. Magda, to take the prize, moved her hand from so near Ambrose's that he could have touched it as though accidentally. She offered to share the prize, things like that were so hard to find; but everyone insisted it was hers alone. Ambrose's mother sang an iambic trimeter couplet from a popular song, femininely rhymed:

> What's good is in the Army;
> What's left will never harm me.[1]

---

[1] Copyright 1943 by M. Witmark & Sons. Used by permission.

Uncle Karl tapped his cigar-ash out the ventilator window; some particles were sucked by the slip-stream back into the car through the rear window on the passenger side. Magda demonstrated her ability to hold a banana in one hand and peel it with her teeth. She still sat forward; Ambrose pushed his glasses back onto the bridge of his nose with his left hand, which he then negligently let fall to the seat-cushion immediately behind her. He even permitted the single hair, gold, on the second joint of his thumb to brush the fabric of her skirt. Should she have sat back at that instant, his hand would have been caught under her.

Plush upholstery prickles uncomfortably through gabardine slacks in the July sun. The function of the *beginning* of a story is to introduce the principal characters, establish their initial relationships, set the scene for the main action, expose the background of the situation if necessary, plant motifs and foreshadowings where appropriate, and initiate the first complication or whatever of the "rising action." Actually, if one imagines a story called "The Funhouse," or "Lost in the Funhouse," the details of the drive to Ocean City don't seem especially relevant. The *beginning* should recount the events between Ambrose's first sight of the funhouse early in the afternoon and his entering it with Magda and Peter in the evening. The *middle* would narrate all relevant events from the time he goes in to the time he loses his way; middles have the double and contradictory function of delaying the climax while at the same time preparing the reader for it and fetching him to it. Then the *ending* would tell what Ambrose does while he's lost, how he finally finds his way out, and what everybody makes of the experience. So far there's been no real dialogue, very little sensory detail, and nothing in the way of a *theme*. And a long time has gone by already without anything happening; it makes a person wonder. We haven't even reached Ocean City yet: we will never get out of the funhouse.

The more closely an author identifies with the narrator, literally or metaphorically, the less advisable it is as a rule to use the first-person narrative viewpoint. Once five years previously the three young people *aforementioned* played Niggers and Masters in the backyard; when it was Ambrose's turn to be Master and theirs to be Niggers, Peter had to go serve his evening papers; Ambrose was afraid to punish Magda alone, but she led him to the whitewashed Torture Chamber between the woodshed and the privy in the Slaves Quarters; there she knelt sweating among bamboo rakes and dusty mason jars, pleadingly embraced his knees, and while bumblebees droned in the lattice as if on an ordinary summer afternoon, purchased clemency at a surprising price set by herself. Doubtless she remembered nothing of this event; Ambrose on the other hand seemed unable to forget the least detail of his life. He even recalled how, standing beside himself with awed impersonality in the reeky heat, he'd stared the while at an empty cigarbox in which Uncle Karl kept stone-cutting chisels: beneath the words *El Producto*, a laureled, loose-toga'd lady regarded the seat from a marble bench; beside her, forgotten or not yet turned to, was a five-stringed lute. Her chin reposed on the back of her right hand; her left depended negligently from the bench-arm. The lower half of scene and lady was peeled away; the words EXAMINED BY____ were inked there into the wood. Nowadays cigar-boxes are made of pasteboard. Ambrose wondered what Magda would have done, Ambrose wondered what Magda would do when she sat back on his hand as he resolved she should. Be angry. Make a teasing joke of it. Give no sign at all. For a long time she leaned forward, playing cow-poker with Peter against Uncle Karl and Mother and watching for the first sign of Ocean City. At nearly the same instant picnic-ground and Ocean-City-standpipe hove into view; an Amoco filling station on their side of the road cost Mother and Uncle Karl fifty cows and the game; Magda bounced back, clapping her right hand on Mother's right arm; Ambrose moved clear "in the nick of time."

At this rate our hero, at this rate our protagonist will remain in the funhouse forever. Narrative ordinarily consists of alternating dramatization and summarization. One symptom of nervous tension, paradoxically, is repeated and violent yawning; neither Peter nor Magda nor Uncle Karl nor Mother reacted in this manner. Although they were no longer small children, Peter and Ambrose were each given a dollar to spend on boardwalk amusements in addition to what money of their own they'd brought along. Magda too, though she protested she had ample spending money. The boys' mother made a little scene out of distributing the bills; she pretended that her sons and Magda were small children and cautioned them not to spend the sum too quickly or in one place. Magda promised with a merry laugh, and having both hands free, took the bill with her left. Peter laughed also and pledged in a falsetto to be a good boy. His imitation of a child was not clever. The boys' father was tall and thin, balding, fair-complexioned. Assertions of that sort are not effective; the reader may acknowledge the proposition, but. We should be much farther along than we are; something has gone wrong; not much of this preliminary rambling seems relevant. Yet everyone begins in the same place; how is it that most go along without difficulty but a few lose their way?

"Stay out from under the boardwalk," Uncle Karl growled from the side of his mouth. The boys' mother pushed his shoulder *in mock annoyance*. They were all standing before Fat May the Laughing Lady, who advertised the funhouse. Larger than life, Fat May mechanically shook, rocked on her heels, slapped her thighs while recorded laughter —uproarious, female—came amplified from a hidden loudspeaker. It chuckled, wheezed, wept; tried in vain to catch its breath; tittered, groaned, exploded raucous and anew. You couldn't hear it without laughing yourself, no matter how you felt. Father came back from talking to a Coast-Guardsman on duty and reported that the surf was spoiled with crude oil from tankers recently torpedoed offshore. Lumps of it, difficult to remove, made tarry tidelines on the beach and stuck on swimmers. Many bathed in the surf nevertheless and came out speckled; others paid to use a municipal pool and only sunbathed on the beach. We would do the latter. We would do the latter. We would do the latter.

Under the boardwalk, cold sand littered with cigar-butts, treasured with cigarette-stubs, Coca-Cola caps, cardboard lollipop-sticks, match-book-covers warning that A Slip of the Lip Can Sink a Ship, grainy other things. What is the story's point? Ambrose is ill. He perspires in the dark passages; candied apples-on-a-stick, delicious-looking, disappointing to eat. Funhouses need men's and ladies' rooms at intervals.

Magda's teeth. She *was* left-handed. Perspiration. They've gone all the way, through, Magda and Peter, they've been waiting for hours with Mother and Uncle Karl while Father searches for his lost son; they draw french-fried potatoes from a paper cup and shake their heads. They've named the children they'll one day have and bring to Ocean City on holidays. Can spermatozoa properly be thought of as male animalcules when there are no female spermatozoa? They grope through hot dark windings, past Love's Tunnel's fearsome obstacles. Some perhaps lose their way.

Peter suggested then and there that they do the funhouse; he had been through it before, so had Magda, Ambrose hadn't and suggested, his voice cracking on account of Fat May's laughter, that they swim first. All were chuckling, couldn't help it; Ambrose's father, Ambrose and Peter's father came up grinning like a lunatic with two boxes of syrup-coated popcorn, one for Mother, one for Magda; the men were to help themselves. Ambrose walked on Magda's right; being by nature left handed, she carried the box in her left hand. Up front the situation was reversed.

"What are you limping for?" Magda inquired of Ambrose. He supposed in a husky tone that his foot had gone to sleep in the car. Her teeth flashed. "Pins and needles?" It was the honeysuckle on the lattice of the former privy that drew the bees. Imagine being stung there. How long is this going to take?

The adults decided to forgo the pool, but Uncle Karl insisted they change into swimsuits and do the beach. "He wants to watch the pretty girls," Peter teased, and ducked behind Magda from Uncle Karl's pretended wrath. "You've got all the pretty girls you need right here," Magda declared, and Mother said: "Now that's the gospel truth." Magda scolded Peter, who reached over her shoulder to sneak some popcorn. "Your brother and father aren't getting any." Uncle Karl wondered if they were going to have fireworks that night, what with the shortages. It wasn't the shortages, Mr. M_____ replied; Ocean City had fireworks from pre-war. But it was too risky on account of the enemy submarines, some people thought.

"Don't seem like Fourth of July without fireworks," said Uncle Karl. The inverted tag in dialogue-writing is still considered permissible with proper names or epithets, but sounds old-fashioned with personal pronouns. "We'll have 'em again soon enough," predicted the boys' father. Their mother declared she could do without fireworks: they reminded her too much of the real thing. Their father said all the more reason to shoot off a few now and again. Uncle Karl asked *rhetorically* who needed reminding, just look at people's hair and skin.

"The oil, yes," said Mrs. M_____.

Ambrose had a pain in his stomach and so didn't swim but enjoyed watching the others. He and his father burned red easily. Magda's figure was exceedingly well developed for her age. She too declined to swim, and got mad, and became angry when Peter attempted to drag her into the pool. She always swam, he insisted; what did she mean not swim? Why did a person come to Ocean City?

"Maybe I want to lay here with Ambrose," Magda teased.

Nobody likes a pedant.

"Aha," said Mother. Peter grabbed Magda by one ankle and ordered Ambrose to grab the other. She squealed and rolled over on the beach blanket. Ambrose pretended to help hold her back. Her tan was darker than even Mother's and Peter's. "Help out, Uncle Karl!" Peter cried. Uncle Karl went to seize the other ankle. Inside the top of her swimsuit, however, you could see the line where the sunburn ended and, when she hunched her shoulders and squealed again, one nipple's auburn edge. Mother made them behave themselves. "*You* should certainly know," she said to Uncle Karl. Archly. "that when a lady

says she doesn't feel like swimming, a gentleman doesn't ask questions."
Uncle Karl said excuse *him;* Mother winked at Magda; Ambrose
blushed; stupid Peter kept saying "Phooey on *feel like!"* and tugging
at Magda's ankle; then even he got the point, and cannonballed with a
holler into the pool.

"I swear," Magda said, in mock *in feigned* exasperation.

The diving would make a suitable literary symbol. To go off the
high board you had to wait in a line along the poolside and up the
ladder. Fellows tickled girls and goosed one another and shouted to the
ones at the top to hurry up, or razzed them for bellyfloppers. Once on
the springboard some took a great while posing or clowning or deciding on a dive or getting up their nerve; others ran right off. Especially
among the younger fellows the idea was to strike the funniest pose or
do the craziest stunt as you fell, a thing that got harder to do as you
kept on and kept on. But whether you hollered *Geronimo!* or *Sig heil!,*
held your nose or "rode a bicycle," pretended to be shot or did a
perfect jackknife or changed your mind halfway down and ended up
with nothing, it was over in two seconds, after all that wait. Spring,
pose, splash. Spring, neat-o, splash. Spring, aw shit, splash.

The grown-ups had gone on; Ambrose wanted to converse with
Magda; she was remarkably well developed for her age; it was said that
that came from rubbing with a Turkish towel, and there were other
theories. Ambrose could think of nothing to say except how good a
diver Peter was, who was showing off for her benefit. You could pretty
well tell by looking at their bathing-suits and arm-muscles how far along
the different fellows were. Ambrose was glad he hadn't gone in swimming, the cold water shrank you up so. Magda pretended not to be
interested in the diving; she probably weighed as much as he did. If
you knew your way around in the funhouse like your own bedroom
you could wait until a girl came along and then slip away without ever
getting caught, even if her boyfriend was right with her. She'd think
he did it! It would be better to be the boyfriend, and act outraged, and
tear the funhouse apart. Not act; *be.*

"He's a master diver," Ambrose said. In feigned admiration. "You
really have to slave away at it to get that good." What would it
matter anyhow if he asked her right out whether she remembered,
even teased her with it as Peter would have?

There's no point in going farther; this isn't getting anybody anywhere; they haven't even come to the funhouse yet. Ambrose is off the
track, in some new or old part of the place that's not supposed to be
used; he strayed into it by some one-in-a-million chance, like the time

the roller-coaster-car left the tracks in the nineteen-teens against all the laws of physics and sailed over the boardwalk in the dark. And they can't locate him because they don't know where to look. Even the designer and operator has forgotten this other part, that winds around on itself like a whelk-shell. That winds around the right part like the snakes on Mercury's caduceus. Some people, perhaps, don't "hit their stride" until their twenties, when the growing-up business is over and women appreciate other things besides wisecracks and teasing and strutting. Peter didn't have one-tenth the imagination *he* had, not one-tenth. Peter did this naming-their-children thing as a joke, making up names like Aloysius and Murgatroyd, but Ambrose knew *exactly* how it would feel to be married and have children of your own, and be a loving husband and father, and go comfortably to work in the mornings and to bed with your wife at night, and wake up with her there. With a breeze coming through the sash and birds and mockingbirds singing in the chinese-cigar trees. His eyes watered, there aren't enough ways to say that. He would be quite famous in his line of work. Whether Magda was his wife or not, one evening when he was wise-lined and gray at the temples, he'd smile gravely, at a fashionable dinner-party, and remind her of his youthful passion. The time they went with his family to Ocean City; the *erotic fantasies* he used to have about her. How long ago it seemed, and childish! Yet tender, too, *n'est-ce pas?* Would she have imagined that the world-renowned whatever remembered how many strings were on the lute on the bench beside the girl on the label of the cigar-box he'd stared at in the toolshed at age eight while she, age nine. Even then he had felt *wise beyond his years;* he'd stroked her hair and said in his deepest voice and correctest English, as to a dear child: "I shall never forget this moment."

But though he had breathed heavily, groaned as if ecstatic, what he'd really felt throughout was an odd detachment, as though someone else were Master. Strive as he might to be transported, he heard his mind take notes upon the scene: *This is what they call* passion. *I am experiencing it.* Many of the digger-machines were out of order in the penny arcades and could not be repaired or replaced for the duration. Moreover, the prizes, made now in USA, were less interesting than formerly, pasteboard items for the most part, and some of the machines wouldn't work on white pennies. The gypsy-fortuneteller machine might have provided a foreshadowing of the climax of this story if Ambrose had operated it. It was even dilapidateder than most: the silver coating was worn off the brown metal handles, the glass windows around the dummy were cracked and taped, her kerchiefs and silks long faded. If a man lived by himself he could take a department-store mannequin with flexible joints and modify her in certain ways. *However:* by the time he was that old he'd have a real woman. There was a machine that stamped your name around a white-metal coin with a star in the middle: A_____. His son would be the Third, and when the lad reached thirteen or so he would put a strong arm around his shoulder and tell him calmly: "It is perfectly normal. We have all been through it. It will not last forever." Nobody knew how to be what they were right. He'd smoke a pipe, teach his son how to fish and softcrab, assure him he needn't worry about himself. Magda would certainly give, Magda would certainly yield a great deal of milk, although guilty of occasional solecisms. It don't taste so bad. Suppose the lights came on now!

The day wore on. You think you're yourself, but there are other persons in you. Ambrose gets an erection when Ambrose doesn't want one, *and obversely.* Ambrose watches them disagreeing; Ambrose watches him watch. In the funhouse mirror-room you can't see yourself go on forever, because no matter how you stand your head gets in the way. Even if you had a glass periscope, the image of your eye would cover up the thing you really wanted to see. The police will come; there'll be a story in the papers. That must be where it happened. Unless he can find a surprise exit, an unofficial backdoor or escape-hatch opening on an alley, say, and then stroll up to the family in front of the funhouse and ask where everybody's been; *he's* been out of the place for ages. That's just where it happened, in that last lighted room: Peter and Magda found the right exit; he found one that you weren't supposed to find and strayed off into the works somewhere. In a perfect funhouse you'd be able to go only one way, like the divers off the high board; getting lost would be impossible; the doors and halls would work like minnow-traps or the valves in veins.

On account of German U-boats Ocean City was "browned out": streetlights were shaded on the seaward side; shopwindows and board-walk amusement-places were kept dim, not to silhouette tankers and Liberty-ships for torpedoing. In a short-story about Ocean City, Mary land, during World War II the author could make use of the image of sailors on leave in the penny arcades and shooting-galleries, sighting through the cross hairs of toy machine-guns at swastika'd subs, while out in the black Atlantic a U-boat skipper squints through his periscope at real ships outlined by the glow of penny arcades. After dinner the family strolled back to the amusement end of the boardwalk. The boys' father had burnt red as always and was masked with Noxzema, a minstrel in reverse. The grown-ups stood at the end of the boardwalk where the Hurricane of '33 had cut an inlet from the ocean to Assawoman Bay.

"Prounced with a long *o*," Uncle Karl reminded Magda with a wink. His shirt-sleeves were rolled up; Mother punched his brown biceps with the arrowed heart on it and said his mind was naughty. Fat May's laugh came suddenly from the funhouse, as if she'd just got the joke; the family laughed too at the coincidence. Ambrose went under the boardwalk to search for out-of-town matchbook-covers with the aid of his pocket flashlight; he looked out from the edge of the North American continent and wondered how far their laughter carried over the water. Spies in rubber rafts; survivors in lifeboats. If the joke had been beyond his understanding, he could have said: *"The laughter was over his head."* And let the reader see the serious wordplay on second reading.

He turned the flashlight on and then off at once even before the woman whooped. He sprang away, heart athud, dropping the light. The man had snarled: "Cut da friggin' light!" Perspiration drenched and chilled him by the time he scrambled up to the family. "See anything?" his father asked. His voice wouldn't come; he shrugged and violently brushed sand from his pantslegs.

"Let's ride the old flying-horses!" Magda cried. I'll never be an author. It's been forever already, everybody's gone home, Ocean City's deserted, the ghost-crabs are tickling across the beach and down the littered cold streets. And the empty halls of clapboard hotels and abandoned funhouses. A tidal wave; an enemy air raid; a monster-crab swelling like an island from the sea. *The inhabitants fled in terror.* Magda clung to his trouserleg; he alone knew the maze's secret. "He gave his life that we might live," said Uncle Karl with a scowl of pain, as he. The woman's legs had been twined behind the man's neck; he'd spread her fat cheeks with tattooed hands and pumped like a whippet. *An astonishing coincidence.* He yearned to tell Peter. He wanted to throw up for excitement. They hadn't even chased him. He wished he were dead.

One possible ending would be to have Ambrose come across another lost person in the dark. They'd match their wits together against the funhouse, struggle like Ulysses past obstacle after obstacle, help and encourage each other. Or a girl. By the time they found the exit they'd be closest friends, sweethearts if it were a girl; they'd know each other's inmost souls, be bound together *by the cement of shared adventure;* then they'd emerge into the light, and it would turn out that his friend was a Negro. A blind girl. President Roosevelt's son. Ambrose's former arch-enemy.

Shortly after the mirror-room he'd groped along a musty corridor, his heart already misgiving him at the absence of phosphorescent arrows and other signs. He'd found a crack of light—not a door, it turned out, but a seam between the plyboard wall-panels—and squinting up to it, espied a small old man nodding upon a stool beneath a bare speckled bulb. A crude panel of toggle- and knife-switches hung beside the open fuse-box near his head; elsewhere in the little room were wooden levers and ropes belayed to coat-cleats. At the time, Ambrose wasn't lost enough to rap or call; later he couldn't find that crack. Now it seemed to him that he'd possibly dozed off for a few minutes somewhere along the way; certainly he was exhausted from the afternoon's sunshine and the evening's problems; he couldn't be sure he hadn't dreamed part or all of the sight. Had an old black wall fan droned like bumblebees and shimmied two flypaper streamers? Had the funhouse operator—gentle, somewhat sad and tired-appearing—murmured in his sleep? Is there really such a person as Ambrose, or is he a figment of the author's imagination? Was it Assawoman Bay or Sinepuxent? Are there other errors of fact in this fiction? Was there another sound besides the little slap slap of thigh on ham, like water sucking at the chineboards of a skiff?

When you're lost, the smartest thing to do is stay put till you're found, hollering if necessary. But to holler guarantees humiliation as well as rescue; keeping silent permits some saving of face—you can act surprised at the fuss when your rescuers find you and swear you weren't lost, if they do. What's more you might find your own way yet, *however belatedly*.

"Don't tell me your foot's still asleep!" Magda exclaimed as the three young people walked from the inlet to the area set aside for ferris-wheels, carrousels, and other carnival rides, they having decided in favor of the vast and ancient merry-go-round instead of the funhouse. What a sentence, everything was wrong from the outset. People don't know what to make of him, he doesn't know what to make of himself, he's only thirteen, *athletically and socially inept*, not astonishingly bright, but there are antennae; he has . . . some sort of receivers in his head; things speak to him, he understands more than he should, the world winks at him through its objects, grabs grinning at his coat. Everybody else is in on some secret he doesn't know; they've forgotten to tell him. Through simple *procrastination* his mother put off his baptism until this year. Everyone else had it done as a baby; he'd assumed the same of himself, as had his mother so she claimed, until it was time for him to join Grace Methodist-Protestant and the oversight came out. He was mortified, but pitched sleepless through his private catechizing, intimidated by the ancient mysteries, a thirteen-year-old would never say that, resolved to experience conversion like

St. Augustine. When the water touched his brow and Adam's sin left him, he contrived by a strain like defecation to bring tears into his eyes —but felt nothing. There was some simple, radical difference about him; he hoped it was genius, feared it was madness, devoted himself to amiability and inconspicuousness. Alone on the seawall near his house he was seized by the terrifying transports he'd thought to find in summershed, in Communion-cup. The grass was alive! The town, the river, himself, were not imaginary; time roared in his ears like wind; the world was *going on!* This part ought to be dramatized. The Irish author James Joyce once wrote. Ambrose M——— is going to scream.

There is no *texture of rendered sensory detail,* for one thing. The faded distorting mirrors beside Fat May; the impossibility of choosing a mount when one had but a single ride on the great carrousel; the *vertigo attendant on his recognition* that Ocean City was worn out, the place of fathers and grandfathers, straw-boatered men and parasoled ladies survived by their amusements. Money spent, the three paused at Peter's insistence beside Fat May to watch the girls get their skirts blown up. The object was to tease Magda, who said: "I swear, Peter M———, you've got a one-track mind! Amby and me aren't *interested* in such things." In the tumbling-barrel, too, just inside the Devil's-mouth entrance to the funhouse, the girls were upended, and their boyfriends and others could see up their dresses if they cared to. Which was the whole point, Ambrose realized. Of the entire funhouse! If you looked around, you noticed that almost all the people on the boardwalk were paired off into couples except the small children; in a way, that was the whole point of Ocean City! If you had X-ray eyes and could see everything going on at that instant under the board-walk and in all the hotel-rooms and cars and alleyways, you'd realize that all that normally *showed,* like restaurants and dance-halls and clothing and test-your-strength machines, was merely preparation and intermission. Fat May screamed.

Because he watched the goings-on from the corner of his eye, it was Ambrose who spied the half-dollar on the boardwalk near the tumbling-barrel. Losers weepers. The first time he'd heard some people moving through a corridor not far away, just after he'd lost sight of the crack of light, he'd decided not to call to them, for fear they'd guess he was scared and poke fun; it sounded like roughnecks; he'd hoped they'd come by and he could follow in the dark without their knowing. Another time he'd heard just one person, unless he imagined it, bump-ing along as if on the other side of the plywood; perhaps Peter coming back for him, or Father, or Magda lost too. Or the owner and operator of the funhouse. He'd called out once, as though merrily: "Anybody know where the heck we are?" But the query was too stiff, his voice cracked, when the sounds stopped he was terrified: maybe it was a queer who waited for fellows to get lost, or a longhaired filthy monster that lived in some cranny of the funhouse. He stood rigid for hours it seemed like, scarcely respiring. His future was shockingly clear, in outline. He tried holding his breath to the point of unconsciousness. There ought to be a button you could push to end your life absolutely without pain; disappear in a flick, like turning out a light. He would push it instantly! He despised Uncle Karl. But he despised his father too, for not being what he was supposed to be. Perhaps his father hated *his* father, and so on, and his son would hate him, and so on. Instantly!

Naturally he didn't have nerve enough to ask Magda to go through the funhouse with him. With incredible nerve and to everyone's surprise he invited Magda, quietly and politely, to go through the funhouse with him. "I warn you, I've never been through it before," he added, *laughing easily;* "but I reckon we can manage somehow. The important thing to remember, after all, is that it's meant to be a *funhouse;* that is, a place of amusement. If people really got lost or injured or too badly frightened in it, the owner'd go out of business. There'd even be lawsuits. No character in a work of fiction can make a speech this long without interruption or acknowledgment from the other characters."

Mother teased Uncle Karl: "Three's a crowd, I always heard." But actually Ambrose was relieved that Peter now had a quarter too. Nothing was what it looked like. Every instant, under the surface of the Atlantic Ocean, millions of living animals devoured one another. Pilots were falling in flames over Europe; women were being forcibly raped in the South Pacific. His father should have taken him aside and said: "There is a simple secret to getting through the funhouse, as simple as being first to see the Towers. Here it is. Peter does not know it, neither does your Uncle Karl. You and I are different. Not surprisingly, you've often wished you weren't. Don't think I haven't noticed how unhappy your childhood has been! But you'll understand, when I tell you, why it had to be kept secret until now. And you won't regret not being like your brother and your uncle. *On the contrary.*" If you knew all the stories behind all the people on the boardwalk you'd see that *nothing* was what it looked like. Husbands and wives often hated each other; parents didn't necessarily love their children; et cetera. A child took things for granted because he had nothing to compare his life to, and everybody acted as if things were as they should be. Therefore each saw himself as the hero of the story, when the truth might turn out to be that he's the villain, or the coward. And there wasn't one thing you could do about it!

Hunchbacks, fat ladies, fools—that no one chose what they were was unbearable. In the movies he'd meet a beautiful young girl in the funhouse; they'd have hairsbreadth escapes from real dangers; he'd do and say the right things; she also; in the end they'd be lovers; their dialogue-lines would match up; he'd be perfectly at ease; she'd not only like him well enough, she'd think he was *marvelous;* she'd lie awake thinking about *him,* instead of vice versa—the way *his* face looked in different lights and how he stood and exactly what he'd said—and yet that would be only one small episode in his wonderful life, among many many others. Not a *turning-point* at all. What had happened in the toolshed was nothing. He hated, he loathed his parents! One reason for not writing a lost-in-the-funhouse story is that either everybody's felt what Ambrose feels, in which case it goes without saying, or else no normal person feels such things, in which case Ambrose is a freak. "Is anything more tiresome, in fiction, than the problems of sensitive adolescents?" And it's all too long and rambling, as if the author. For all a person knows the first time through, the end could be just around any corner; perhaps, *not impossibly* it's been within reach any number of times. On the other hand he may be scarcely past the start, with everything yet to get through, an intolerable idea.

Fill in: His father's raised eyebrows when he announced his decision to do the funhouse with Magda. Ambrose understands now, but didn't then, that his father was wondering whether he knew what the funhouse was *for*—especially since he didn't object, as he should have, when Peter decided to come along too. The ticket-woman, witchlike, mortifying him when inadvertently he gave her his name-coin instead of the half-dollar, then unkindly calling Magda's attention to the birthmark on his temple: "Watch out for him, girlie, he's a marked man!" She wasn't even cruel, he understood, only vulgar and insensitive. Somewhere in the world there was a young woman with such splendid understanding that she'd see him entire, like a poem or story, and find his words so valuable after all that when he confessed his apprehensions she would explain why they were in fact the very things that made him precious to her . . . and to Western Civilization! There was no such girl, the simple truth being. Violent yawns as they approached the mouth. Whispered advice from an old-timer on a bench near the barrel: "Go crabwise and ye'll get an eyeful without upsetting!" Composure vanished at the first pitch: Peter hollered joyously, Magda tumbled,

shrieked, clutched her skirt; Ambrose scrambled crabwise, tightlipped
with terror, was soon out, watched his dropped name-coin slide among
the couples. Shamefaced he saw that to get through expeditiously was
not the point; Peter feigned assistance in order to trip Magda up,
shouted "I see Christmas!" when her legs went flying. The old man,
his latest betrayer, cacked approval. A dim hall then of blackthread
cobwebs and recorded gibber: he took Magda's elbow to steady her
against revolving discs set in the slanted floor to throw your feet out
from under, and explained to her in a calm deep voice his theory that
each phase of the funhouse was triggered either automatically, by a
series of photoelectric devices, or else manually by operators stationed
at peepholes. But he lost his voice thrice as the discs unbalanced him;
Magda was anyhow squealing; but at one point she clutched him
about the waist to keep from falling, and her right cheek pressed
for a moment against his belt-buckle. Heroically he drew her up,
it was his chance to clutch her close as if for support and say: "I
love you." He even put an arm lightly about the small of her back
before a sailor-and-girl pitched into them from behind, sorely treading
his left big toe and knocking Magda asprawl with them. The sailor's
girl was a string-haired hussy with a loud laugh and light-blue drawers;
Ambrose realized that he wouldn't have said "I love you" anyhow, and
was smitten with self-contempt. How much better it would be to be
that common sailor! A wiry little Seaman 3rd, the fellow squeezed a
girl to each side and stumbled hilarious into the mirror-room, closer
to Magda in thirty seconds than Ambrose had got in thirteen years.
She giggled at something the fellow said to Peter; she drew her hair
from her eyes with a movement so womanly it struck Ambrose's heart;
Peter's smacking her backside then seemed particularly coarse. But
Magda made a pleased indignant face and cried, "All right for *you,*
mister!" and pursued Peter into the maze without a backward glance.
The sailor followed after, leisurelily, drawing his girl against his hip;
Ambrose understood not only that they were all so relieved to be rid
of his burdensome company that they didn't even notice his absence,
but that he himself shared their relief. Stepping from the treacherous
passage at last into the mirror-maze, he saw once again, more clearly
than ever, how readily he deceived himself into supposing he was a
person. He even foresaw, wincing at his dreadful self-knowledge, that
he would repeat the deception, at ever-rarer intervals, all his wretched
life, so fearful were the alternatives. Fame, madness, suicide; perhaps
all three. It's not believable that so young a boy could articulate that
reflection, and in fiction the merely true must always yield to the

plausible. Yet Ambrose M——— understood, as few adults do, that the famous loneliness of the great was no popular myth but a general truth —and moreover, that it was as much cause as effect.

All the preceding except the last few sentences is exposition that should've been done earlier or interspersed with the present action instead of lumped together. No reader would put up with so much with such *prolixity*. It's interesting that Ambrose's father, though presumably an intelligent man (as indicated by his role as high-school teacher), neither encouraged nor discouraged his children at all in any way—as if he either didn't care about them or cared all right but didn't know how to act. If this fact should contribute to one of his children's becoming a celebrated but wretchedly unhappy scientist, was it a good thing or not? He too might someday face that question; it would be useful to know whether it had tortured his father for years, for example, or never once crossed his mind.

In the mirror-maze two important things happened. First, our hero found a name-coin someone else had lost or discarded: *AMBROSE*, suggestive of the famous lightship and of his father's favorite dessert, which his mother prepared on special occasions out of coconut, oranges, grapes, and what else. Second, as he wondered at the endless replication of his image in the mirrors—second, as he *lost himself in the reflection* that the necessity for an observer makes perfect observation impossible, better make him eighteen at least, yet that would render other things unlikely, he heard Peter and Magda chuckling somewhere in the maze. "Here!" "No, here!" they shouted to each other; Peter said, "Where's Amby?" Magda murmured. "Amb?" Peter called. In a pleased, friendly voice. He didn't reply. The truth was, his brother was a *happy-go-lucky youngster* who'd've been better off with a regular brother of his own, but who seldom complained of his lot and was generally cordial. Ambrose's throat ached; there aren't enough different ways to say that. He stood quietly while the two young people giggled and thumped through the glittering maze, hurrah'd their discovery of its exit, cried out in joyful alarm at what next beset them. Then he set his mouth and followed after, as he supposed, took a wrong turn, strayed into the pass *wherein he lingers yet*.

The action of conventional dramatic narrative may be represented by a diagram called Freitag's Triangle— $A \overset{B}{\diagup}\diagdown_C$ —or more accurately by a variant of that diagram— $A \underset{B}{\rule{1cm}{0.4pt}} \overset{C}{\diagdown}_D$ —in which *AB* represents the exposition, *B* the introduction of conflict, *BC* the "rising action," complication, or development of the conflict, *C* the climax or turn of the action, *CD* the *dénouement* or resolution of the conflict.

While there is no reason to regard this pattern as an absolute necessity, like many other conventions it became conventional because great numbers of people over great numbers of years learned by trial and error that it was effective; one ought not to forsake it, therefore, unless one wishes to forsake as well the effect of drama or has clear cause to feel that deliberate violation of the "normal" pattern can better can better effect that effect. This can't go on much longer; it can go on forever. He died telling stories to himself in the dark; years later, when that vast unsuspected area of the funhouse came to light, the first expedition found his skeleton in one of its labyrinthine corridors and mistook it for part of the entertainment. He died of starvation telling himself stories in the dark; but unbeknownst unbeknownst to him, an assistant operator of the funhouse, happening to overhear him, crouched just behind the plyboard partition and wrote down his every word. The operator's daughter, an exquisite young woman with a figure unusually well developed for her age, crouched just behind the partition and transcribed his every word. Though she had never laid eyes on him, she recognized that here was one of Western Culture's truly great imaginations, the eloquence of whose suffering would be an inspiration to unnumbered. And her heart was torn between her love for the misfortunate young man (yes, she loved him, though she had never laid though she knew him only—but how well!—through his words, and the deep, calm voice in which he spoke them) between her love et cetera and her woman's intuition that only in suffering and isolation could he give voice et cetera. Lone dark dying. Quietly she kissed the rough plyboard, and a tear fell upon the page. Where she had written in shorthand *Where she had written in shorthand* Where she had written in shorthand *Where she* et cetera. A long time ago we should have passed the apex of Freitag's Triangle and made brief work of the *dénouement;* the plot doesn't rise by meaningful steps but winds upon itself, digresses, retreats, hesitates, sighs, collapses, expires. The climax of the story must be its protagonist's discovery of a way to get through the funhouse. But he has found none, may have ceased to search.

What relevance does the war have to the story? Should there be fireworks outside or not?

Ambrose wandered, languished, dozed. Now and then he fell into his habit of rehearsing to himself the unadventurous story of his life, narrated from the third-person point of view, from his earliest memory parenthesis of maple-leaves stirring in the summer breath of tidewater

Maryland end of parenthesis to the present moment. Its principal events, on this telling, would appear to have been *A, B, C,* and *D.*

He imagined himself years hence, successful, married, at ease in the world, the trials of his adolescence far behind him. He has come to the seashore with his family for the holiday: how Ocean City has changed! But at one seldom at one ill-frequented end of the boardwalk a few derelict amusements survive from times gone by: the great carrousel from the turn of the century, with itts monstrous griffins and mechanical concert-band; the roller-coaster rumored since 1916 to have been condemned; the mechanical shooting-gallery in which only the image of our enemies changed. His own son laughs with Fat May and wants to know what a funhouse is; Ambrose hugs the sturdy lad close and smiles around his pipestem at his wife.

The family's going home. Mother sits between Father and Uncle Karl, who teases him goodnaturedly who chuckles over the fact that the comrade with whom he'd fought his way shoulder to shoulder through the funhouse had turned out to be a colored boy—to their mutual discomfort, as they'd opened their souls. But such are the walls of custom, which even. Whose arm is where? How must it feel. He dreams of a funhouse vaster by far than any yet constructed; but by then they may be out of fashion, like steamboats and excursion-trains. Already quaint and seedy: the draperied ladies on the frieze of the carrousel are his father's father's mooncheeked dreams; if he thinks of it more he will vomit his apple-on-a-stick.

He wonders: will he become a regular person? Something has gone wrong; his vaccination didn't take; at the Boy-Scout initiation campfire he only pretended to be deeply moved, as he pretends to this hour that it is not so bad after all in the funhouse, and that he has a little limp. How long will it last? He envisions a truly astonishing funhouse, incredibly complex yet utterly controlled from a great central switchboard like the console of a pipe-organ. Nobody had enough imagination. He could design such a place himself, wiring and all, and he's only thirteen years old. He would be its operator: panel-lights would show what was up in every cranny of its cunning of its multifarious vastness; a switch-flick would ease this fellow's way, complicate that's, to balance things out; if anyone seemed lost or frightened, all the operator had to do was.

He wishes he had never entered the funhouse. No: he wishes he had never been born. But he was. Then he wishes he were dead. But he's not. Therefore he will construct funhouses for others and be their secret operator—though he would rather be among the lovers for whom funhouses are designed.

City Life

1

Elsa and Ramona entered the complicated city. They found an apartment without much trouble, several rooms on Porter Street. Curtains were hung. Bright paper things from a Japanese store were placed here and there.

—You'd better tell Charles that he can't come to see us until everything is ready.

Ramona thought: I don't want him to come at all. He will go into a room with Elsa and close the door. I will be sitting outside reading the business news. Britain Weighs Economic Curbs. Bond Rate Serge Looms. Time will pass. Then they will emerge. Acting as if nothing had happened. Elsa will make coffee. Charles will put brandy from his flat silver flask in the coffee. We will all drink the coffee with the brandy in it. Ugh!

—Where shall we put the telephone books?

—Put them over there by the telephone.

Elsa and Ramona went to the $2 plant store. A man stood outside selling individual peacock feathers. Elsa and Ramona bought several hanging plants in white plastic pots. The proprietor put the plants in brown paper bags.

—Water them every other day, girls. Keep them wet.

—We will.

Elsa uttered a melancholy reflection on life: It goes faster and faster! Ramona said: It's so difficult!

Charles accepted a position with greater responsibilities in another city.

—I'll be able to get in on weekends sometimes.

—Is this a real job?

—Of course, Elsa. You don't think I'd fool you, do you?

Clad in an extremely dark gray, if not completely black, suit, he had shaved his mustache.

—This outfit doesn't let you wear them.

Ramona heard Elsa sobbing in the back bedroom. I suppose I should sympathize with her. But I don't.

2

Ramona received the following letter from Charles:

DEAR RAMONA—

Thank you, Ramona, for your interesting and curious letter. It is true that I have noticed you sitting there, in the living room, when I visit Elsa. I have many times made mental notes about your appearance, which I consider in no wise inferior to that of Elsa herself. I get a pretty electric reaction to your taste in clothes, too. Those upper legs have not been lost on me. But the trouble is, when two girls are living together, one must make a choice. One can't have them both, in our society. This prohibition is enforced by you girls, chiefly, together with older ladies, who if the truth were known probably don't care but nevertheless feel that standards must be upheld, somewhere. I have Elsa, therefore I can't have you. (I know that there is a philosophical problem about "being" and "having" but I can't discuss that now because I'm a little rushed due to the pressures of my new assignment.) So that's what obtains at the moment, most excellent Ramona. That's where we stand. Of course the future may be different. It not infrequently is.

Hastily,
CHARLES

—What are you reading?

—Oh, it's just a letter.

—Who is it from?

—Oh, just somebody I know.

—Who?

—Oh, nobody.

—Oh.

Ramona's mother and father came to town from Montana. Ramona's thin father stood on the Porter Street sidewalk wearing a business suit and a white cowboy hat. He was watching his car. He watched from the steps of the house for a while, and then watched from the sidewalk a little, and then watched from the steps again. Ramona's mother looked in the suitcases for the present she had brought.

—Mother! You shouldn't have brought me such an expensive present!

—Oh, it wasn't all that expensive. We wanted you to have something for the new apartment.

—An original gravure by René Magritte!

—Well, it isn't very big. It's just a small one.

Whenever Ramona received a letter forwarded to her from her Montana home, the letter had been opened and the words "Oops! Opened by mistake!" written on the envelope. But she forgot that in gazing at the handsome new Magritte print, a picture of a tree with a crescent moon cut out of it.

—It's fantastically beautiful! Where shall we hang it?

—How about on the wall?

3

At the University the two girls enrolled in the Law School.

—I hear the Law School's tough, Elsa stated, but that's what we want, a tough challenge.

—You are the only two girls ever to be admitted to our Law School, the Dean observed. Mostly, we have men. A few foreigners. Now I am going to tell you three things to keep an eye on: (1) Don't try to go too far too fast. (2) Wear plain clothes. And (3) Keep your notes clean. And if I hear the words "Yoo hoo' echoing across the quadrangle, you will be sent down instantly. We don't use those words in this school.

—I like what I already know, Ramona said under her breath.

Savoring their matriculation, the two girls wandered out to sample the joys of Pascin Street. They were closer together at this time than they had ever been. Of course, they didn't want to get too close together. They were afraid to get too close together.

Elsa met Jacques. He was deeply involved in the struggle.

—What is this struggle about, exactly, Jacques?

—My God, Elsa, your eyes! I have never seen that shade of umber in anyone's eyes before. Ever.

Jacques took Elsa to a Mexican restaurant. Elsa cut into her *cabrito con queso*.

—To think that this food was once a baby goat!

Elsa, Ramona, and Jacques looked at the dawn coming up over the hanging plants. Patterns of silver light and so forth.

—You're not afraid that Charles will bust in here unexpectedly and find us?

—Charles is in Cleveland. Besides, I'd say you were with Ramona. Elsa giggled.

Ramona burst into tears.

Elsa and Jacques tried to comfort Ramona.

—Why don't you take a 21-day excursion-fare trip to "preserves of nature"?

—If I went to a "preserve of nature," it would turn out to be nothing but a terrible fen!

Ramona thought: He will go into a room with Elsa and close the door. Time will pass. Then they will emerge, acting as if nothing had happened. Then the coffee. Ugh!

4

Charles in Cleveland.
    "Whiteness"
    "Vital skepticism"
Charles advanced very rapidly in the Cleveland hierarchy. That sort of situation that develops sometimes wherin managers feel threatened by gifted subordinates and do not assign them really meaningful duties but instead shunt them aside into dead areas where their human potential is wasted did not develop in Charles' case. His devoted heart lifted him to the highest levels. It was Charles who pointed out that certain operations had been carried out more efficiently "when the cathedrals were white," and in time the entire Cleveland structure was organized around his notions: "whiteness," "vital skepticism."

Two men held Charles down on the floor and a third slipped a needle into his hip.

He awakened in a vaguely familiar room.

—Where am I? he asked the nurse-like person who appeared to answer his ring.

Porter Street, this creature said. Mlle. Ramona will see you shortly. In the meantime, drink some of this orange juice.

Well, Charles thought to himself, I cannot but admire the guts and address of his brave girl, who wanted me so much that she engineered this whole affair—my abduction from Cleveland and removal to these beloved rooms, where once I was entertained by the beautiful Elsa. And now I must see whether my key concepts can get me out of this "fix," for "fix" it is. I shouldn't have written that letter. Perhaps if I wrote another letter? A followup?

Charles formed the letter to Ramona in his mind.

DEAR RAMONA—

Now that I am back in your house, tied down to this bed with these steel bands around my ankles, I understand that perhaps my earlier letter to you was subject to misinterpretation etc, etc.

Elsa entered the room and saw Charles tied down on the bed.

—That's against the law!

—Sit down, Elsa. Just because you are a law student you want to proclaim the rule of law everywhere. But some things don't have to do with the law. Some things have to do with the heart. The heart, which was our great emblem and cockade, when the cathedrals were white.

—I'm worried about Ramona, Elsa said. She has been missing lectures. And she has been engaging in hilarity at the expense of the law.

—Jokes?

—Gibes. And now this extra-legality. Your sequestration.

Charles and Elsa looked out of the window at the good day.

—See that blue in the sky. How wonderful. After all the gray we've had.

5

Elsa and Ramona watched the Motorola television set in their pajamas.

—What else is on? Elsa asked.

Ramona looked in the newspaper.

—On 7 there's "Johnny Allegro" with George Raft and Nina Foch. On 9 "Johnny Angel" with George Raft and Claire Trevor. On 11 there's "Johnny Apollo" with Tyrone Power and Dorothey Lamour. On 13 is "Johnny Concho" with Frank Sinatra and Phyllis Kirk. On 2 is "Johnny Dark" with Tony Curtis and Piper Laurie. On 4 is "Johnny Eager" with Robert Taylor and Lana Turner. On 5 is "Johnny O'Clock" with Dick Powell and Evelyn Keyes. On 31 is "Johnny Trouble" with Stuart Whitman and Ethel Barrymore.

—What's this one we're watching?

—What time is it?

—Eleven-thirty-five.
—"Johnny Guitar" with Joan Crawford and Sterling Hayden.

6

Jacques, Elsa, Charles, and Ramona sat in a row at the sun dance. Jacques was setting next to Elsa and Charles was sitting next to Ramona. Of course Charles was also sitting next to Elsa but he was leaning toward Ramona mostly. It was hard to tell what his intentions were. He kept his hands in his pockets.
—How is the struggle coming, Jacques?
—Quite well, actually. Since the Declaration of Rye we have accumulated many hundreds of new members.
Elsa leaned across Charles to say something to Ramona.
—Did you water the plants?
The sun dancers were beating the ground with sheaves of wheat.
—Is that supposed to make the sun shine, or what? Ramona asked.
—Oh, I think it's just sort of to . . . honor the sun. I don't think it's supposed to make it do anything.
Elsa stood up.
—That's against the law!
—Sit down, Elsa.
Elsa became pregnant.

7

"This young man, a man though only eighteen . . ."
A large wedding scene.
Charles measures the church
    Elsa and Jacques bombarded with flowers
    Fathers and mothers riding on the city railway
    The minister raises his hand
    Evacuation of the sacristy: bomb threat
    Black limousines with ribbons tied to their aerials
    Several men on balconies who appear to be signaling, or applauding
    Traffic lights
    Pieces of blue cake
    Champagne

8

Well, Ramona, I am glad we came to the city. In spite of everything.
—Yes, Elsa, it has turned out well for you. You are Mrs. Jacques Tope now. And soon there will be a little one.

—Not so soon. Not for eight months. I am sorry, though, about one thing. I hate to give up Law School.

—Don't be sorry. The Law needs knowledgeable civilians as well as practioners. Your training will not be wasted.

—That's dear of you. Well, goodbye.

Elsa and Jacques and Charles went into the back bedroom. Ramona remained outside with the newspaper.

—Well, I suppose I might as well put the coffee on, she said to herself. Rats!

SAUL BELLOW

Mosby's Memoirs

The birds chirped away. Fweet, Fweet, Bootchee-Fweet. Doing all the things naturalists say they do. Expressing abysmal depths of aggression, which only Man—Stupid Man—heard as innocence. We feel everything is so innocent—because our wickedness is so fearful. Oh, very fearful!

Mr. Willis Mosby, after his siesta, gazing down-mountain at the town of Oaxaca where all were snoozing still—mouths, rumps, long black Indian hair, the antique beauty photographically celebrated by Eisenstein in *Thunder over Mexico*. Mr. Mosby—Dr. Mosby really; erudite, maybe even profound; thought much, accomplished much—had made some of the most interesting mistakes a man could make in the twentieth century. He was in Oaxaca now to write his memoirs. He had a grant for the purpose, from the Guggenheim Foundation. And why not?

Bougainvillaea poured down the hillside, and the hummingbirds were spinning. Mosby felt ill with all this whirling, these colors, fragrances, ready to topple on him. Liveliness, beauty, seemed very dangerous. Mortal danger. Maybe he had drunk too much mescal at lunch (beer, also). Behind the green and red of Nature, dull black seemed to be thickly laid like mirror backing.

Mosby did not feel quite well; his teeth, gripped tight, made the muscles stand out in his handsome, elderly tanned jaws. He had fine blue eyes, light-pained, direct, intelligent, disbelieving; hair still thick, parted in the middle; and strong vertical grooves between the brows, beneath the nostrils, and at the back of the neck.

The time had come to put some humor into the memoirs. So far it had been: Fundamentalist family in Missouri—Father the successful builder—Early schooling—The State University—Rhodes Scholarship —Intellectual friendships—What I learned from Professor Collingwood —Empire and the mental vigor of Britain—My unorthodox interpretation of John Locke—I work for William Randolph Hearst in Spain —The personality of General Franco—Radical friendships in New York—Wartime service with the O.S.S.—The limited vision of Franklin D. Roosevelt—Comte, Proudhon, and Marx revisited—De Tocqueville once again.

Nothing very funny here. And yet thousands of students and others would tell you, "Mosby had a great sense of humor." Would tell their children, "This Mosby in the O.S.S.," or "Willis Mosby, who was in Toledo with me when the Alcázar fell, made me die laughing." "I shall never forget Mosby's observations on Harold Laski." "On packing the Supreme Court." "On the Russian purge trials." "On Hitler."

So it was certainly high time to do something. He had given it some consideration. He would say, when they sent down his ice from the hotel bar (he was in a cottage below the main building, flowers heaped upon it; envying a little the unencumbered mountains of the Sierra Madre) and when he had chilled his mescal—warm, it tasted rotten— he would write that in 1947, when he was living in Paris, he knew any number of singular people. He knew the Comte de la Mine-Crevée, who sheltered Gary Davis the World Citizen after the World Citizen had burnt his passport publicly. He knew Mr. Julian Huxley at UNESCO. He discussed social theory with Mr. Lévi-Straus but was not invited to dinner—they ate at the Musée de l'Homme. Sartre refused to meet with him; he thought all Americans, Negroes excepted, were secret agents. Mosby for his part suspected all Russians abroad of working for the G.P.U. Mosby knew French well; extremely fluent in Spanish; quite good in German. But the French cannot identify originality in foreigners. That is the curse of an old civilization. It is a heavier planet. Its best minds must double their horsepower to overcome the gravitational field of tradition. Only a few will ever fly. To fly away from Descartes. To fly away from the political anachronisms of left, center, and right persisting since 1789. Mosby found these French exceedingly banal. These French found him lean and tight. In well-tailored clothes, elegant and dry, his good Western skin, pale eyes, strong nose, handsome mouth, and virile creases. *Un type sec.*

Both sides—Mosby and the French, that is—with highly developed attitudes. Both, he was lately beginning to concede, quite wrong. Possibly equidistant from the truth, but lying in different sectors of error. The French were worse off because their errors were collective. Mine, Mosby believed, were at least peculiar. The French were furious over the collapse in 1940 of *La France Pourrie,* their lack of military will, the extensive collaboration, the massive deportations unopposed (the Danes, even the *Bulgarians* resisted Jewish deportations), and, finally, over the humiliation of liberation by the Allies. Mosby, in the O.S.S., had information to support such views. Within the State Department, too, he had university colleagues—former students and old acquaintances. He had expected a high post-war appointment, for which, as director of counter-espionage in Latin America, he was ideally qualified. But Dean Acheson personally disliked him. Nor did Dulles approve. Mosby, a fanatic about *ideas,* displeased the institutional gentry. He had said that the Foreign Service was staffed by rejects of the power structure. Young gentlemen from good Eastern colleges who couldn't make it as Wall Street lawyers were allowed to interpret the alleged interests of their class in the State Department bureaucracy. In foreign consulates they could be rude to D.P.s and indulge their country-club anti-Semitism, which was dying out even in the country clubs. Besides, Mosby had sympathized with the Burnham position on managerialism, declaring, during the war, that the Nazis were winning because they had made their managerial revolution first. No Allied combination could conquer, with its obsolete industrialism, a nation which had reached a new state of history and tapped the power of the inevitable, etc. And then Mosby, holding forth in Washington, among the elite Scotch drinkers, stated absolutely that however deplorable the concentration camps had been, they showed at least the rationality of German political ideas. The Americans had no such ideas. They didn't know what they were doing. No design existed. The British were not much better. The Hamburg fire-bombing, he argued in his clipped style, in full declarative phrases, betrayed the idiotic emptiness and planlessness of Western leadership. Finally, he said that when Acheson blew his nose there were maggots in his handkerchief.

Among the defeated French, Mosby admitted that he had a galled spirit. (His jokes were not too bad.) And of course he drank a lot. He worked on Marx and Tocqueville, and he drank. He would not cease from mental strife. The Comte de la Mine-Crevée (Mosby's own improvisation on a noble and ancient name) kept him in PX booze and exchanged his money on the black market for him. He described his swindles and was very entertaining.

Mosby now wished to say, in the vein of Sir Harold Nicolson or Santayana or Betrand Russell, writers for whose memoirs he had the greatest admiration, that Paris in 1947, like half a Noah's Ark, was waiting for the second of each kind to arrive. There was one of every-thing. Something of this sort. Especially among Americans. The city was very bitter, grim; the Seine looked and smelled like medicine. At an American party, a former student of French from Minnesota, now running a shady enterprise, an agency which specialized in bribery, private undercover investigations, and procuring broads for V.I.P.s, said something highly emotional about the City of Man, about the meaning of Europe for Americans, the American failure to preserve human scale. Not omitting to work in Man the Measure. And every other tag he could bring back from Randall's *Making of the Modern Mind* or *Readings in the Intellectual History of Europe.* "I was tempted," Mosby meant to say (the ice arrived in a glass jar with tongs; the natives no longer wore the dirty white drawers of the past). "Tempted . . ." He rubbed his forehead, which projected like the back of an observation car. "To tell this sententious little drunkard and gyp artist, formerly a pacifist and vegetarian, follower of Gandhi at the University of Minnesota, now driving a very handsome Bentley to the Tour d'Argent to eat duck *à l'orange.* Tempted to say, 'Yes, but we come here across the Atlantic to relax a bit in the past. To recall what Ezra Pound had once said. That we would make another Venice, just for the hell of it, in the Jersey marshes any time we liked. Toying. To divert ourselves in the time of colossal mastery to come. Reproduc-ing anything, for fun. Baboons trained to row will bring us in gondolas to discussions of astrophysics. Where folks burn garbage now, and fatten pigs and junk their old machines, we will debark to hear a concert.' "

Mosby the thinker, like other busy men, never had time for music. Poetry was not his cup of tea. Members of Congress, Cabinet officers, Organization Men, Pentagon planners, Party leaders, Presidents had no such interest. They could not be what they were and read Eliot, hear Vivaldi, Cimarosa. But they planned that others might enjoy these things and benefit by their power. Mosby perhaps had more in common with political leaders and Joint Chiefs and Presidents. At least, they were in his thoughts more often than Cimarosa and Eliot. With hate, he pondered their mistakes, their shallowness. Lectured on Locke to show them up. Except by the will of the majority, unam-biguously expressed, there was no legitimate power. The only absolute democrat in America (perhaps in the world—although who can know what there is in the world, among so many billions of minds and souls) was Willis Mosby. Notwithstanding his terse, dry, intolerant style of conversation (more precisely, examination), his lank dignity of person, his aristocratic bones. Dark long nostrils hinting at the afflictions that needed the strength you could see in his jaws. And, finally, the light-pained eyes.

A most peculiar, ingenious, hungry, aspiring, and heartbroken animal, who, by calling himself Man, thinks he can escape being what he really is. Not a matter of his definition, in the last analysis, but of his being. Let him say what he likes.

> Kingdoms are clay: our dungy earth alike
> Feeds beast as man; the nobleness of life
> Is to do thus.

Thus being love. Or any other sublime option. (Mosby knew his Shakespeare anyway. *There* was a difference from the President. And of the Vice-President he said, "I wouldn't trust him to make me a pill. A has-been druggist!")

With sober lips he sipped the mescal, the servant in the coarse orange shirt enriched by metal buttons reminding him that the car was coming at four o'clock to take him to Mitla, to visit the ruins.

"*Yo mismo soy una ruina*," Mosby joked.

The stout Indian, giving only so much of a smile—no more—withdrew with quiet courtesy. Perhaps I was fishing, Mosby considered. Wanted him to say I was *not* a ruin. But how could he? Seeing that for him I *am* one.

Perhaps Mosby did not have a light touch. Still, he thought he did have an eye for certain kinds of comedy. And he *must* find a way to relieve the rigor of this account of his mental wars. Besides, he could really remember that in Paris at that time people, one after another, revealed themselves in a comic light. He was then seeing things that way. Rue Jacob, Rue Bonaparte, Rue du Bac, Rue de Verneuil, Hôtel de l'Université—filled with funny people.

He began by setting down a name: Lustgarten. Yes, there was the man he wanted. Hymen Lustgarten, a Marxist, or former Marxist, from New Jersey. From Newark, I think. He had been a shoe salesman, and belonged to any number of heretical, fanatical, bolshevistic groups. He had been a Leninist, a Trotskyist, then a follower of Hugo Oehler, then of Thomas Stamm, and finally of an Italian named Salemme who gave up politics to become a painter, an abstractionist. Lustgarten also gave up politics. He wanted now to be successful in business—rich. Believing that the nights he had spent poring over *Das Kapital* and

Lenin's *State and Revolution* would give him an edge in business dealings. We were staying in the same hotel. I couldn't at first make out what he and his wife were doing. Presently I understood. The black market. This was not then reprehensible. Postwar Europe was like that. Refugees, adventurers, G.I.s. Even the Comte de la M.-C. Europe still shuddering from the blows it had received. Governments new, uncertain, infirm. No reason to respect their authority. American soldiers led the way. Flamboyant business schemes. Machines, whole factories, stolen, treasures shipped home. An American colonel in the lumber business started to saw up the Black Forest and send it to Wisconsin. And, of course, Nazis concealing their concentration-camp loot. Jewels sunk in Austrian lakes. Art works hidden. Gold extracted from teeth in extermination camps, melted into ingots and mortared like bricks into the walls of houses. Incredibly huge fortunes to be made, and Lustgarten intended to make one of them. Unfortunately, he was incompetent.

You could see at once that there was no harm in him. Despite the bold revolutionary associations, and fierceness of doctrine. Theoretical willingness to slay class enemies. But Lustgarten could not even hold his own with pushy people in a *pissoir*. Strangely meek, stout, swarthy, kindly, grinning with mulberry lips, a froggy, curving mouth which produced wrinkles like gills between the ears and the grin. And perhaps, Mosby thought, he comes to mind in Mexico because of his Toltec, Mixtec, Zapotec look, squat and black-haired, the tip of his nose turned downward and the black nostrils shyly widening when his friendly smile was accepted. And a bit sick with the wickedness, the awfulness of life but, respectfully persistent, bound to get his share. Efficiency was his style—action, determination, but a traitorous incompetence trembled within. Wrong calling. Wrong choice. A bad mistake. But he was persistent.

His conversation amused me, in the dining room. He was proud of his revolutionary activities, which had consisted mainly of cranking the mimeograph machine. Internal Bulletins. Thousands of pages of recondite examination of fine points of doctrine for the membership. Whether the American working class should give *material* aid to the Loyalist Government of Spain, controlled as that was by Stalinists and other class enemies and traitors. You had to fight Franco, and you had to fight Stalin as well. There was, of course, no material aid to give. But *had* there been any, *should* it have been given? This purely theoretical problem caused splits and expulsions. I always kept myself informed of these curious agonies of sectarianism, Mosby wrote. The single effort made by Spanish Republicans to purchase arms in the

United States was thwarted by that friend of liberty Franklin Delano Roosevelt, who allowed one ship, the *Mar Cantábrico,* to be loaded but set the Coast Guard after it to turn it back to port. It was, I believe, that *genius* of diplomacy, Mr. Cordell Hull, who was responsible, but the decision, of course, was referred to F.D.R., whom Huey Long amusingly called Franklin de la *No!* But perhaps the most refined of these internal discussions left of left, the documents for which were turned out on the machine by that Jimmy Higgins, the tubby devoted party-worker Mr. Lustgarten, had to do with the Finnish War. Here the painful point of doctrine to be resolved was whether a Workers' State like the Soviet Union, even if it was a *degenerate* Workers' State, a product of the Thermidorian Reaction following the glorious Proletarian Revolution of 1917, could wage an Imperialistic War. For only the *bourgeoisie* could be Imperialistic. Technically, Stalinism could not be Imperialism. By definition. What then should a Revolutionary Party say to the Finns? Should they resist Russia or not? The Russians were monsters but they would expropriate the Mannerheim White-Guardist landowners and move, painful though it might be, in the correct historical direction. This, as a sect-watcher, I greatly relished. But it was too foreign a sublety for many of the sectarians. Who were, after all, Americans. Pragmatists at heart. It was *too* far out for Lustgarten. He decided, after the war, to become (it shouldn't be hard) a rich man. Took his savings and, I believe his wife said, his mother's savings, and went abroad to build a fortune.

Within a year he had lost it all. He was cheated. By a German partner, in particular. But also he was caught smuggling by Belgian authorities.

When Mosby met him (Mosby speaking of himself in the third person as Henry Adams had done in *The Education of Henry Adams*) —when Mosby met him, Lustgarten was working for the American Army, employed by Graves Registration. Something to do with the procurement of crosses. Or with supervision of the lawns. Official employment gave Lustgarten PX privileges. He was rebuilding his financial foundations by the illegal sale of cigarettes. He dealt also in gas-ration coupons which the French Government, anxious to obtain dollars, would give you if you exchanged your money at the legal rate. The gas coupons were sold on the black market. The Lustgartens, husband and wife, persuaded Mosby to do this once. For them, he cashed his dollars at the bank, not with la Mine-Crevée. The occasion seemed important. Mosby gathered that Lustgarten had to drive at once to Munich. He had gone into the dental-supply business there with a German dentist who now denied that they had ever been partners.

Many consultations between Lustgarten (in his international in-
triguer's trenchcoat, ill-fitting; head, neck, and shoulders sloping backward in a froggy curve) and his wife, a young woman in an eyelet-lace
blouse and black velveteen skirt, a velveteen ribbon tied on her round,
healthy neck. Lustgarten, on the circular floor of the bank, explaining
as they stood apart. And sweating blood; being reasonable with Trudy,
detail by tortuous detail. It grated away poor Lustgarten's patience.
Hands feebly remonstrating. For she asked female questions or raised
objections which gave him agonies of patient rationality. Only there
was nothing rational to begin with. That is, he had had no legal right
to go into business with the German. All such arrangements had to be
licensed by Military Government. It was a black-market partnership
and when it began to show a profit, the German threw Lustgarten
out. With what they call impunity. Germany as a whole having
discerned the limits of all civilized systems of punishment as compared
with the unbounded possibilities of crime. The bank in Paris, where
these explanations between Lustgarten and Trudy were taking place,
had an inferior of some sort of red porphyry. Like raw meat. A color
which bourgeois France seemed to have vested with ideas of potency,
mettle, and grandeur. In the Invalides also, Napoleon's sarcophagus was
of polished red stone, a great, swooping, polished cradle containing the
little green corpse. (We have the testimony of M. Rideau, the Bon-
partist historian, as to the color.) As for the living Bonaparte, Mosby
felt, with Auguste Comte, that he had been an anachronism. The Revolution was historically necessary. It was socially justified. Politically,
economically, it was a move toward industrial democracy. But the
Napoleonic drama itself belonged to an archaic category of personal
ambitions, feudal ideas of war. Older than feudalism. Older than Rome.
The commander at the head of armies—nothing rational to recommend it. Society, increasingly rational in its organization, did not need
it. But humankind evidently desired it. War is a luxurious pleasure.
Grant the first premise of hedonism and you must accept the rest also.
Rational foundations of modernity are cunningly accepted by man
as the launching platform of ever wilder irrationalities.

Mosby, noting these reflections in a blue-green color of ink which
might have been extracted from the landscape. As his liquor had been
extracted from the green spikes of the mescal, the curious sharp,
dark-green fleshy limbs of the plant covering the fields.

The dollars, the francs, the gas rations, the bank like the beefsteak
mine in which W. C. Fields invested, and shrinking but persistent dark
Lustgarten getting into his little car on the sodden Parisian street.
There were few cars then in Paris. Plenty of parking space. And the
streets were so yellow, gray, wrinkled, dismal. But the French were

even then ferociously telling the world that they had the *savoir-vivre*, the *gai savoir*. Especially Americans, haunted by their Protestant Ethic, had to hear this. My God—sit down, sip wine, taste cheese, break bread, hear music, know love, stop running, and learn ancient life-wisdom from Europe. At any rate, Lustgarten buckled up his trench-coat, pulled down his big hoodlum's fedora. He was bunched up in the seat. Small brown hands holding the steering wheel of the Simca Huit, and the grinning despair with which he waved.

"*Bon voyage*, Lustgarten."

His Zapotec nose, his teeth like white pomegranate seeds. With a sob of the gears he took off for devastated Germany.

Reconstruction is big business. You demolish a society, you decrease the population, and off you go again. New fortunes. Lustgarten may have felt, *qua* Jew, that he had a right to grow rich in the German boom. That all Jews had natural claims beyond the Rhine. On land enriched by Jewish ashes. And you never could be sure, seated on a sofa, that it was not stuffed or upholstered with Jewish hair. And he would not use German soap. He washed his hands, Trudy told Mosby, with Lifebuoy from the PX.

Trudy, a graduate of Montclair Teachers' College in New Jersey, knew French, studied composition, had hoped to work with someone like Nadia Boulanger, but was obliged to settle for less. From the bank, as Lustgarten drove away in a kind of doomed, latently tearful daring in the rain-drenched street, Trudy invited Mosby to the Salle Pleyel, to hear a Czech pianist performing Schönberg. This man, with muscular baldness, worked very hard upon the keys. The difficulty of his enterprise alone came through—the labor of culture, the trouble it took to preserve art in tragic Europe, the devoted drill. Trudy had a nice face for concerts. Her odor was agreeable. She shone. In the left half of her countenance, one eye kept wondering. Stone-hearted Mosby, making fun of flesh and blood, of these little humanities with their short inventories of bad and good. The poor Czech in his blazer with chased buttons and the muscles of his forehead rising in protest against *tabula rasa*—the bare skull.

Mosby could abstract himself on such occasions. Shut out the piano. Continue thinking about Comte. Begone, old priests and feudal soldiers! Go, with Theology and Metaphysics! And in the Positive Epoch Enlightened Woman would begin to play her part, vigilant, preventing the managers of the new society from abusing their powers. Over Labor, the supreme good.

Embroidering the trees, the birds of Mexico, looking at Mosby, and the hummingbird, so neat in its lust, vibrating tinily, and the lizard on the soil drinking heat with its belly. To bless small creatures is supposed to be real good.

Yes, this Lustgarten was a funny man. Cheated in Germany, licked by the partner, and impatient with his slow progress in Graves Registration, he decided to import a Cadillac. Among the new postwar millionaires of Europe there was a big demand for Cadillacs. The French Government, moving slowly, had not yet taken measures against such imports for rapid resale. In 1947, no tax prevented such transactions. Lustgarten got his family in Newark to ship a new Cadillac. Something like four thousand dollars was raised by his brother, his mother, his mother's brother for the purpose. The car was sent. The customer was waiting. A down payment had already been given. A double profit was expected. Only, on the day the car was unloaded at Le Havre new regulations went into effect. The Cadillac could not be sold. Lustgarten was stuck with it. He couldn't even afford to buy gas. The Lustgartens were seen one day moving out of the hotel, into the car. Mrs. Lustgarten went to live with musical friends. Mosby offered Lustgarten the use of his sink for washing and shaving. Weary Lustgarten, defeated, depressed, frightened at last by his own plunging, scraped at his bristles, mornings, with a modest cricket noise, while sighing. All that money—mother's savings, brother's pension. No wonder his eyelids turned blue. And his smile, like a spinster's sachet, the last fragrance ebbed out long ago in the trousseau never used. But the long batrachian lips continued smiling.

Mosby realized that compassion should be felt. But passing in the night the locked, gleaming car, and seeing huddled Lustgarten, sleeping, covered with two coats, on the majestic seat, like Jonah inside Leviathan, Mosby could not say in candor that what he experienced was sympathy. Rather he reflected that this shoe salesman, in America attached to foreign doctrines, who could not relinquish Europe in the New World, was now, in Paris, sleeping in the Cadillac, encased in this gorgeous Fisher Body from Detroit. At home exotic, in Europe a Yankee. His timing was off. He recognized this himself. But believed, in general, that he was too early. A pioneer. For instance, he said, in a voice that creaked with shy assertiveness, the French were only now beginning to be Marxians. He had gone through it all years ago. What did these people know! Ask them about the Shakhty Engineers! About Lenin's Democratic Centralism! About the Moscow Trials! About "Social Fascism"! They were ignorant. The Revolution having been totally betrayed, these Europeans suddenly discovered Marx and Lenin. "Eureka!" he said in a high voice. And it was the Cold War, beneath it all. For should America lose, the French intellectuals were preparing to collaborate with Russia. And should America win they could still be free, defiant radicals under American protection.

"You sound like a patriot," said Mosby.

"Well, in a way I am," said Lustgarten. "But I am getting to be objective. Sometimes I say to myself, 'If you were outside the world, if you, Lustgarten, didn't exist as a man, what would your opinion be of this or that?' "

"Disembodied truth."

"I guess that's what it is."

"And what are you going to do about the Cadillac?" said Mosby.

"I'm sending it to Spain. We can sell it in Barcelona."

"But you have to get it there."

"Through Andorra. It's all arranged. Klonsky is driving it."

Klonsky was a Polish Belgian in the hotel. One of Lustgarten's associates, congenitally dishonest, Mosby thought. Kinky hair, wrinkled eyes like Greek olives, and a cat nose and cat lips. He wore Russian boots.

But no sooner had Klonsky departed for Andorra, than Lustgarten received a marvelous offer for the car. A capitalist in Utrecht wanted it at once and would take care of all excise problems. He had all the necessary *tuyaux*, unlimited drag. Lustgarten wired Klonsky in Andorra to stop. He raced down on the night train, recovered the Cadillac, and started driving back at once. There was no time to lose. But after sitting up all night on the *rapide*, Lustgarten was drowsy in the warmth of the Pyrenees and fell asleep at the wheel. He was lucky, he said later, for the car went down a mountainside and might have missed the stone wall that stopped it. He was only a foot or two from death when he was awakened by the crash. The car was destroyed. It was not insured.

Still faintly smiling, Lustgarten, with his sling and cane, came to Mosby's café table on the Boulevard Saint-Germain. Sat down. Removed his hat from dazzling black hair. Asked permission to rest his injured foot on a chair. "Is this a private conversation?" he said.

Mosby had been chatting with Alfred Ruskin, an American poet. Ruskin, though some of his front teeth were missing, spoke very clearly and swiftly. A perfectly charming man. Inveterately theoretical. He had been saying, for instance, that France had shot its collaborationist poets. America, which had no poets to spare, put Ezra Pound in Saint Elizabeth's. He then went on to say, barely acknowledging Lustgarten, that America had had no history, was not a historical society. His proof was from Hegel. According to Hegel, history was the history of wars and revolutions. The United States had had only one revolution and very few wars. Therefore it was historically empty. Practically a vacuum.

Ruskin also used Mosby's conveniences at the hotel, being too fastidious for his own latrine in the Algerian backstreets of the Left Bank. And when he emerged from the bathroom he invariably had a topic sentence.

"I have discovered the main defect of Kierkegaard."

Or, "Pascal was terrified by universal emptiness, but Valéry says the difference between empty space and space in a bottle is only quantitative, and there is nothing intrinsically terrifying about quantity. What is your view?"

We do not live in bottles—Mosby's reply.

Lustgarten said when Ruskin left us, "Who is that fellow? He mooched you for the coffee."

"Ruskin," said Mosby.

"*That* is Ruskin?"

"Yes, why?"

"I hear my wife was going out with Ruskin while I was in the hospital."

"Oh, I wouldn't believe such rumors," said Mosby. "A cup of coffee, an apéritif together, maybe."

"When a man is down on his luck," said Lustgarten, "it's the rare woman who won't give him hell in addition."

"Sorry to hear it," Mosby replied.

And then, as Mosby in Oaxaca recalled, shifting his seat from the sun—for he was already far too red, and his face, bones, eyes, seemed curiously thirsty—Lustgarten had said, "It's been a terrible experience."

"Undoubtedly so, Lustgarten. It must have been frightening."

"What crashed was my last stake. It involved family. Too bad in a way that I wasn't killed. My insurance would at least have covered my kid brother's loss. And my mother and uncle."

Mosby had no wish to see a man in tears. He did not care to sit through these moments of suffering. Such unmastered emotion was abhorrent. Though perhaps the violence of this abomination might have told Mosby something about his own moral constitution. Perhaps Lustgarten did not want his face to be working. Or tried to subdue his agitation, seeing from Mosby's austere, though not unkind, silence that this was not his way. Mosby was by taste a Senecan. At least he admired Spanish masculinity—the *varonil* of Lorca. The *clavel varonil*, the manly red carnation, the clear classic hardness of honorable control.

"You sold the wreck for junk, I assume?"

"Klonsky took care of it. Now look, Mosby. I'm through with that. I was reading, thinking in the hospital. I came over to make a pile. Like the gold rush. I really don't know what got into me. Trudy and I were just sitting around during the war. I was too old for the draft. And we both wanted action. She in music. Or life. Excitement. You know, dreaming at Montclair Teachers' College of the Big Time. I wanted to make it possible for her. Keep up with the world, or something. But really—in my hospital bed I realized—I was right the first time. I am a Socialist. A natural idealist. Reading about Attlee, I felt at home again. It became clear that I am still a political animal."

Mosby wished to say, "No, Lustgarten. You're a dandler of swarthy little babies. You're a piggyback man—a giddyap horsie. You're a sweet old Jewish Daddy." But he said nothing.

"And I also read," said Lustgarten, "about Tito. Maybe the Tito alternative is the real one. Perhaps there is hope for Socialism somewhere between the Labour Party and the Yugoslav type of leadership. I feel it my duty," Lustgarten told Mosby, "to investigate. I'm thinking of going to Belgrade."

"As what?"

"As a matter of fact, that's where you could come in," said Lustgarten. "If you would be so kind. You're not *just* a scholar. You wrote a book on Plato, I've been told."

"On the *Laws*."

"And other books. But in addition you know the Movement. Lots of people. More connections than a switchboard. . . ."

The slang of the forties.

"You know people at the *New Leader?*"

"Not my type of paper," said Mosby. "I'm actually a political conservative. Not what you would call a Rotten Liberal but an out-and-out conservative. I shook Franco's hand, you know."

"Did you?"

"This very hand shook the hand of the Caudillo. Would you like to touch it for yourself?"

"Why should I?"

"Go on," said Mosby. "It may mean something. Shake the hand that shook the hand."

Very strangely, then, Lustgarten extended padded, swarthy fingers. He looked partly subtle, partly ill. Grinning, he said, "Now I've made contact with real politics at last. But I'm serious about the *New Leader*. You probably know Bohn. I need credentials for Yugoslavia."

"Have you ever written for the papers?"

"For the *Militant*."

"What did you write?"

Guilty Lustgarten did not lie well. It was heartless of Mosby to amuse himself in this way.

"I have a scrapbook somewhere," said Lustgarten.

But it was not necessary to write to the *New Leader.* Lustgarten, encountered two days later on the Boulevard, near the pork butcher, had taken off the sling and scarcely needed the cane. He said, "I'm going to Yugoslavia. I've been invited."

"By whom?"

"Tito. The Government. They're asking interested people to come as guests to tour the country and see how they're building Socialism. Oh, I know," he quickly said, anticipating standard doctrinal objection, "you don't build Socialism in one country, but it's no longer the same situation. And I really believe Tito may redeem Marxism by actually transforming the dictatorship of the proletariat. This brings me back to my first love—the radical movement. I was never meant to be an entrepreneur."

"Probably not."

"I feel some hope," Lustgarten shyly said. "And then also, it's getting to be spring." He was wearing his heavy moose-colored bristling hat, and bore many other signs of interminable winter. A candidate for resurrection. An opportunity for the grace of life to reveal itself. But perhaps, Mosby thought, a man like Lustgarten would never, except with supernatural aid, exist in a suitable form.

"Also," said Lustgarten touchingly, "this will give Trudy time to reconsider."

"Is that the way things are with you two? I'm sorry."

"I wish I could take her with me, but I can't swing that with the Yugoslavs. It's sort of a V.I.P. deal. I guess they want to affect foreign radicals. There'll be seminars in dialectics, and so on. I love it. But it's not Trudy's dish."

Steady-handed, Mosby on his patio took ice with tongs, and poured more mescal flavored with *gusano de maguey*—a worm or slug of delicate flavor. These notes on Lustgarten pleased him. It was essential, at this point in his memoirs, to disclose new depths. The preceding chapters had been heavy. Many unconventional things were said about the state of political theory. The weakness of conservative doctrine, the lack, in America, of conservative alternatives, of resistance to the prevailing liberalism. As one who had personally tried to create a more rigorous environment for slovenly intellectuals, to force them to do their homework, to harden the categories of political thought, he was aware that on the Right as on the Left the results were barren.

Absurdly, the college-bred dunces of America had longed for a true Left Wing movement on the European model. They still dreamed of it. No less absurd were the Right Wing idiots. You cannot grow a rose in a coal mine. Mosby's own Right Wing graduate students had disappointed him. Jut a lot of television actors. Bad guys for the Susskind interview programs. They had transformed the master's manner of acid elegance, logical tightness, factual punctiliousness, and merciless laceration in debate into a sort of shallow Noël Coward style. The real, the original Mosby approach brought Mosby hatred, got Mosby fired. Princeton University had offered Mosby a lump sum to retire seven years early. One hundred and forty thousand dollars. Because his mode of discourse was so upsetting to the academic community. Mosby was invited to no television programs. He was like the Guerrilla Mosby of the Civil War. When he galloped in, all were slaughtered.

Most carefully, Mosby had studied the memoirs of Santayana, Malraux, Sartre, Lord Russell, and others. Unfortunately, no one was reliably or consistently great. Men whose lives had been devoted to thought, who had tried mightily to govern the disorder of public life, to put it under some sort of intellectual authority, to get ideas to save mankind or to offer it mental aid in saving itself, would suddenly turn into gruesome idiots. Wanting to kill everyone. For instance, Sartre calling for the Russians to drop A-bombs on American bases in the Pacific because America was now presumably monstrous. And exhorting the Blacks to butcher the Whites. This moral philosopher! Or Russell, the Pacifist of World War I, urging the West to annihilate Russia after World War II. And sometimes, in his memoirs—perhaps he was gaga—strangely illogical. When, over London, a Zeppelin was shot down, the bodies of Germans were seen to fall, and the brutal men in the street horribly cheered, Russell wept, and had there not been a beautiful woman to console him in bed that night, this heartlessness of mankind would have broken him utterly. What was omitted was the fact that these same Germans who fell from the Zeppelin had come to bomb the city. They were going to blow up the brutes in the street, explode the lovers. This Mosby saw.

It was earnestly to be hoped—this was the mescal attempting to invade his language—that Mosby would avoid the common fate of intellectuals. The Lustgarten digression should help. The correction of pride by laughter.

There were twenty minutes yet before the chauffeur came to take the party to Mitla, to the ruins. Mosby had time to continue. To say that in September the Lustgarten who reappeared looked frightful.

He had lost no less than fifty pounds. Sun-blackened, creased, in a filthy stained suit, his eyes infected. He said he had had diarrhea all summer.

"What did they feed their foreign V.I.P.s?"

And Lustgarten shyly bitter—the lean face and inflamed eyes materializing from a spiritual region very different from any heretofore associated with Lustgarten by Mosby—said, "It was just a chain gang. It was hard labor. I didn't understand the deal. I thought we were invited, as I told you. But we turned out to be foreign volunteers of construction. A labor brigade. And up in the mountains. Never saw the Dalmatian coast. Hardly even shelter for the night. We slept on the ground and ate shit fried in rancid oil."

"Why didn't you run away?" asked Mosby.

"How? Where?"

"Back to Belgrade. To the American Embassy at least?"

"How could I? I was a guest. Came at their expense. They held the return ticket."

"And no money?"

"Are you kidding? Dead broke. In Macedonia. Near Skoplje. Bug-stung, starved, and running to the latrine all night. Laboring on the roads all day, with pus in my eyes, too."

"No first aid?"

"They may have had the first, but they didn't have the second."

Mosby thought it best to say nothing of Trudy. She had divorced him.

Commiseration, of course.

Mosby shaking his head.

Lustgarten with a certain skinny dignity walking away. He himself seemed amused by his encounters with Capitalism and Socialism.

The end? Not quite. There was a coda: The thing had quite good form.

Lustgarten and Mosby met again. Five years later. Mosby enters an elevator in New York. Express to the forty-seventh floor, the executive dining room of the Rangeley Foundation. There is one other passenger, and it is Lustgarten. Grinning. He is himself again, filled out once more.

"Lustgarten!"

"Willis Mosby!"

"How are you, Lustgarten?"

"I'm great. Things are completely different. I'm happy. Successful. Married. Children."

"In New York?"

"Wouldn't live in the U.S. again. It's godawful. Inhuman. I'm visiting."

Without a blink in its brilliancy, without a hitch in its smooth, regulated power, the elevator containing only the two of us was going up. The same Lustgarten. Strong words, vocal insufficiency, the Zapotec nose, and under it the frog smile, the kindly gills.

"Where are you going now?"

"Up to *Fortune*," said Lustgarten. "I want to sell them a story."

He was on the wrong elevator. This one was not going to *Fortune*. I told him so. Perhaps I had not changed either. A voice which for many years had informed people of their errors said, "You'll have to go down again. The other bank of elevators."

At the forty-seventh floor we emerged together.

"Where are you settled now?"

"In Algiers," said Lustgarten. "We have a Laundromat there."

"We?"

"Klonsky and I. You remember Klonsky?"

They had gone legitimate. They were washing burnooses. He was married to Klonsky's sister. I saw her picture. The image of Klonsky, a cat-faced woman, head ferociously encased in kinky hair, Picasso eyes at different levels, sharp teeth. If fish, dozing in the reefs, had nightmares, they would be of such teeth. The children also were young Klonskys. Lustgarten had the snapshots in his wallet of North African leather. As he beamed, Mosby recognized that pride in his success was Lustgarten's opiate, his artificial paradise.

"I thought," said Lustgarten, "that *Fortune* might like a piece on how we made it in North America."

We then shook hands again. Mine the hand that had shaken Franco's hand—his that had slept on the wheel of the Cadillac. The lighted case opened for him. He entered in. It shut.

Thereafter, of course, the Algerians threw out the French, expelled the Jews. And Jewish-Daddy-Lustgarten must have moved on. Passionate fatherhood. He loved those children. For Plato this childbreeding is the lowest level of creativity.

Still, Mosby thought, under the influence of mescal, my parents begot me like a committee of two.

From a feeling of remotion, though he realized that the car for Mitla had arrived, a shining conveyance waited, he noted the following as he gazed at the afternoon mountains:

> Until he was some years old
> People took care of him
> Cooled his soup, sang, chirked,

Drew on his long stockings,
Carried him upstairs sleeping.
He recalls at the green lakeside
His father's solemn navel,
Nipples like dog's eyes in the hair
Mother's thigh with wisteria of blue veins.

After they retired to death,
He conducted his own business
Not too modestly, not too well.
But here he is, smoking in Mexico
Considering the brown mountains
Whose fat laps are rolling
On the skulls of whole families.

Two Welsh women were his companions. One was very ancient,
lank. The Wellington of lady travelers. Or like C. Aubrey Smith, the
actor who used to command Gurkha regiments in movies about India.
A great nose, a gaunt jaw, a pleated lip, a considerable mustache. The
other was younger. She had a small dewlap, but her cheeks were round
and dark eyes witty. A very satisfactory pair. Decent was the word.
English traits. Like many Americans, Mosby desired such traits for
himself. Yes, he was pleased with the Welsh ladies. Though the guide
was unsuitable. Overweening. His fat cheeks a red pottery color. And
he drove too fast.

The first stop was at Tule. They got out to inspect the celebrated
Tule tree in the churchyard. This monument of vegetation, intricately
and densely convolved, a green cypress, more than two thousand years
old, roots in a vanished lake bottom, older than the religion of this
little heap of white and gloom, this charming peasant church. In the
comfortable dust, a dog slept. Disrespectful. But unconscious. The old
lady, quietly dauntless, tied on a scarf and entered the church. Her stiff
genuflection had real quality. She must be Christian. Mosby looked into
the depths of the Tule. A world in itself! It could contain communities.
In fact, if he recalled his Gerald Heard, there was supposed to be a
primal tree occupied by early ancestors, the human horde housed in
such appealing, dappled, commodious, altogether beautiful organisms.
The facts seemed not to support this golden myth of an encompassing
paradise. Earliest man probably ran about on the ground, horribly
violent, killing everything. Still, this dream of gentleness, this aspiration
for arboreal peace was no small achievement for the descendants of so
many killers. For his religion, this tree would do, thought Mosby. No
church for him.

He was sorry to go. *He* could have lived up there. On top, of course.
The excrements would drop on you below. But the Welsh ladies were

already in the car, and the bossy guide began to toot the horn. Waiting
was hot.

The road to Mitla was empty. The heat made the landscape beauti-
fully crooked. The driver knew geology, archaeology. He was quite
ugly with his information. The Water Table, the Caverns, the Triassic
Period. Inform me no further! Vex not my soul with more detail. I
cannot use what I have! And now Mitla appeared. The right fork continued to Tehuantepec. The left brought you to the Town of Souls.
Old Mrs. Parsons (Elsie Clews Parsons, as Mosby's mental retrieval
system told him) had done ethnography here, studied the Indians in
these baked streets of adobe and fruit garbage. In the shade, a dark
urinous tang. A longlegged pig struggling on a tether. A sow. From
behind, observant Mosby identified its pink small female opening. The
dungy earth feeding beast as man.

But here were the fascinating temples, almost intact. This place the
Spanish priests had not destroyed. All others they had razed, building
churches on the same sites, using the same stones.

A tourist market. Coarse cotton dresses, Indian embroidery, hung
under flour-white tarpaulins, the dust settling on the pottery of the
region, black saxophones, black trays of glazed clay.

Following the British travelers and the guide, Mosby was going once
more through an odd and complex fantasy. It was that he was dead. He
had died. He continued, however, to live. His doom was to live life to
the end as Mosby. In the fantasy, he considered this his purgatory. And
when had death occurred? In a collision years ago. He had thought it
a near thing then. The cars were demolished. The actual Mosby was
killed. But another Mosby was pulled from the car. A trooper asked,
"You okay?"

Yes, he was okay. Walked away from the wreck. But he still had the
whole thing to do, step by step, moment by moment. And now he
heard a parrot blabbing, and children panhandled him and women
made their pitch, and he was getting his shoes covered with dust. He
had been working at his memoirs and had provided a diverting recollec-
tion of a funny man—Lustgarten. In the manner of Sir Harold Nicolson. Much less polished, admittedly, but in accordance with a certain
protocol, the language of diplomacy, of mandarin irony. However
certain facts had been omitted. Mosby had arranged, for instance, that
Trudy should be seen with Alfred Ruskin. For when Lustgarten was
crossing the Rhine, Mosby was embracing Trudy in bed. Unlike Lord
Russell's beautiful friend, she did not comfort Mosby for the disasters
he had (by intellectual commitment) to confront. But Mosby had not
advised her about leaving Lustgarten. He did not mean to interfere.

However, his vision of Lustgarten as a funny man was transmitted to
Trudy. She could not be the wife of such a funny man. But he *was*, he
was a funny man! He was, like Napoleon in the eyes of Comte, an
anachronism. Inept, he wished to be a colossus, something of a Napoleon
himself, make millions, conquer Europe, retrieve from Hitler's fall a
colossal fortune. Poorly imagined, unoriginal, the rerun of old ideas,
and so inefficient. Lustgarten didn't have to happen. And so he *was*
funny. Trudy too was funny, however. What a large belly she had.
Since individuals are sometimes born from a twin impregnation, the
organism carrying the undeveloped brother or sister in vestigial form—
at times no more than an extra organ, a rudimentary eye buried in the
leg, or a kidney or the beginnings of an ear somewhere in the back—
Mosby often thought that Trudy had a little sister inside her. And to
him she was a clown. This need not mean contempt. No, he liked her.
The eye seemed to wander in one hemisphere. She did not know how
to use perfume. Her atonal compositions were foolish.

At this time, Mosby had been making fun of people.

"Why?"

"Because he had needed to."

"Why?"

"Because!"

The guide explained that the buildings were raised without mortar.
The mathematical calculations of the priests had been perfect. The
precision of the cut stone was absolute. After centuries you could not
find a chink, you could not insert a razor blade anywhere. These geo-
metrical masses were balanced by their own weight. Here the priests
lived. The walls had been dyed. The cochineal or cactus louse provided
the dye. Here were the altars. Spectators sat where you are standing.
The priests used obsidian knives. The beautiful youths played on flutes.
Then the flutes were broken. The bloody knife was wiped on the head
of the executioner. Hair must have been clotted. And here, the tombs
of the nobles. Stairs leading down. The Zapotecs, late in the day, had
practiced this form of sacrifice, under Aztec influence.

How game this Welsh crone was. She was beautiful. Getting in and
out of these pits, she required no assistance.

Of course you cannot make yourself an agreeable, desirable person.
You can't will yourself into it without regard to the things to be done.
Imperative tasks. Imperative comprehensions, monstrous compulsions
of duty which deform. Men will grow ugly under such necessities. This
one a director of espionage. That one a killer.

Mosby had evoked, to lighten the dense texture of his memoirs, a
Lustgarten whose doom was this gaping comedy. A Lustgarten who

didn't have to happen. But himself, Mosby, also a separate creation, a finished product, standing under the sun on large blocks of stone, on the stairs descending into this pit, he was complete. He had completed himself in this cogitating, unlaughing, stone, iron, nonsensical form.

Having disposed of all things human, he should have encountered God.

Would this occur?

But having so disposed, what God was there to encounter?

But they had now been led below, into the tomb. There was a heavy grille, the gate. The stones were huge. The vault was close. He was oppressed. He was afraid. It was very damp. On the elaborately zigzag-carved walls were thin, thin pipings of fluorescent light. Flat boxes of ground lime were here to absorb moisture. His heart was paralyzed. His lungs would not draw. Jesus! I cannot catch my breath! To be shut in here! To be dead here! Suppose one were! Not as in accidents which ended, but did not quite end, existence. *Dead*-dead. Stooping, he looked for daylight. Yes, it was there. The light was there. The grace of life still there. Or, if not grace, air. Go while you can.

"I must get out," he told the guide. "Ladies, I find it very hard to breathe."

ELIZABETH BISHOP

Rainy Season—Sub-Tropics

GIANT TOAD:

I am too big, too big by far. Pity me.

My eyes bulge and hurt. They are my one great beauty, even so. They see too much, above, below, and yet there is not much to see. The rain has stopped. The mist is gathering on my skin in drops. The drops run down my back, run from the corners of my down-turned mouth, run down my sides and drip beneath my belly. Perhaps the droplets on my mottled hide are pretty, like dewdrops, silver on a moldering leaf? They chill me through and through. I feel my colors changing now, my pigments gradually shudder and shift over.

Now I shall get beneath that overhanging ledge. Slowly. Hop. Two or three times more, silently. That was too far. I'm standing up. The lichen's gray, and rough to my front feet. Get down. Turn facing out, it's safer. Don't breathe until the snail gets by. But we go traveling the same weathers.

Swallow the air and mouthfuls of cold mist. Give voice, just once. O how it echoed from the rock! What a profound, angelic bell I rang!

I live, I breathe, by swallowing. Once, some naughty children picked me up, me and two brothers. They set us down again somewhere and in our mouths they put lit cigarettes. We could not help but smoke them, to the end. I thought it was the death of me, but when I was entirely filled with smoke, when my slack mouth was burning, and all my tripes were hot and dry, they let us go. But I was sick for days.

I have big shoulders, like a boxer. They are not muscle, however, and their color is dark. They are my sacs of poison, the almost unused poison that I bear, my burden and my great responsibility. Big wings of poison, folded on my back. Beware. I am an angel in disguise; my wings are evil, but not deadly. If I will it, the poison could break through, blue-black, and dangerous to all. Blue-black fumes would rise upon the air. Beware, you frivolous crab.

STRAYED CRAB:

This is not my home. How did I get so far from water? It must be over that way somewhere.

I am the color of wine, of *tinta*. The inside of my powerful right claw is saffron-yellow. See, I see it now; I wave it like a flag. I am dapper and elegant; I move with great precision, cleverly managing all my smaller yellow claws. I believe in the oblique, the indirect approach, and I keep my feelings to myself.

But on this strange, smooth surface I am making too much noise. I wasn't meant for this. If I maneuver a bit and keep a sharp lookout, I shall find my pool again. Watch out for my right claw, all passers-by! This place is too hard. The rain has stopped, and it is damp, but still not wet enough to please me.

My eyes are good, though small; my shell is tough and tight. In my own pool are many small gray fish. I see right through them. Only their large eyes are opaque, and twitch at me. They are hard to catch, but I, I catch them quickly in my arms and eat them up.

What is that big soft monster, like a yellow cloud, stifling and warm? What is it doing? It pats my back. Out, claw. There, I have frightened it away. It's sitting down, pretending nothing's happened. I'll skirt it. It's still pretending not to see me. Out of my way, O monster. I own a pool, all the little fish that swim in it, and all the skittering waterbugs that smell like rotten apples.

Cheer up, O grievous snail. I tap your shell, encouragingly, not that you will ever know about it.

And I want nothing to do with you, either, sulking toad. Imagine, at least four times my size and yet so vulnerable . . . I could open your belly with my claw. You glare and bulge, a watchdog near my pool; you make a loud and hollow noise. I do not care for such stupidity. I admire compression, lightness, and agility, all rare in this loose world.

GIANT SNAIL:

The rain has stopped. The waterfall will roar like that all night. I have come out to take a walk and feed. My body—foot, that is—is wet and cold and covered with sharp gravel. It is white, the size of a dinner plate. I have set myself a goal, a certain rock, but it may well be dawn before I get there. Although I move ghostlike and my floating edges barely graze the ground, I am heavy, heavy, heavy. My white muscles are already tired. I give the impression of mysterious ease, but it is only with the greatest effort of my will that I can rise above the smallest stones and sticks. And I must not let myself be distracted by those rough spears of grass. Don't touch them. Draw back. Withdrawal is always best.

The rain has stopped. The waterfall makes such a noise! (And what if I fall over it?) The mountains of black rock give off such clouds of steam! Shiny streamers are hanging down their sides. When this occurs, we have a saying that the Snail Gods have come down in haste. *I* could never descend such steep escarpments, much less dream of climbing them.

That toad was too big, like me. His eyes beseeched my love. Our proportions horrify our neighbors.

Rest a minute; relax. Flattened to the ground, my body is like a pallid, decomposing leaf. What's that tapping on my shell? Nothing. Let's go on.

My sides move in rhythmic waves, just off the ground, from front to back, the wake of a ship, wax-white water, or a partly frozen ice floe. I am cold, cold, cold as ice. My blind, white bull's head was a Cretan scare-head; degenerate, my four horns that can't attack. The sides of my mouth are now my hands. They press the earth and suck it hard. Ah, but I know my shell is beautiful, and high, and glazed, and shining. I know it well, although I have not seen it. Its curled white lip is of the finest enamel. Inside, it is as smooth as silk, and I, I fill it to perfection.

My wide wake shines, now it is growing dark. I leave a lovely opalescent ribbon: I know this.

But O! I am too big. I feel it. Pity me.

If and when I reach the rock, I shall go into a certain crack there for the night. The waterfall below will vibrate through my shell and body all night long. In that steady pulsing I can rest. All night I shall be like a sleeping ear.

RICHARD BRAUTIGAN

A Note on the Camping Craze
That Is Currently Sweeping America

As much as anything else, the Coleman lantern is the symbol of the camping craze that is currently sweeping America, with its unholy white light burning in the forests of America.

Last summer, a Mr. Norris was drinking at a bar in San Francisco. It was Sunday night and he'd had six or seven. Turning to the guy on the next stool, he said, "What are you up to?"

"Just having a few," the guy said.

"That's what I'm doing," Mr. Norris said. "I like it."

"I know what you mean," the guy said. "I had to lay off for a couple years. I'm just starting up again."

"What was wrong?" Mr. Norris said.

"I had a hole in my liver," the guy said.

"In your liver?"

"Yeah, the doctor said it was big enough to wave a flag in. It's better now. I can have a couple once in a while. I'm not supposed to, but it won't kill me."

"Well, I'm thirty-two years old," Mr. Norris said. "I've had three wives and I can't remember the names of my children."

The guy on the next stool, like a bird on the next island, took a sip from his Scotch and soda. The guy liked the sound of the alcohol in his drink. He put the glass back on the bar.

"That's no problem," he said to Mr. Norris. "The best thing I know for remembering the names of children from previous marriages, is to go out camping, try a little trout fishing. Trout fishing is one of the best things in the world for remembering children's names."

"Is that right?" Mr. Norris said.

"Yeah," the guy said.

"That sounds like an idea," Mr. Norris said. "I've got to do something. Sometimes I think one of them is named Carl, but that's impossible. My third-ex hated the name Carl."

"You try some camping and that trout fishing," the guy on the next stool said. "And you'll remember the names of your unborn children."

"Carl! Carl! Your mother wants you!" Mr. Norris yelled as a kind of joke, then he realized that it wasn't very funny. He was getting there.

He'd have a couple more and then his head would always fall forward and hit the bar like a gunshot. He'd always miss his glass, so he wouldn't cut his face. His head would always jump up and look startled around the bar, people staring at it. He'd get up then, and take it home.

The next morning Mr. Norris went down to a sporting goods store and charged his equipment. He charged a 9 x 9 foot dry finish tent with an aluminum center pole. Then he charged an Arctic sleeping bag filled with eiderdown and an air mattress and an air pillow to go with the sleeping bag. He also charged an air alarm clock to go along with the idea of night and waking in the morning.

He charged a two-burner Coleman stove and a Coleman lantern and a folding aluminum table and a big set of interlocking aluminum cookware and a portable ice box.

The last things he charged were his fishing tackle and a bottle of insect repellent.

He left the next day for the mountains.

Hours later, when he arrived in the mountains, the first sixteen campgrounds he stopped at were filled with people. He was a little surprised. He had no idea the mountains would be so crowded.

At the seventeenth campground, a man had just died of a heart attack and the ambulance attendants were taking down his tent. They lowered the center pole and then pulled up the corner stakes. They folded the tent neatly and put it in the back of the ambulance, right beside the man's body.

They drove off down the road, leaving behind them in the air, a cloud of brilliant white dust. The dust looked like the light from a Coleman lantern.

Mr. Norris pitched his tent right there and set up all his equipment and soon had it all going at once. After he finished eating a dehydrated beef Stroganoff dinner, he turned off all his equipment with the master air switch and went to sleep, for it was now dark.

It was about midnight when they brought the body and placed it beside the tent, less than a foot away from where Mr. Norris was sleeping in his Arctic sleeping bag.

He was awakened when they brought the body. They weren't exactly the quietest body bringers in the world. Mr. Norris could see the bulge of the body against the side of the tent. The only thing that separated him from the dead body was a thin layer of 6 oz. water resistant and mildew resistant DRY FINISH green AMERIFLEX poplin.

Mr. Norris un-zipped his sleeping bag and went outside with a gigantic hound-like flashlight. He saw the body bringers walking down the path toward the creek.

"Hey, you guys!" Mr. Norris shouted. "Come back here. You forgot something."

"What do you mean?" one of them said. They both looked very sheepish, caught in the teeth of the flashlight.

"You know what I mean," Mr. Norris said. "Right now!"

The body bringers shrugged their shoulders, looked at each other and then reluctantly went back, dragging their feet like children all the way. They picked up the body. It was heavy and one of them had trouble getting hold of the feet.

That one said, kind of hopelessly to Mr. Norris, "You won't change your mind?"

"Goodnight and good-bye," Mr. Norris said.

They went off down the path toward the creek, carrying the body between them. Mr. Norris turned his flashlight off and he could hear them, stumbling over the rocks along the bank of the creek. He could hear them swearing at each other. He heard one of them say, "Hold your end up." Then he couldn't hear anything.

About ten minutes later he saw all sorts of lights go on at another campsite down along the creek. He heard a distant voice shouting, "The answer is no! You already woke up the kids. They have to have their rest. We're going on a four-mile hike tomorrow up to Fish Konk Lake. Try someplace else."

WILLIAM BURROUGHS

From *A Distant Hand Lifted*

A note on the method used in this text

Since work in progress tentatively titled *a distant hand lifted* consists of walky talky messages between remote posts of interplanetary war the cut up and fold in method here used as a decoding operation. For example agent K9 types out a page of random impressions from whatever is presented to him at the moment::street sounds, phrases from newspapers or magazine, objects in the room Ect. He then folds this page down the middle and places it on another page of typewriter messages and where the shift from one text to another is made/marks the spot. The method can approximate walky talky immediacy so that the writer writes in present time : : : : remember/my/messages between remote posts of/exploded star/fold in/distant sky/example agent K9 types out a/distant hand lifted/there on/whatever is presented to him/sad boy speaking/from magasine/this page/filtered back 'adios' and death/message/from his gun/is/buried in sand/hear this dry/walky talky/post erased/"You hear now?"/writer writes in present time/drifting/messages/on a windy street/to scan out your message as it were/said/the operation consisting : : : : : : "You are yourself Mr. Bradly Mr. Martin/of course"/who else?/your first arrest wasn't it?/the point is/

past time whistling/message that *is* you/to scan out your message as it were: : : : : : : *'a distant hand lifted'*/: : : :"You/and I/sad old/ broken film/knife/cough/it lands in/cough/present time/long cough/ decoding arrest/wasn't it? : : : : : : cough/immediacy/cough/empty arteries must tell you/cough/'adios'/who else?/cough/drew Sept 17, 1899 over New York? ? ?

Mr. Bradly Mr. Martin stood there after/the order to drop the atom bomb/wasn't anything to say/house keeper makes a statement/: "hollow/still East Texas afternoon/fried fragments/I wiped away vapor/ looking through the smoke/"

"no feelings/may I venture?/that's *your* Martin/irrevocably committed to/a long/existence/So called/the necessary/uh fabrication organism/to interfere/:we of the nova police/"

"was a boy/I own cops out of Hell/all the Grey Guards"/said Martin softly/a faint odor of/nova/in the air/as it were/summoned/his saddle/ uh belated/there/in/cigarette smoke drifting/no more/peg to hang it on/like where?/"Well, Martin I/tell you just where/I start/: the uh 'public' cooling system under/survey./"

"That's mighty close, Clem/well/I/closed down./"

"may I venture/'Big Red'/because you had no choice? that your/old signal/irrevocably committed to/uh rather special/uh cooling system/: *sizzling there naked that young officer????????????????????????* "I start blind/had no choice/that/pinpoint/existence/sizzling/rays of negation and death/only exist/after the fact of nova"/"Haven't you forgotten / some / harder names / back from Hell? / put down / plain Mr. Jones/or Mr. J/if you prefer/the Inferential Kid/exploded the/uh 'public' cooling system/there/in/cigarette smoke drifting/grey ash of Pluto/blown from/empty sleeve/which is precisely how my/uh presence is/uh belatedly/infered/you???/*officer*???/precisely/to use/ soiled clothes / of / fabrication organism??? / appears / necessary / to / uh flash you the grey/nova/police/lack of you/may infer/belated/a little smarter/clutch/your/parenthetically dying/finger nail of Nagasaki/ light system/Martin/"

"And parenthetically/in all this/my name was/'Fried Fragments'/??? Well? Martin?/Just/no/trials in human beings/you can look any place/ they all went away/no good/no bueno/clom Fliday/" "Big Red?/ please/remember/there naked/that/young/officer/special/uh flashyou understand/from/special/uh/police/no/more/peg/to/hang/it/on/Martin/and parenthetically/a gun/defined/the statement./'Big/'Red'/you are/no/where/you/left/there/naked/that/young/officer/because/you/ had no choice?/that forgotten/boy/cops out/his existence/sizzling/to/ nova?????????????? nova police/sizzling to interfere/in such pain/as it were/summoned/a lot of/harder names/haven't you forgotten/some/ boy/own/cops/out of Hell/now? Add it all/up now/against harder names/from/uh special police/uh/literally/uh/sizzling/parenthetically /to interfere./a young cop drew the curtains.

"nova heat bugging all of us. You know how laws are. Once they start asking questions there's no end to it??????????????????? Few things in my own past I'd just as soon forget."

"You/left/there/naked/that young/officer/*because you had not choice???????????????here*/Ring those screaming fragments: : : : : : : : :/"Mr. Bradley/I/*here/burning/burning*/rockets across the valley/ *whole sky burning*" You call that young officer "Operation Expendable??????????????Servants who did what you you were afraid to do yourself just so many bangs of heavy metal junk????????/"Medics broke out 'the boy who paid'and we all took a shot"/"I may venture that/the/uh/quivering excuse for being/for these/uh/'fire works'/ the/uh/'public cooling system'????????????? " "My confessions have finished off three hardened police inspectors remember?????????????/ memory hit the old detective like a knife/"God/I remember"/(who else?/your first arrest wasn't it?) Just old moonshiners you might say setting on our dead heavy metal ass condensing the cold heavy silver water of exploding stars. dry county you understand/you hear that dry desert?/Just as cool *there* as it is hot *here*. A word to the wise guy.: : : : : : : : : : : : :/buy a Martin Frgididaire/

"Keep the home fires burning because they burn cool blue to me/you remember me? Honest Mart The Working Man's Friend? I pushed the best cap in/New Orleans used to cap it in those days remember? Later it was all packs and a nickle cap strictly from milk sugar, You going to miss me honey/old friend you know/the oldest/A chorous of sincere homosexual foot ball coaches sing: "In the sweet bye and bye"/An old junky selling Christmas seals on North Clark Street/"Fight tuberculosis, folks/cough/lake wind hit the old junky like a knife/The Priest they called him/just an old friend left/between worlds.

"Should auld aquaintance be forgot and never brought to mind??????????????????????????

We'll take a cup of kindness yet for the sake of auld
lang syne/////Bradly stands there in the empty ball
room/"after the ball is over"/under streamers of cold
grey ash

"What an old corn ball. Just hope he can drag it out till I get my
bags packed. Oh, don't bother with all that junk, John. John this is *nova
heat.*"

"Hell, Arch,/message from boy's magasine/drew iron tears down
Pluto's cheek. I don't like welchers, Martin. You pulled an oven in the
wrong company. Chilie house it all up Martin and laugh out a few
more cobble stone streets"/And since you not always remember ash
blown from my sleeve was war and death/Bradly's broken junk of
exploded star/twilight train whistles in a distant sky/cigarette smoke
drifting far away and long ago/a distant hand lifted/there on a windy
street/half buried in sand/sad calm boy speaking here on the farthest
shore/dead stars splash his cheek bone with silver ash/a transitory
magasine filtered back 'adios' and death/The soldier?/to him my
question ???? from his gun distant smoke/from his gun a dusty answer/
half buried in sand/hear this dry desert/blocade exploded/last gun
post erased/You hear now that hideous electric/whisper of/last young
officer/naked/there/screaming/hand lifted/*for you*????????? Blood I
created paid? Martin/clear as the white hot sky/*Don't ever call me
again, Martin*"/

Mr. Bradly Mr. Martin said/the empty room said/the cigarette smoke
behind him said/: : : : : : : : : "You are yourself Mr. Bradly Mr.
Martin who never existed at all/Who else? Your first arrest wasn't it?
Well remember a young cop walking down past time whistling Annie
Laurie twirling his club drew Sept 17, 1899 over New York.

ash/streaking his cheek bones/on the face/"Klinker is dead/Major Ash
is dead."/a silver adios from/this shattered/grey hand/brought/train
whistles to a distant/window/tracks/half buried in sand/on lonely
sidings/blurred/boy speaking here/a million/dead stars splash his cheek
bones/like flint sparks/"18" he said/waiting/in the clinic/on/the name/
Honest Mart/far away pushed the best cap in New Orleans/hands
shaking/a blackened spoon/remember?/'state of vision' he said/in
oriental eyes/a cruel unreasoning hate/you, writer/yes, I can hear
you/might close/the soldier's words/like a knife/feeling for/a distant/
cough/spitting blood/on white steps of the sea wall/wounded street
boy/must tell you/and I/sad old/broken film/giving you my/toy
soldiers/put away/in the haunted attic/see this refuse/Bradley's broken

junk of exploded star/far away/a blackened gun/half buried in sand/ You may infer/my/typewriter/and so/there on/sad old tunes/sad old showmen/peanuts/in 1920 movie/you may infer/books and toys/put away/in the past/waiting the touch/of a distant hand/half buried in sand/twisted coat on a bench/cough/a trail of blood down white steps of the sea wall/knife and empty arteries/must tell you/: : : : "You are yourself 'Mr. Bradly Mr. Martin'/cough/who else?/cough/trailing knife/cough/it lands in an alley/cough/the sea ahead/cough/way long /cough/steps few/cough/Twisted/falls/remember?/your first arrest wasn't it?/: : : : : you never existed at all/He could not choose his own place where the story ended/the appropriate button/past time whistling 'Annie Laurie"/Sept. 17, 1899 over New York/a distant hand lifted.

KEITH COHEN

The Balustrade

This is a street that tries our credulity. A caterpillar truck has just overturned, arching its middle into the air. The neighbors appear. The driver wriggles out unhurt. The rain didn't stop. Frère Lubin flies down the adjacent street, gathering up his skirts several inches below the crotch. The debris is removed.

The tub occupies the far left-hand corner of the *salle de bain*. A shower attachment fits onto the main nozzle, and the shower head is suspended from a plastic hook on the wall by the circular formation at its head. When the door has been closed, a chair is revealed in the near left-hand corner and to its side on the wall three rows of towels hanging vertically. The seat of the chair is made of wicker, while its back consists of three parallel, slightly curved panels. The extreme right side of the room is taken up by a small sink and a large table next to it. Flat and round soaps lie at different points on the ledge at the back of the sink. The plug, attached by a chain just below this ledge, sits near some soap, a little off-center of the drain. At the end of the table nearest the sink, a short circular tin box stands apart from a jumbled assortment of combs, brushes, and stained pink plastic containers. Inside is a kind of mint candy known as pastilles. In the center of the room is a small white rug in the form of an oval.

A war memorial to the Canadian dead. The evanescent and pale petal nymphs, dead wives of the dead soldiers' uncles, would come each year, carrying in their cupped hands the water of the warm Artois. They danced slowly up the steps toward the central statue and stretched out their arms and bent their backs. The white light of the ground lights and the white light of the moon lit up their figures, which, like the statue, glowed in the night. They swarmed across the darkened fields and filled the white pavilion like comets entering a brighter galaxy. At the foot of the statue, they let the water drop, as if from their eyes. Once tired of their fête, the nymphs climbed up the statue and perched themselves all along its giant portions. As they came to rest, they instantly melted into the marble. None of the powerful spotlights had failed to work, none of them faltered.

Thesis is the point to be discussed or, in argument, maintained. It is usually stated in sentences at or near the outset. In logic, it can be an affirmation either to be proved or advanced without proof (a postulate). Otherwise, thesis is often considered a theme, composition, or essay. In such structures as these, thesis, in the sense of the point to be discussed, is conscientiously sought. When it is discovered, it is like a prize or a treasure. In other structures, thesis concerns the absence of thesis. Certain theses, thus, could be the union of two antithetical notions or the assemblage of purposefully bizarre propositions. In general, we come to regard thesis as an essential structure that disappears or denies a duality.

Thus we leave this subject at a most exciting stage of development, when discoveries of moment seem most imminent. The subject will not, as is often feared, flag with our withdrawal; rather, it will lie fallow for a time to rise once again and flourish. It is as though these soldiers guarded the subject, waving their flags one way and another, the colors red, white, and blue equally combined in each flag. Children stop to watch. Some ask what it's about. When they receive no answer, they pass along, seeming to forget. Straight red and yellow tulips wave in the air. A man honks his horn as he comes by in his car. Now the field is empty.

A face appears from behind a slightly opened door on the upper floor of the inner court. Each side of the building is of equal length. The dark court is reached by a large opening on the side bordering the street, past a high gate that is usually left open. To the left, on the ground floor, is the entrance to the upper chambers and to the office. At the far end of the court is another door. Shutters flank the entire length of most of the windows on the second story. Other smaller windows appear here and there along the otherwise uninterrupted inside wall. Ivy covers most of the wall area below the lower windows and stretches in some places up beyond the second panes.

After dinner, the boys would disperse. Some of them, unable, or simply disinclined, to wait any longer, flew up to their bedrooms. The majority, however, made for the streets with equally interesting projects in mind, to find a snack-bar to work behind and take over, to convert swan boats into submarines for the Seine, to have the hat-check girls join the floor show, to call forth all the domes, or to meet their favorite famous man, such as Jean-Jacques Rousseau, in his own street. Then they returned, some having succeeded, some having failed.

While performing the experiment, utmost care was taken that no vital data of the participants should be revealed to the proctors and that similarly no vital data of the plant formations should be revealed to the participants. Different sections of the photographs were ex-amined by each of the participants in succession, who were then asked to check their particular reaction. Results were generated more or less as expected, except for one photographic section that showed the very base of a flower surrounded, where it entered the ground, by dead leaves. The experiment was repeated several times for verification, and always they concluded with the same astounding fact: that women see no stem in it.

Here is the call we had expected. Pedestrians, wandering slowly by the grand gates, stop now and then to look through. Now they sud-denly turn their heads. What passes is not the peace that surpasses understanding, but a bread and pastry truck that seems about to lose its cargo. Tartes aux fraises, tartes aux mirabelles, tartes aux cerises, tartes aux abricots, mille-feuilles, éclairs. Deep in the garden mademoi-selle refuses and monsieur insists. What passes between them is not the peace that surpasses understanding, but a figure like the dove that Gradgeon released from the castle tower early this morning and that Piero della Francesca painted in similar lines.

The grounds are proportioned in the French manner. To each side of the central walkway are rectangular plots, varying in individual area, but corresponding from one side to the other. At certain junc-tions of these plots, patios are located that depict a story or saying in mosaic or surround a small fountain. High hedges are the divisions between sections that are not naturally separated by a narrow path-way. Though in most respects only functional, these hedges are seen to form curves in two places where no other decoration exists. The curving hedges rise up and down and fill these land areas with intricately sculptured designs.

Night fell, and the castle spirits fled into the park. All day they had heard about the mischief carried on by a few of the wood spirits. They searched now through every bower and grove and at last came upon their comrades the wood spirits dancing merrily around a man and a woman who did not move. These two beings seemed frozen at the point of an action. The man, supporting himself with one foot against the stone bench where the woman sat, held one hand toward the woman's bared shoulder which he was an inch from touching. The woman, her hands folded in her lap, directed her head slightly away though her eyes were turned in the direction of the man. The wood spirits, who had seen their chance, transfixed the couple at this moment and waited for the time of day more suitable for the anticipated action. Now they were ready to unloosen their victims' muscles and proceed to watch the fascinating results. They danced furiously around the couple, intoning their magic songs to erase the enchantment. But the man and woman remained immobile. Only the woman's hair changed: it stopped waving in the night breeze. The wood spirits were bewildered and vexed, the castle spirits indignant. In a last fit of frenzy, the wood spirits, begging the castle spirits to join in, threw themselves against the fixed couple. As each spirit smacked against what was now cold marble, it vanished entirely. All that moved was the night breeze.

Out in the fields, Ted goes on with the weed clearance. He performs his duty with a sickle, an instrument consisting of a curved metal blade with a handle fitted onto a tang or some similar projecting shank. The blade, whose sharp edge is on the inner part of the curve, meets each weed at or near its base, depending on the arm-length Ted proportions from his elbows, and cuts cleanly through its width so that the weed falls to the ground. The curvature of this instrument, besides being convenient for the easily repeated motion it permits, is also dangerous, because its proximity to the worker with each circuit of cutting it apt to incur nicks to the lower leg. In such cases, Ted razes the weeds, and the sickle (weed-ax) pecks Ted.

C'est la photo parfaite. I'm keeping it hidden. It's of me and you: I'm beautiful and so are you. You don't know when it was taken—it's exquisite. I don't want you to see it now. But one day you can see it. It's of me and you, une vraie photo.

Inside the church is a replica in miniature of the outside. It appears above the gate-like formation that separates the nave from the transept and altar areas. The spires here include all the careful decoration, the lattice work, the buttressing, of the actual outer walls. The pinnacles are proportionately equidistant from the wall surface, and the ribs, transverse and diagonal, cut across each other to form the same angles. Behind these miniature stone carvings is the empty transept.

At the playground, the children are having a good time. Elyce asks herself one question: Is it right for her to interfere with the game and tell the other children that Ronnie is cheating? The ball flies through the woods and lands at the dead end, from which point it rolls down the street till it comes to the front yard. Dr. Little turns away from Uncle to look at something in the street and then, turning back, says, "You're a father to all the children."

Thanks to the sequence of all things living, we no longer doubt a time in which all was infinity. We look around and suddenly find manholes, chalk dust, lakes, and firing pins. What was once a fence is now a needle, and through that organ of life, the eye, passes a whole masquerade. Behind the most translucent of things, a deep-pitched tuning fork is beginning to vibrate of its own accord. This is magic, though not mysterious.

The backyard of this house was equally grave. Yellow rectangles and greenish circles spread out over the ground as grass. A bleached green hose lay coiled up against the house. Russel continued working on the big hole dug into the bank at the end of the yard marked by barbed wire. The great stone had been removed. He heard the flapping of the screen door, but went on with the digging. The hose had been dragged across the length of the yard. He turned on the spigot, ran to the edge of the pit, and waited. Trees fell in adjacent woods. The water spurted from the hose, and he directed its flow. The hole was filled.

The lighting is blue. This is a temporary museum. The handicapped lady is informative. The statues are polychromatically glazed wood. The windows are long and blue. A virgin and child, chipped cheeks, the butcher, a saint bathing, fingerless, another halo, felony, education, three meters, three musicians, a monocle, incapacity, and early flowers. Out in the square they refer to the fair taking place before their eyes. Another crowd takes over. In smaller streets, shops close down and shadows diminish. These streets, if pulled tight from either end of the town, snap. Ice cream is sold.

And so on through the forests of Fontainebleau. The gods had neither plan nor project. When they reached a sharp ridge that looked out over a dying savannah, they covered themselves with gauze and danced fiercely over the region. When they came to a family picnic, they blew the tires and tilted the land and enchanted the kickball. All around, the trees were full with the syrup of the gods. Bees came to the gods and pricked them one by one over and over, filling their veins with more of the same liquor. The forest became hotter and steamed like jungles. Heaps of pine needles fumed a luxuriant vapor. The bark oozed, and the most delicate of the flowers wilted. It was not that all the people froze into statues and that all the statues came to life. There was none of these. It was just the gods who swept across the arid clearings and through the heavy copses. It was nothing to bend one's belief.

Now you could see as far as Boulevard Richard Wallace. The trees were all flattened. They were cutting them down one by one for the new supermarket. Yellow bulldozers were already leveling some of the hills, and the last tree crashes were drowned out by the roar of the swathed and cushioned machines that stalked here as they had in the front yard the week before in order to take down, chop up, and cart away the unusually thick tree. Just on this side of the barbed wire Uncle was pushing the mower up the embankment of tough weeds. Here and there he was suddenly stopped by too large a clump of weeds. At the spot from which the immense rock had been moved, he pushed the mower freely and let it roll back down as the blades were still spinning. Somewhere in the midst of the action was the spark of a rock hit or of a wire cut.

This is a sky that suggests eyes down. A black road approaches this fence from far in the distance and veers off again. It is slowly covered with snow. Snow is everywhere, and the children's coats, too, lose their coloring. It is as if this fence unfolded with each successive coating of snow. Questions are asked and left in the air like smoke rings. Along the road comes a black limousine. "Madame?" For the window is rolled down, and no snow is getting in. The car stops. " 'Squeek'—that's no name." The fingers of the nun press against the children's necks as she leads them to the car. The snow didn't stop. "That's not a name."

A discussion ensues with the opponents. Is a ball that is relayed just as it touches the boundary line considered "out"? The puff of chalk dust, it is argued first of all, is evidence that the ball did hit the line. There is no doubting that. A lineman of the red team rubs a red sock on the opposite calf in readiness to kick in the out-of-bounds ball. The wooden wagon wheel on which he is obliged to stand slowly sinks in the muddy ditch. The discussion goes on. The umpire is non-committal, and the decision, like a ball, bounces from one side to the other. Questions become exclamations, arguments become threats, diagrams become punches, and victory unconsciousness. The game ends, and the lineman sinks slowly away.

Thus kingdoms expand. A mirror speaks. A song-bird is cut off, and generations of princes celebrate speechlessness. Each end suggests reverie and seriousness, each beginning the same. Each middle is peopled with inter-planetary storms and concepts, which liberal princes generally advocate. We hear that bird universally thought dead and then bear something forth in imitation. Other princes go on advocating these customs like so many clouds, and geese and pigeons squabble in the courtyard. A mirror speaks, saying "The palace shakes." In the tumult that follows, the mirror is shattered and the entire kingdom swallowed up.

Elyce stands up among the trees and the children who form a large circle around her and says, "This is no game for the sake of anything you could have horses for or singing bobsleds in a pinch I want to make it clear whatever you go on to do in sequence after sequence a game or the idea of a game always to promote good cheer among future children explaining why dust and locust filled the air one summer without rules but just to stick to what you're told and re-member to connect up the one half that goes with the other to play the way that makes good never crossing but repeating even forever when necessary or blue fingers make you scared or cold as I do such things myself not for anyone's sake near the water tower when they leave the gate open but to continue a kind of multiplication table that gets to two and three digits after pulling your pants up you think up a higher form and remember a sweeter sound."

Deep in the gardens mademoiselle unbends and monsieur relaxes. One recalls a group of little elves, the other the branches. Not very far away the ground slopes down sharply. A fat pot hangs over a dead fire. Above, the trees seem to reign over the clouding sky. They had shed all their leaves during the night. A garden gate falls over. Some-body has picked it up, or rather, somebody must have, for it is back in place. And the castle: mademoiselle walks slowly again through the first seven chambers of the western wing, hoping this time to reach an eighth; monsieur again lets down the bridge over the moat and watches the rabbits hop away on the far bank.

The castle has not always been this way. Here warriors died inside heavy metal and under red and yellow flags. Over here some ruler decreed on what is now fragmented paper. Down here some poet hid from the rest of the court. It is as though these things made the castle, but of course these things appeared only as a result of the castle. Tapestries were hung out and made to graze the tips of grass. Flagons were filled and emptied with the regularity of rain. Blade edges were shined and sharpened on a kind of stationary stone. Satin cushions were depressed under elbows that supported fingers plucking the strings of lyres. It is as though these things died away as a result of the castle, but of course these things possessed an intrinsic end. At night torches glided over the pathways, their flames beating against the air. Gauze draperies puffed out beyond the windows and flew over the balconies. The blare of the great dining hall horns seemed to have a counterpart in the depth of the woods. Then, as if in the same chambered flower bed under the same arbor, Gradgeon released the dove, and Regalo looked through a tiny piece of curved glass, and new blood was shed in the Red Sea.

Mademoiselle walks slowly again through the first seven chambers of the western wing. As usual, off several of the chambers, she passes small anterooms whose entry is barred. In the first of these anterooms, the King has just been killed. He lies on the black-and-white tiled floor in a pool of blood. There is no bed, but only a dark oven and a hearth and a window whose shutters, like saloon doors, are swinging back and forth in smaller and smaller arcs, though never stopping. Another anteroom leads into a long narrow passageway that the Queen is backing down. Her hands sporadically fly up into the air above her. The further down she goes, the closer she seems to falling back against a wall or onto the floor. In another of the barred anterooms two knights divest themselves of their mail. Wearing only Maltese crosses around their necks, they set to polishing a coat of armor posed in the center of the room. They begin at the feet and vigorously work up to the empty helmet, climbing onto the shoulders when necessary. As the armor gets more and more brilliant, it begins to move, leading the knights by the slow action of its limbs. It then moves more quickly and in long steady sweeps, as the two knights begin gradually to disappear, first the feet, then upwards to the head. In another anteroom a friar steps from a bathtub onto a small white rug in the form of an oval. He takes from a tin box on the table several small pieces of candy. He returns to the tub, and, once having finished the candies, steps out again and goes back over to the table. Off the seventh chamber is an anteroom from which music issues. In the center of the room is a huge circular bed surrounded by torches. To one side of the bed is a tall-backed straight chair with a dark velvet covering, and to the other side is a chair with a deep cushion whose back, in the form of an undulated shell, curls back at its greatest height. Here mademoiselle stops and goes no further.

Monsieur again lets down the bridge over the moat. From the center of the area that many rabbits suddenly quit, a small jester rises, crosses the moat, and enters the Great Hall where he calls forth his actors. The two Kings confer. The Prince approaches them naked and then assumes his royal robes. One hands him a scepter, the other a sword. They prompt him with his lines and all goes well. There follows a procession down the Great Hallway that leads to the dining hall. Members of the courts and clowns participate. At the end of the passage the Prince sits down between two princesses who are engaged in conversation. He speaks to one, the more slender of the two, who turns and lowers her eyes to the ground. He then places his lips against her cheek and holds them there for a moment. In the Great Feast Room the wines and meats are spilling over the tables. The Prince awakens aside of the slender princess and goes to the jester for refreshment. The jester tells the Prince to get the cheeses from the kitchen. The cheeses are huge and slippery, and the Prince must grasp them securely against his chest. He manages to prevent them from sliding over the limits of his arms as he returns through the long dank hallways. The foundation arches deepen as the hallways turn into the Feast Room, and within the compartments thus formed, shielded by the series of columns that outlines the hall, are small musical ensembles, jack-in-the-boxes, card games, and giant picture books. Monsieur draws up the bridge whose clanks echo throughout the lower castle.

This is a climb that defies our stamina. Frère Lubin gave two beeps on his horn—*pour sauler*—and drove on toward Gèrardmer. The pinball machines light up and clack by themselves. Soon the rain will get heavier. The telepherique wires shine like so many uncoiled pinball rebounders, and no one feels safe about taking a ride. The red earth sends its drippings down the mounting roadway. The mountain remains stationary.

When the bottle is broken, its contents spread through the table cloth. The breaking is instantaneous, the spreading gradual. Even after the glass remnants of the bottle seem empty, the tinted surfaces continue to pale and the stain borders continue, as in time-lapse photography, to push out over the cloth. It is as though this continent were ruled by a maniac, shattered by the lay of the land and labeled a nothing. And it is as though this maniac-King were actually ruled by the tide, forever extending his empire involuntarily. And it is as though his castle were whole, untouched, and far away. Several pieces of the bottle hang onto the moistened label, which remains intact as part of the unbroken base. When these are pulled away, like scabs, from the label, they are, though still sharp, rather clouded by the thin glue applied long before.

A farm passes by, and still it is not clear about the owner of this region. Fresh milk can be gotten at the farm, and chocolate can be added if desired. All around are deep ravines and sharp cliffs. The only workers are the cows. Flies hover nearby as witnesses. The milk is warm. Soon the day will be over, and a fresh question will arise. The first star passes by.

Animus is the animating or actuating spirit; in Latin, simply the mind. In a less specific way, it refers to the disposition or intention to do something. Traditionally, this disposition or intention is always very strong. For this reason, the term animus has also come to denote a feeling of hostility or hatred, resulting, for example, when the original animus is countered or challenged. Such animi resist most salves, whether in the form of materials or of love. Sometimes, however, a well-meaning animus, in the original sense, satisfies the sorest animi.

At the center of the house, Uncle sinks back in a livingroom easy chair to doze. He meant to call up about going back to the city but forgot. His drivers have come anyway, or else have just stopped by on their way. The funny lady they visited in the house had never been seen there before. She wore an old print dress that had a tie around the waist and bareheeled slippers. When she asked Uncle for some extra molding, he searched under all the cabinets. Though there was no molding, there were many other things:

    two sets of rewinds
    paper cups
    rough planks
    busted light bulbs
    three half-used paint cans: gray, cream, and white
    Elyce and Russell
    sealing tape
    Contact ("Pennsylvania Dutch")
    a broken hair drier

Uncle finally felt anxious about the city departure and knew that all the presents being carried up and down the steps were for the children. One is always in the process of getting dressed in such instances. The presents were explicitly marked for Uncle. He thought the people

would never get to the living room. And once they were there and
had gotten their coats, he could only lead them out to the front yard.
He leaned with one hand against the lawn mower as they left.

Out in the woods, Elyce is thinking of the bedroom. There she tells
about another house, different from this one. It was Elyce's first house,
a house of foreigners. There were so many people that some had to
sleep outside in the back yard. And since they had no clothes, they
slept naked, a man and a woman in each sleeping bag. They were the
first people to have moved into the neighborhood, and they'd brought
with them a black dog. They loved the dog so much that they took
movies of it every day. But one day the dog wandered into a tunnel
constructed for the subway, which was having a trial run in the
neighborhood before going to the city. When the train came along,
the dog was scooped up by the front car. The train continued through
a maze of tunnels, nosing up and down, swerving right and left. Eventually, it came out of the ground onto a trestle that ran alongside a
river. Then the black dog was thrown off the train and into the river.
Elyce asks Russell one question: Was it right for them not to be
allowed to watch the movies they had taken of the black dog?

Out in the fields, Ted tightens the shank of the sickle. It has taken
him so long to return from the tool shed that it is now almost dark
and snow is imminent. He is annoyed to have lost valuable working
time, but it was imperative that he get the first-aid kit from the tool
shed to bandage his nicked leg. He had lost his way when he headed
back and couldn't find the exact spot where he had left off working.
Instead, he came to an asphalt roadway that led through the woods to
a fenced-in area. There, a boy and girl were playing together. Ted
didn't get close enough to recognize the faces of the children, since
he knew by this time that he was way off track. As he turned back
down the roadway, trucks were being stopped and asked to contribute
to local charities. Ted wandered through the fields and finally spotted
his pitchfork leaning against a heavy, low-branched tree. Nearby were
his sickle and the fading line of uncut weeds. Now they are slowly
covered with snow. Snow is everywhere, and Ted's face, too, loses
its coloring. He has barely gotten up from under the branches before
he goes inside.

The hole in the backyard is filled with water, and now the pro-
duction can begin. Russell directs his actors through the air. The
Queen soon lies slain on the ground. Russell approaches the embankment at the end of the yard and, as he falls down on it, delivers his
main line: "I am the cruelest man." Lying there in the loose dirt, he
worries about remembering the rest of his lines. He had pressed the

buzzer and was climbing up the stairway in Elyce's apartment building because she hadn't been at the door to meet him. As he wondered if he'd like to live in a place like this, the steps became carpeted. This flight led to Elyce's apartment, but Russell decided to go back down and wait for her at the door. On one landing that he passed he noticed a straight-edged razor blade. When he got to the stoop, Elyce and all their friends were there waiting. Over the intercom Elyce's mother repeated the same question over and over: "Why didn't you come all the way up?"

This is a factory that threatens the sky. The little managers are conferring on the lawn. What was yesterday's quota? Which way is the Quai d'Orléans? Slowly the sprinkler shoots its streams to the south and to the north. One of the managers points with his cigar. Other sprinklers begin to sway. Somewhere the grass was licked. Along the sidewalk stand sparkling plastic letters ten feet high: RENAU and so on. The blue bricks are scraped of their soot, and the white windows fog up.

When the green lights go on, not only are the branches and leaves given new luster, but also the ceiling of the night sky realizes a different height. The dust in the air passes in pensive sheets. Each leaf, as it waves, reveals the now sharply shadowed veins of its underside. Its tips are patterned perfectly against the tree trunk, and the ruined rocks pale at the spectacle. It is as though some urchin child were shining a flashlight at his most recent bit of mischievousness. And it is as though the act itself were quaking from exposure. And it is as though everyone else looked on approvingly or else aesthetically. The atmosphere is thick. The trees respond to more breeze than there is.

The horses enter the simulated park by way of the cobblestone pathways. Their hoofs resound against the Roman ruins that rise in front, as they gallop among the background trees. When the green lights come up their riders are revealed. These are the ghosts from Roman times disguised as German knights of the Middle Ages. They swarm across the lighted area, screaming and gesticulating toward the hill as if women, agoras, temples, and tribunals were all there. The great Prince approaches them and turns them all into rock. He enters the cave thus formed and loses his way forever.

Most important in this study is the question of color intensification. Dr. Little reports that the participants in the experiment repeatedly note that the color red, for example, gets brighter as successively greater amounts of heat are directed at it. (He goes on to prove a corresponding theory that actual intensification of a color generates greater heat, which can be measured tactually.) Nevertheless, scientists hold to the incontestable fact that additions of heat do not change, in any detectable way, the molecular composition of the light rays that make up the color. Tests have even been conducted in association with Dr. Little where the samples to which the participants react are measured as the heat is added. According to the marks on the response sheets, the red shades consistently grow brighter with greater additions of heat. The problem remains: must we offer a thesis of fact or read that the reds intensify?

Across from this funeral the artists have arranged an open-air show. Many of the paintings are hung from trees by wire, and others are set up on artificial easels. The artists lie down on rugs they have brought with them. Under the ground the dead man is cool. It is as if these pall bearers and holy men were preparing to launch an artistic career, fingering dust and watching the sway of new canvases. Little bands of children stray from the art show and stand on the edge of the road watching the funeral. A woman calls to her son to come and see a picture. Little girls ask what it's about. Straight red and yellow tulips, like so many girls or so many paintings, wave in the air.

At the central station art lovers from all around fill the platforms as they transfer to the train that will take them to their favorite part of the exhibition. Ladies with wide-brimmed hats crowd in front of the information kiosk to the point of obstructing the view, so that others must squeeze between them and stoop under the railing to get a look at the list.

Oils	Forest line
Watercolors	Sun lake line
Pen and Ink	Central pool local
Sculpture: marble	West hill roundabout
Sculpture: plaster	Lawn elevator
Sculpture: metal	Tower express
Sculpture: "furniture"	Highway local
Collages	Fruit and grain elevator
Constructions: wood	Insect line
Constructions: metal	Dome passage
Constructions: plastic	Refreshment-stand express

Lines grow before the elevators that carry the people from level to level. Trains puff slowly over the greens and under the bridges and into the woods. Various colored flagstones stipple the lawns and parks, leading the visitors on special tours. Here the pathway passes a brook where a car factory has been constructed out of inflated plastic. Here the pathway crosses metal grass. Another pathway leads to where some artist is lying.

A man honks his horn as he comes by in his car. At the same time, he swerves and just misses hitting several children who are on the point of crossing the road. The children wander back to the paintings. The man, lifting his right arm slightly into the air, turns toward the back seat and, with his lips curled, says something to the three people sitting there. It is at this moment that the car crashes. It runs head-long into a tree trunk, that makes up part of the art-show border, and bursts into flames. Leaves and bodies ignite. People from all over the countryside gather around and shade their sparkling eyes with saluting hands.

The helicopters came to bring first-aid supplies. They leveled off slowly, maneuvering between the trees of the countryside. Their soft whirring stopped only when their flat landing supports were planted firmly on the ground. From among the mass of onlookers, several artists stepped forth to unload the supplies and to perform the immediate surgery required. They devoted their entire energies to this delicate task. Women called to their children to come away. Holy men carefully crossed the road. Much of the surgery was performed, and many of the unlucky passengers remained alive for awhile, but by the time the helicopters, like so many balloons or so many ghosts, rose up slowly over the trees, the last of the victims died. They were raised forthwith on canvas stretchers and carried across the road where the prematurely abandoned funeral was taken up again. The holy men and pall bearers, rising to the occasion, gave out careful directions and managed the burials. The artists returned to their canvases. The people and the tow-truck moved slowly away from the charred tree. Not long before the sun set, the last special express pulled off for the central station. Now the field was empty.

This is a city that spreads its sensation, belonging indoors, out to every structure. It is Friday, the day of departure. Clouds gang together from peak to peak and hang still, as if suspended from the Haute Ecole de Meteorologie. Picnickers lie down on their checkered cloths. They are wearing watch bands of camouflage canvas, which fade into the landscape perfectly. Desserts are bought from the eighteen shops that dot the city's straight streets. The rain didn't stop. One of the picnickers, a blond girl whose name sounds like glazed pears, motions toward something and says, "These are Caesar's." The sound that repeats itself in the distance reminds one of the "mysteries" of the Isère, which makes more than one street bend. Another of the picnickers, a young man with glasses and a nose to support them, looks up and says, "Is it really six o'clock?" It is. A third, a poet who is eating a chicken leg, says, "Richesse, mon oncle, quelle est la vraie saison?" They are all sacrificed to the city. On the opposite mountain, signals are exchanged between two outposts.

It was certain that there would be a window opened. Near that window, apart from the leaning shelves, the concave ground, and the broken tea cups, there was a photograph of a blond girl pinned to the wall. The smile on her face was so candid that, like panoramic travel posters, it seemed to make a hole in the wall that it lay against. When the two of them, late at night, came through the window, they landed on the oil-stained linoleum floor almost soundlessly. The Danish girl in the photograph, if she was there, took them for officials. They had what they wanted and then left just as quickly, though not by the window. The impression that remained, both in the wall and in the mind, was one of murder, rape, and deceit. Off in the distance of the photograph, another figure was discovered that resolved whatever mystery there was. The Dane was again seen at Bellegarde.

The lake spirits, with the sun, leak slowly away from the Lac de Paladru to join their friends the river spirits. The rectangles that command the area, the mooring station, the Place de Verdun, the Place Victor Hugo, and the public swimming pool, are, for a moment, all the same. Then the water changes, and the first legions of lake spirit soldiers, to the river spirits, appear. By the time all the lake spirits, the bridegroom's entourage, have assembled near the mooring stations, the lake prince and the river princess are next to each other and surrounded by musicians. Currents encircle their heads. The kings and queens gather together in front of the couple and, touching their scepters all at once, the river stops flowing. Up and down the shores, the reeds freeze and the moist earth dries up. Wooden piers cake. Foam disappears. The prince and princess then are joined, and the river comes to life again. The spirits disperse, the lake spirits returning upstream, and the mooring station brightens.

This is the season's end of dull sensations. Inward the blade has fallen, and the wires have criss-crossed. Money collects at every aperture and clogs the motion. Broken white lines divide the avenues of insubordinance; acquiescence crosses minds everywhere. What was once most resented is now resented and cherished; what was most at odds is corrupt and congruent. A certain height is attained on this mountain, and the clouds vanish. Here on the table some bread sits, insatiable. Lands end and will not ever restructure.

As the moderator draws to a conclusion, Dr. Little leafs hurriedly through the stack of papers he has with him. Graphs and diagrams fly by in the dim light of the auditorium wings. He now reshuffles several sets of these papers. He begins going through them from the top one by one, as if counting them, but stops after a dozen or so. He looks around him, under the chair, near the thick wires. He checks his pockets and brief case. The moderator backs up from the lectern and carefully makes his way down the small steps to its side. It is at this moment that someone approaches Dr. Little, says something smiling, and guides him toward the entry to the stage. Dr. Little places his pile of papers and his small notebooks on the lectern and consults his watch. Graphs and diagrams are mounted across the air. The audience looks.

"Experiments were then performed by raising and lowering patients, while they were sleeping. Of course, these patients would be informed about the operating of the experiment before they went to sleep. They were shown a short film that depicted the elevator mechanism, the mirror arrangement between sleeping room and data room, and the various instruments that were set up on very sensitive tripods around each bed. In several cases, technicians actually entered the sleeping rooms to measure with small, intricate instruments, such things as ear pressure and muscle tone. They were all fed the same special meals during twenty-four hours in our own cafeteria. In short, all variables were scrupulously kept to a minimum. The results were, in general, that lowering seemed most often to suggest to the patient's dream undressing or embarrassment resulting from some kind of immodesty. Raising, on the other hand, usually meant being threatened by some unnameable source and often choked. Some patients, however, did not reflect in the slightest way these movements during their hours of sleep. While most whose dreams were affected said that they remembered being aware of some motion during the night, these others claimed to remember no such movements. What is remarkable is that most of these latter cases did nonetheless have peculiar dreams. Their dreams characteristically included all the elements of the experiment, but as they actually existed (as they saw them in the film) and not as the patients were affected by them. One patient, for example, saw many of his friends in an elevator. He was asked by an important person about a broken mirror and went to the other side of town to borrow a tripod. The overwhelming anxiety that marks such dreams as these, according to the patients, is having to recall accurately the effects of the experiment."

Definition is the explanation of a meaning or the formulation of this meaning. It is used for words, concepts, and processes, and is one of the basic operations in scientific deduction. Definition is also the act or power of making clear or of bringing into sharp relief. In this sense, we refer, for example, to the distinctness of outline in a picture as good definition. In most cases, however, the goodness or badness of definition cannot be measured by visual clarity. Definitions of words, for example, depend on the accuracy and forethought with which they are composed. They also depend on which meaning of the word is being treated. Some people think that a particular definition, whether accurate or imperfect, predicts and forms the whole process that follows. Others think that any definition, no matter how composed, may either reveal an already existing meaning or else imply a meaning that altogether alters the underlying idea.

DATA REPORT

The major part of these results have, of course, never heretofore been published. I must therefore begin by thanking all those assistants, technicians and patients who made the experiments possible. Never before have we come up with such singularly revealing results. Probably the most significant aspect of these results is the manner in which they give us insights into the sleeping man. All the doors are wide open now. There is more room for expansion and exploration than ever before. For man is not always a particularly mobile and sensate animal—at least not always in the same way. Each time he sleeps he enters a new world of motion which he has created for himself. External motion has been seen in these experiments to be often important in sleep behavior, though not always in dream content. Variations in

CONFESSION

Heretofore where do four lost papers from the major part graphed data cycles of repitition indications of tardy schedules the train was therefore—thanking the Negro woman technical probability getting it getting run over getting it assist me possibility reveal dark—the popsicle wrapper is it probably written without ancestors leading to a different sight the bridal veil and the ear examiner what I see naked or posing is it in—what I think wider elevator shifts before fudged data mechanism new areas withdrawal swimming sighting watching in mirrors walking tasting gaining access the same cafeteria never before floor never before food never before world into long-distance moving pianos shoulders clocks tripods setting up model room in the sleeping room naked is it in the ear hears behavior signs of pos-

physiological processes cannot always accurately describe the interior world the sleeping man is experiencing. Rather, this world becomes the ruler of the body and, in many cases, of the mind as well.

ing to be content pose naked sublimations contortion on the carpet interior search "checking" pays the movers finds out pays "publishing" other reports world diagram how big lay the graphs discover the pages "inventing" for train screw find.

We are the ones that were found here. All over the red rocks, all through the jasmin crop, all over the road. The girls were going only to a nearby lake which was well known. The boys were going down to the seashore. The sun questioned both groups, approaching from behind. Deep in the cool water the coral formations crossed, and there were bubbles around them. Each jasmin bloom, like a small planet that turns slowly, swayed in the wind. Each is plucked. They have met here, the girls who were found on the main square buying garlic and the boys who checked each of the sea-front hotels for employment, to pick the crop. We are the ones to hold out each basket and to wait for its slow load. From deep in the middle of the house the cry of breakfast is heard. Then they will leave, the girls returning to the seaside restaurant for fried fish and the boys to the station for the Paris train.

The meadows grow silent. A face appears again in an upstairs window of the police station that hugs the edge of a road. "The base of my right shoe broke." Near the bright sand concrete of the new locks under construction a man quietly puts his melon crop out for sale. There are sharp knives. At the waterfall young girls are drinking. It is the waterfall by the old Roman aqueduct. "The base of my right shoe broke." Metal cylinders are ground into shape, files line the deck. The sun, still bright, dries up the discarded melon seeds. Other melons split open wide. A large shadow covers over the police station, and the long grass bends. A face reappears. The gleaming locks are checked, first tightened, then unloosened.

At the furthest reach of the argument, a specific concern, a central point even, was discovered. It had not been previously hidden, but merely prepared for with great elaboration and minute explication. It was as if these houses, built by various city people who could afford a summer home, outlined this point and cultivated it and made it habitable. Children played on the beaches at the edges of the point, as well as on the playgrounds of the grassy middle strips. Once when

the ball flew from the playground down the street to the front yard,
Dr. Little turned back to Uncle, saying, "You're a father to all the
children." For most of the year, however, the point was without
people. For months the sun was never hot on the red rocks, and the
coral grew dull. The grass, for some time at least, would become
weeded and wild and eventually overgrow all its boundaries. The point
was of course attached to the mainland, but often at this time thick
fogs mounted from the sea in such a way that the mainland was in-
distinguishable or else seemed very remote. The houses remained
there, shut up, and occasionally a falling limb would break a window.
This and other such anonymous incidents were easily reckoned with
once the people returned and set up house again for a small portion of
the year. They set at once to gardening and mending. They took
great pride in their land segments on the point and helped each other
to maintain them. It was as if they were making a point of giving an
overall impression of fine cultivation, a concern that would require
many related queries and counterarguments.

And then a screen is a partition or curtain that cuts off incon-
venience, injury, or danger. Sometimes it is almost entirely opaque,
such as when made of a meshed fabric and used to separate coarser
from finer parts. At other times it is simply some sort of protective
barrier whose material may be a perforated plate or the more elaborate
criss-crossing of wood or metal segments. In the case of metal screen-
ing, long sheets of very regular meshing are often manufactured to
be fitted into a wooden doorframe, which acts as an outer door. This
frame is painted white and half-way up its length has a simple metal
latch, which is released by the hand of Mademoiselle, who, in doing
so, steps out onto the sunny patio. The extremities of the patio cannot
be seen because of the thick heat, and, as she lets the screen-door go
and proceeds across the cement, Mademoiselle similarly loses sight
of the castle walls. The wind off the sea blows some of the heat at her;
she turns toward the sea, which is also at present invisible, and then
goes on. She advances to where some high hedges, a sort of barrier
between the patio and the marshes, are providing shade. At the other
end of the patio Monsieur lies out on a long cushioned chair. The sun
starts setting, and the air is filled with heavy red colors. Monsieur's
chair forms a long shadow that starts expanding across the patio
toward Mademoiselle. All around the woods darken and the bogs
humidify and the castle fades.

They have now all descended. The air between objects drums with
them. Minor stratospheres are built up above the grass, above the pave-

ments, above the water. The sea spirits roll in slowly with the fog that thickens over the beaches. The river spirits splash higher and higher as the currents lash out. The lake spirits rise across the rays of reflected light. The marsh spirits dive between high stalks and floating blossoms. The forest spirits buzz around the branches and load the pathways through the thick trunks. The field spirits form informal regiments in a billowing patchwork. The castle spirits hover over lattices and around turrets. The statue spirits reverberate with the white glow of the marble. They have all descended; at last they have a project. Enchantment and excitation are now old habits, and trickery is set aside for the moment. They cover every realm, and, with their infinite powers of measurement, will extract the pattern of nature. Now as the sun starts setting and the ground seems everywhere to have just been pounded across by a single speeding horse and the oceans seem set to boil by the fires at the pit of the earth, a universal pulse is taken. The spirits fan out and record. They exist, like a tuning fork, around and in-between each thing. They intersect and separate.

For a long time the spirits had been developing this project. They had extraordinary powers, of course, from the very beginning, but they were manifested, like a firecracker, in every direction at once without covering the widest of ranges. They wanted to be everywhere at the same time, and in a sense, they were. But they could never coordinate all their effects and observations. So they decided to take hold of their powers and to direct them with a purpose. At first there were arguments as to what their purpose was, but then they agreed that it was total, uncompromising report of nature that they sought. They figured that, by taking precise stock of their strength, they would be able perpetually to reflect the odd sense of being that they experienced all around them.

Thus did these discriminations prove interesting. Trees bent against the forces of the wind. Bricks were cemented in more or less straight lines. Songbirds sang out in the night, and people were observed listening to them. Mirrors reflected faces, objects, and actions. Princes shifted scepters. Blacktops slowly caved in. Large machines oozed specks of grease at their joints. The land expanded and retracted. And above all, there was nothing to bend one's belief. But before very long, the spirits grew tired of sensing and knowing everything around them. Their infinite intersections and separations were exquisite but, like a molecular catalogue, already explored. Their work, in its extreme closeness, became, just as they had expected, entirely patterned, and, as if owing to it, nothing ever went wrong. This made it seem at the beginning that the spirits were in control of something magnificently balanced, but actually they were simply noting it.

The spirits fan out and record. The pattern rises and reduplicates, like so many wave lengths of sound or of light. Deep within the bonded structure of their operations and far outside the gigantic manifestation of their total activity, all goes well. But slowly the spirits are developing another project, a project that entirely supercedes their previous one. Their functioning has become almost automatic, and now they relax and direct their attention to what they are actually doing from moment to moment. They suddenly recall their rash, splendid beginning, their remarkable power poured into everything around them. They get drunk with themselves and their manipulations. It is as though some generator were operated like a planet on the quantum-reversal rule. And it is as though the turning cranks, like so many irritated people, started coming to life all at once. And it is as though each revolution provoked an impression of disintegration, though nothing ever changed. Tapestries, statues, and clocks all confer with the spirits. The perfect-pitched tuning fork suggests a thousand tones, each of which is rejected, though not unheeded.

ROBERT CREELEY

The Unsuccessful Husband

Such a day of peace it was, so calm and quiet, with the haze at the window, beginning, and from there going far out over the fields to the river beyond, a morning haze, such as the sun soon burns and has done with. Yet all through that day there was quiet and the haze of calm. It was not the first of many such days. None followed. But it became the reminder of something somewhat better than what one had, the stasis of peace, which, once found, can always remind one and even be found again. Such a day, a peaceful day, so calm and quiet, one is never done with, no matter how long . . .

We were married fifteen years ago at a quiet ceremony attended by a very few people, close friends, and following the ceremony we travelled to a place where I had not been since my childhood but where, as it were, I had always lived or at least wanted to. My wife was then a very pretty woman, a quiet face with a smile of destructive calm, and a figure which, at the very least, provoked one to thoughts not quite in keeping with a usual intention. I cannot say how it was but it was simply that she could not be won, not in the usual manner. Although I do not remember it as deliberate, still I can see now that it was a matter of giving in the old sense such as I had believed no longer to exist. Nothing so much suggested it as when, after we had eaten and had spent what was left of the evening reading, perhaps, with some time of quiet conversation, she would at last turn to me with an air of permission and would then rise and set about the task of going to bed. What I had expected was not necessarily something more, but certainly something different, and when on that first night I was so permitted, I saw that nothing again would ever be as I intended it, never what I had hoped for.

I am not a successful man in any sense of the word and if my wife has permitted me in her own way, the rest of the world has allowed me to live in another. I have never been openly molested, not with intention of the sort I might imagine for myself. I have often thought that an open attack might be fairer for all concerned but I can see now that I was only thinking of myself. Others seemed not to care that much and I suppose that they had every right not to. I have annoyed them but, after all, I have never essentially disturbed their lives. Let live, they say, and they know what they are doing.

The fact of my failure can be seen in many instances but it is not so much this fact as the other of my not having been a success. Because, after all, I haven't failed if it was my own intention not to be successful, although to anyone else it would seem so. I will allow that I am not successful but I confess it is more difficult to admit of my failure. I agree to the compromise but must reserve the choice for myself.

When it was that I first gave evidence of my intention to be an unsuccessful man, I do not remember. In any event it was a long time ago and quite probably not long after our marriage. Before that time I was not quite so sure as I am now of the fact that it is at all costs necessary to oppose oneself to the determinations of one's destroyers. I had not then thought that my wife would be in some sense their general. But it turned out so and soon after I began the task of opposition on whatever level they should choose. Though I have never been successful, even in this, I have the eventual satisfaction of a life so empty that even they will be hard put to it for praises.

At the time of our marriage my wife had a small sum of money with which we intended to make our start. This sum she put at my disposal, to use in whatever way I thought best. She had given me this sum or rather she had given me a check on her bank for the amount and told me that it was now mine to do with as I pleased. So, taking the check, I set out toward the business district of the town and when I had come to the first bank, I went in and deposited the check in her name. And there it has been ever since.

This gesture, which was, to be sure, very much a gesture, began the understanding between my wife and myself which was never obscured in all our years of living together, which did, in fact, survive those years more gracefully than we ourselves. It was an altogether simple act, half-understood and at best angry, but it served us better than any of the more deliberate ones that followed. Nothing made it quite so plain to each of us where the other stood and there never was a better reminder.

I would often say to my wife who was not so well controlled that she could forbear mention of the money at all times, that when I had at last made my fortune, this money we would use to make a wonderful time for ourselves, spending it on a trip to the Bahamas or some such nonsensical place. On such occasions she would smile and laugh a little but the success of my wit had really more to do with the fact of my certainty that even should I have had those tickets in my hand at that very moment, she would have laughed just as delightfully and would not have moved one inch from her chair. The surety with which we grew to deal with one another was actually what delighted us and we always knew exactly what to say. If it had not been for the money to begin with, it would not have been so easy and this first gesture of mine served as model for many more. Still, if my gesture seemed the first, and the money the source of all our understanding, as time passed I began to understand my wife a little more acutely than at first and also to see that if it was I who had put the money to such good use, it was, nevertheless, she who had had the good sense to give it to me.

In past years I have often had called to my attention the constant infidelities of husbands and wives which marked them much more than they would have, had they been confined to the flesh only. Because flesh is at best flesh and would look as poor as any hanging in a butcher's window. But these whom I have watched were dealing primarily with other values, with lives in a more total sense, and they could only be condemned for their lack of understanding. Their bickering was constant, never-ending, and the wives waited only for the moment when their husbands would return from their various jobs so that it could all begin again. And I suspect that even the husbands hurried a little faster on their way home from work, to get at it and to miss as little as they possibly could. For myself, perhaps a month or two would pass before either my wife or myself was aware of our differences. Perhaps they were not even differences but rather our unholy similarities, our understandings. We were not thought to be unhappy, to be fighting all of the time, and to tell the truth we weren't.

But I suspect that each of us was sure that there was, after all something better though we had long since given up trying to think about it. It was the suggestion of this which reminded us, which gave us all our pleasure.

Yet we did live together in a way which few people do nowadays. We dealt with one another constantly and were never put off, never refused unless it were a condition of our understanding that was in question. We knew one another as well as anyone ever knew another and, if it had not been for our loathing, we should have been happy.

Other people, although I don't for a moment believe that what they say is true, at least claim a continuity in their lives, a going up or a coming down. The rise or fall which they maintain is their way of saying that they have lived and even those who stay in the middle suppose that they narrowly missed worse or very nearly achieved better. For me this does not apply, and I find it very hard to believe that it does even for others. If I say that I got to know my wife better during the time we lived together, what I intend to say is that after a time I knew her whereas before that time she was no better for my uses than an utter stranger. Neither of us lived for much more than ourselves, one another, though not in the usual sense. God knows we lived long enough, both of us, though I can't say we grew older or younger or that we grew at all. If one lives at all, one lives for the kind of things that my wife and I lived for, understandings, the security of knowledge. One certainly does not live to grow old.

But now for my purposes it is necessary to suppose a continuity although none comes readily to hand. What my wife said a year ago is no more to the point than what she said on our wedding night. There is nothing to suggest that we have lived in between. No, for both of us, it was like going past some beautiful spot, stopping to look, and then never leaving, always looking to see more and more and more. We never tired of one another and we spent our lives in such looking though at times we might wish to be gone. But still we stayed where we were.

Taken only as years our life seems very uneventful. After our marriage we settled in the town where we spent the days of our honeymoon, an acquiescence on the part of my wife which I was then still too confused to understand. Now I see that it was for her purposes, not mine, that we settled there for it was intended that I should fail on home-ground, so to speak. It was to be the place of my failure or at least the place of my giving proof. But my failure was never what they intended or, because they so deliberately intended it, it was not really mine. I was an unsuccessful man to be sure, but the failure was all theirs. Had they intended my success, it would have been something else again but, as it was, the failure belonged to them.

I can remember the occasions of the first trials quite well just as I can remember almost all of my relations with my wife. A friend would sponsor me, set me up in business, and then quite quietly I would fail. It was always the same, always followed by the half-expressed reproaches from the friend. They could never say that I did not try because I did but what they forgot was my own intelligence which made each of my efforts consistently contributive to my ruin. It was a way I had about which they really knew nothing. My wife knew though, perhaps, not as well as I, but it was for her own purposes that she never said anything and always expressed her confidence in me with the same sure tone, just as if nothing had happened. If at first I was tempted to tell her why I so often failed, I soon saw that she knew quite well without my telling and it was better for all concerned to keep silent.

Such conduct on my part was never very simple and I always envied my wife her own part. She was never obliged to come and go as I was, never forced into tedious misrepresentations, never compelled to show failure if not actually to fail. On some evenings I came home as tired as any honest man, no matter what I had been up to, but never was there anything more than what I had left in the morning. Gently my wife would question me about the day's work and I would answer that it had gone well and that I was sure that soon everything would be all right. It was our particular joke, this question and answer and it never failed to bring a smile from my wife. But it was never quite so simple for me because there were those evenings when I wished that my own work had gone for something more than jokes whose humor was not always so apparent.

It was wrong of me to worry and I did worry quite often during the middle of our life together. At that time it became more difficult than I had thought possible for me to keep my own attitude free of the suggestion of failure directed at me from every side. My wife's friends came frequently to call during that time, and when I came in from work I found them there with my wife, waiting no less than she to see how my day had gone. Perhaps my wife agreed after awhile to the more private engagement I had intended because after some time had passed, her friends were no longer there when I came in and once again it was only my wife I had to face. To me this seemed fairer and moreover it was she whom they had chosen.

It was wrong of me to worry because, as we went on, I began to see that I had very nearly won, at least so far as my wife was concerned. Perhaps it was that her questions concerning the businesses I so carefully guided into failure seemed more genuine, more tired. My own answers were never more cheerful, more full of hope, and I told her each day that perhaps tomorrow would see the final victory and, I would add with a smile, the long-promised trip to the Bahamas. I don't know if it was wrong to take advantage of her growing weakness but I was sure that if it had been I who had been first to give in, she would have been no less kind. There was little chance to do more than I had always done, those things upon which we had so long ago agreed, and I am even enclined to think that my wife would never have respected a response to her own weakness. And I wonder even now if her weakness, so persuasive in its own way, was not, after all, just another trick.

In any event the time after that was a great deal easier for me because I could begin to relax though not too much at first. I had lived with my wife too long not to realize the infinite resources at her disposal and I could suspect with some justice that at any time, a time when I should least suspect it, she would again attack and my long-built defences would fall in ruins. In consequence, I was careful, very careful, at first and then I did relax a little but she gave no sign that she noticed it, my relaxing, until at last I was almost sure that what I did no longer concerned her and my time of trial was at an end.

One evening I came home as usual with much the same news and, when I came into the house, I called to her but she did not answer. It did not surprise me very much because she had begun to show signs of deafness and, although I was not altogether convinced that it was not her last attempt to defeat me, it did seem that she could not hear as well as she once had. Calling again, I went into the room where she spent most of her time and there she was, sitting in her chair. But I could see immediately from the slack position of her hands, fallen beyond the arms of her chair, that she was not well and then, when I came closer, I saw that she was dead.

The next day I have already spoken of, such a calm and peaceful day, and I spent the greater part of it arranging for her funeral. Needless to say, I had only to express a few brief wishes and the rest of the matter was taken out of my hands. The day of her funeral passed without event and I found myself watching her go into the ground without much feeling of any kind. I knew that her part in it was over and my own very nearly so. In any event it was something to think about.

ANDRE DUBUS

The Doctor

In late March, the snow began to melt. First it ran off the slopes and roads, and the brooks started flowing. Finally there were only low, shaded patches in the woods. In April, there were four days of warm sun, and on the first day Art Castagnetto told Maxine she could put away his pajamas until next year. That night he slept in a T-shirt, and next morning, when he noticed the pots on the radiators were dry, he left them empty.

Maxine didn't believe in the first day, or the second, either. But on the third afternoon, wearing shorts and a sweatshirt, she got the charcoal grill from the garage, put it in the back yard, and broiled steaks. She even told Art to get some tonic and limes for the gin. It was a Saturday afternoon; they sat outside in canvas lawn chairs and told Tina, their four-year-old girl, that it was all right to watch the charcoal but she musn't touch it, because it was burning even if it didn't look like it. When the steaks were ready, the sun was behind the woods in back of the house; Maxine brought sweaters to Art and the four children so they could eat outside.

Monday it snowed. The snow was damp at first, melting on the dead grass, but the flakes got heavier and fell as slowly as tiny leaves and covered the ground. In another two days the snow melted, and each gray cool day was warmer than the one before. Saturday afternoon the sky started clearing; there was a sunset, and before going to bed Art went outside and looked up at the stars. In the morning, he woke to a bedroom of sunlight. He left Maxine sleeping, put on a T-shirt, trunks, and tennis shoes, and carrying his sweatsuit he went downstairs, tiptoeing because the children slept so lightly on weekends. He dropped his sweatsuit into the basket for dirty clothes; he was finished with it until next fall.

He did side-straddle hops on the front lawn and then ran on the shoulder of the road, which for the first half mile was bordered by woods, so that he breathed the scent of pines and, he believed, the sunlight in the air. Then he passed the Whitfords' house. He had never seen the man and woman but had read their name on the mailbox and connected it with the children who usually played in the road in front of the small graying house set back in the trees. Its dirt yard was just large enough to contain it and a rusting Ford and an elm tree with a tire-and-rope swing hanging from one of its branches. The house now was still and dark, as though asleep. He went around the bend and, looking ahead, saw three of the Whitford boys standing by the brook.

It was a shallow brook, which had its prettiest days in winter when it was frozen; in the first weeks of spring, it ran clearly, but after that it became stagnant and around July it dried. This brook was a landmark he used when he directed friends to his house. "You get to a brook with a stone bridge," he'd say. The bridge wasn't really stone; its guard walls were made of rectangular concrete slabs, stacked about three feet high, but he liked stone fences and stone bridges and he called it one. On a slope above the brook, there was a red house. A young childless couple lived there, and now the man, who sold life insurance in Boston, was driving off with a boat and trailer hitched to his car. His wife waved goodbye from the driveway, and the Whitford boys stopped throwing rocks into the brook long enough to wave, too. They heard Art's feet on the blacktop and turned to watch him. When he reached the bridge, one of them said "Hi, Doctor," and Art smiled and said "Hello" to them as he passed. Crossing the bridge, he looked down at the brook. It was moving, slow and shallow, into the dark shade of the woods.

About a mile past the brook, there were several houses, with short stretches of woods between them. At the first house, a family was sitting at a picnic table in the side yard, reading the Sunday paper. They did not hear him, and he felt like a spy as he passed. The next family, about a hundred yards up the road, was working. Two little girls were picking up trash, and the man and woman were digging a flower bed. The parents turned and waved, and the man called, "It's a good day for it!" At the next house, a young couple were washing their Volkswagen, the girl using the hose, the man scrubbing away the dirt of winter. They looked up and waved. By now Art's T-shirt was damp and cool, and he had his second wind.

All up the road it was like that: people cleaning their lawns, washing cars, some just sitting under the bright sky; one large bald man lifted a beer can and grinned. In front of one house, two teen-age boys were throwing a Frisbee; farther up the road, a man was gently pitching a softball to his small son, who wore a baseball cap and choked up high on the bat. A boy and girl passed Art in a polished green M.G., the top down, the girl's unscarfed hair blowing across her cheeks as she leaned over and quickly kissed the boy's ear. All the lawn people waved at Art, though none of them knew him; they only knew he was the obstetrician who lived in the big house in the woods. When he turned and jogged back down the road, they waved or spoke again; this time they were not as spontaneous but more casual, more familiar. He rounded a curve a quarter of a mile from the brook; the woman was back in her house and the Whitford boys were gone, too. On this length of road he was alone, and ahead of him squirrels and chipmunks fled into the woods.

Then something was wrong—he felt it before he knew it. When the two boys ran up from the brook into his vision, he started sprinting and had a grateful instant when he felt the strength left in his legs, though still he didn't know if there was any reason for strength and speed. He pounded over the blacktop as the boys scrambled up the lawn, toward the red house, and as he reached the bridge he shouted.

They didn't stop until he shouted again, and now they turned, their faces pale and openmouthed, and pointed at the brook and then ran back toward it. Art pivoted off the road, leaning backward as he descended the short rocky bank, around the end of the bridge, seeing first the white rectangle of concrete lying in the slow water. And again he felt before he knew: he was in the water to his knees, bent over the slab and getting his fingers into the sand beneath it before he looked down at the face and shoulders and chest. Then he saw the arms, too, thrashing under water as though diggin out of caved-in snow. The boy's pale hands did not quite reach the surface.

In perhaps five seconds, Art realized he could not lift the slab. Then he was running up the lawn to the red house, up the steps and shoving open the side door and yelling as he bumped into the kitchen table, pointing one hand at the phone on the wall and the other at the woman in a bright-yellow halter as she backed away, her arms raised before her face.

"Fire Department! A boy's drowning!" Pointing behind him now toward the brook.

She was fast; her face changed fears and she moved toward the phone, and that was enough. He was outside again, sprinting out of a stumble as he left the steps, darting between the two boys, who stood mute at the brook's edge. He refused to believe it was this simple and this impossible. He thrust his hands under the slab, lifting with legs and arms, and now he heard one of the boys moaning behind him, "It fell on Terry, it fell on Terry." Squatting in the water, he held a hand over the Whitford boy's mouth and pinched his nostrils together; then he groaned, for now his own hand was killing the child. He took his hand away. The boy's arms had stopped moving—they seemed to be resting at his sides—and Art reached down and felt the right one and then jerked his own hand out of the water. The small arm was hard and tight and quivering. Art touched the left one, running his hand the length of it, and felt the boy's fingers against the slab, pushing.

The sky changed, was shattered by a smoke-gray sound of winter nights—the fire horn—and in the quiet that followed he heard a woman's voice, speaking to children. He turned and looked at her standing beside him in the water, and he suddenly wanted to be held, his breast against hers, but her eyes shrieked at him to do something and he bent over and tried again to lift the slab. Then she was beside him, and they kept trying until ten minutes later, when four volunteer firemen descended out of the dying groan of the siren and splashed into the brook.

No one knew why the slab had fallen. Throughout the afternoon, whenever Art tried to understand it, he felt his brain go taut and he tried to stop but couldn't. After three drinks, he thought of the slab as he always thought of cancer: that it had the volition of a killer. And he spoke of it like that until Maxine said, "There was nothing you could do. It took five men and a woman to lift it."

They were sitting in the back yard, their lawn chairs touching, and Maxine was holding his hand. The children were playing in front of the house, because Maxine had told them what happened, told them Daddy had been through the worst day of his life, and they must leave him alone for a while. She kept his glass filled with gin-and-tonic and once, when Tina started screaming in the front yard, he jumped out of the chair, but she grabbed his wrist and held it tightly and said, "It's nothing, I'll take care of it." She went around the house, and soon Tina stopped crying, and Maxine came back and said she'd fallen down in the driveway and skinned her elbow. Art was trembling.

"Shouldn't you get some sedatives?" she said.

He shook his head, then started to cry.

Monday morning an answer—or at least a possibility—was waiting for him, at though it had actually chosen to enter his mind now, with the buzzing of the alarm clock. He got up quickly and stood in a shaft of sunlight on the floor. Maxine had rolled away from the clock and was still asleep.

He put on trousers and moccasins and went downstairs and then outside and down the road toward the brook. He wanted to run but he kept walking. Before reaching the Whitfords' house, he crossed to the opposite side of the road. Back in the trees, their house was shadowed and quiet. He walked all the way to the bridge before he stopped and looked up at the red house. Then he saw it, and he didn't know (and would never know) whether he had seen it yesterday, too, as he ran to the door or if he just thought he had seen it. But it was there: a bright-green garden hose, coiled in the sunlight beside the house.

He walked home. He went to the side yard where his own hose had lain all winter, screwed to the faucet. He stood looking at it, and then he went inside and quietly climbed the stairs, into the sounds of breathing, and got his pocketknife. Now he moved faster, down the stairs and outside, and he picked up the nozzle end of the hose and cut it off. Farther down, he cut the hose again. He put his knife away and then stuck one end of the short piece of hose in his mouth, pressed his nostrils between two fingers, and breathed.

He looked up through a bare maple tree at the sky. Then he walked around the house to the Buick, got the key out of the ignition, and opened the trunk. His fingers were trembling as he lowered the piece of hose and placed it beside his first-aid kit, in front of a bucket of sand and a small snow shovel he had carried all through the winter.

GEORGE P. ELLIOTT

In a hole

I am in a hole. At first I did not want to get out of the hole. It was a
sort of relief to be in it. In my city we are prepared for cataclysms.
You cannot be sure which kind of destruction is going to catch you,
but one or another is pretty sure to. In fact, I am lucky. I am nearly
forty and this is the first one to catch me. Properly speaking, I am not
caught yet, for I am still alive and not even injured. When I first came
to in this hole and realized what had happened and where I was, I had
no impulse to get out. I was afraid of finding the city in rubble, even
though I knew we were a tough people and would rebuild it as we had
done more than once before. My first thought was: caught at last.
Perhaps the shock had stunned me. In any case, I certainly felt relieved
of anxiety, my worry about how and when trouble was going to find
me was over.

Our city is great and strong. Yet when it was founded over three
hundred years ago, our forefathers were warned against the location.
We are at the tip of a promontory at the extreme west of the continent, situated on a geological fault— typhoons rake us—the land is
sterile, everything worth having must be brought to us from outside—
our people are immigrants, dissatisfied and ambitious, we have not
brought many of our ancestors' myths with us, we are eager to rid

ourselves of customs, we are unruly and rely on police to keep us in order—no matter how rich we are, no matter how hard we work, we are always overcrowded—despite the researches of our dieticians, we have many nutritional ailments, new ones springing up among us as fast as the old ones are cured. Perhaps the hardships of our location have tested us and made us tough, and our founding fathers knew this would be the case. They were stubborn in choosing this raw location. We question their wisdom, we grumble, we analyze the possibilities. But we do not seriously complain, we have no real intention of rebelling, even if we did it is dangerous to say anything but what is expected. We are too rich from trade, we are richer than we can explain, we are envied by outsiders who do not appreciate the extent and nature of our troubles. They have no idea how troubling it is not to know when and how you will be caught. One can never forget it here for long. Perhaps because of our difficulty with food, threats are always alive in our minds, ready to leap at us. No matter how much we eat, no matter what our dieticians do, no matter what chefs we import to make our food savory, we suffer from malnutrition. We are fat and undernourished. The stupid are luckiest for they do not know they lack. The wise suffer most. There are a few who make a virtue of fasting and austerity; they say they are at peace; but I have never seen one look me in the eye when he said it. They look up at the sky or out to sea, and talk of love and peace and truth. Their strict diet makes their skin rough and scaly, their nails thicken and turn blue, their eyes become vague. They do not bother people much, nobody cares enough to restrain them. We keep on trying to improve our diet, we hold conferences and symposiums on the subject, it has become the subject of our most intensive experiments.

An earthquake caught me. It was quite a severe one, but I don't think it was as bad as the one that killed a third of our people when I was a young man. I was nimble and quick, and came through with nothing worse than a few bruises. In that one, great chasms opened, whereas the hole I am in now is not more than twenty feet deep. This one caught me just as I was coming out of the telephone building.

I had gone there to argue about a mistake on my bill. They had charged me for two long distance calls to Rome the month before. Absurd! Neither my wife nor I would dream of talking with anyone at such a distance. Overseas connections are notoriously unreliable, even with our communications system, our greatest civic pride—we would be able to talk with the moon if there were anyone there to talk to. Neither my wife nor I have any friends in Rome. It is true that I have corresponded for years with a numismatist in Rome—I

collect old coins—but our common interest conceals the profoundest
disagreement. I would do much to avoid meeting him in person,
should he ever propose such a thing, as he has never shown the
slightest sign of doing. To him ancient coins are objects of trade, their
value varies from time to time but at any given moment it can be
agreed upon, they are commodities. I would never expose to him the
slightest edge of what they mean to me, of the speculations they excite
in me. (A drachma which was worth many loaves of bread two thousand years ago is now worth nothing—except to a few antiquarians
like me, to whom it means a hundred times more than it did then. I
look at it unable to comprehend. If I did comprehend, it would cease
to be worth even a slice of bread to me. Do all those to whom it is
worthless understand something that eludes me?) The numismatist and
I share no language but the code of catalogues. We would not be able
to talk to one another face to face, much less over the telephone. And
the length of time these supposed long distance calls went on! One
lasted an hour, the other nearly as long. I went to the telephone building to complain, politely of course, but firmly. They had to prove
that my wife or I had made such preposterous calls. They said they
would find out who it was the call had gone to—both calls to Rome
were to the same number. I saw they did not believe me. I knew that
legally they could not force me to pay if I denied responsibility. All
the same, I was not feeling cleanly victorious as I left the building.

I was thrown to the street. I remember seeing the facade of the
telephone building topple out towards me in one slab, then crack and
buckle. When I came to my senses, I was in this hole. There was still
dust in the air. I stood up, coughed, and wiped my eyes. The rubble
at the bottom of the hole was all small stuff, no boulders or big chunks
of material. There was a good deal of light coming down the chimney
above me; it could not be late in the day; I had not been out long. I
got up, stiff, creaking a bit, but uninjured, and I inspected the hole I
was in. It was shaped like a funnel, big end down. The bottom of the
chimney was at least five feet above my head, and the chimney itself
appeared to extend up another eight or nine feet. The walls of the cone
I was in were of chunks of rock propped on one another. To remove
one would risk making the whole haphazard structure fall in. I yelled.
There was no answer, no answering noise, no noise of any sort. I
whistled and shouted. The echo hurt my ears. I collapsed. At that
moment I realized I did not want to get out. Not till light returned
next morning did my forces rally.

Hunger drove me. At first, choked with dust, I suffered badly from
thirst. But during the night it rained, and enough rain water dripped

down for me to refresh my mouth and rinse my face. Then hunger pulled me up from my lethargy. I determined not to die alone. I would get out if I could.

But how? I yelled for help, there was no response. Once I got up into the chimney above me, I would be able to brace myself back and knees like a mountain climber and inch my way up. But getting myself into the chimney, that was the problem. The walls sloped back, only an experienced mountain climber with equipment would even try to climb them. There was nothing else to be done— I would have to build a pile of rocks to climb up on so that I could insert my body into the chimney. I tried to pull one of the boulders free but it was lodged too tight to budge. Another was as tight; another, another. Then one moved a little as I pulled and pushed. But when it moved, there were ominous shiftings in the wall above me, and a stone as big as my fist sprang out from just over my head, narrowly missing me. All the other boulders I could reach were wedged tight. I pulled at the loose one again. Suddenly half of it broke free and I fell on my back. It was of rotten stone, it crumbled, I had gained nothing.

I complained. If there had been anyone to hear me I would never have been so self-indulgent as to complain. But I was alone and not quite hopeless. I stood with legs spread, raised my fists, and spoke in a loud clear voice as though I were addressing myself to someone who would have understood me if he had heard me. "I have not been unwilling to be destroyed, I know how to resign myself to destruction. But why must I exhaust myself laboring to return to a world which may be in ruins and where, if it is still standing, I will be even more fearful than I was before?" As I finished speaking, a fair-sized piece of stone fell from the wall high above me onto the floor of the hole. I waited to see what else might happen. Nothing happened. I complained again, watchfully. Another rock fell. The sound of my voice was dislodging some of the upper rocks without causing the whole pile to shatter down onto me. I sang, hummed, yelled, whooped, wailed: nothing happened. I went back to complaining, in a loud clear voice and complete, rather formal sentences. Another rock fell. One of the fallen boulders was too big for me to lift, but I could roll it into place. They were of irregular shapes and would not pile easily and securely. I was going to need a great many pieces of stone of this size. I am healthy and my gardening has kept me in good condition; nevertheless, I felt myself weaker after each complaining and rock-piling episode and had to rest for longer and longer periods. My predicament did not allow me to complain mildly. I am reserved by temperament, I tried to hold back both out of inclination and out of a desire to save my strength, but I found that I could give each complaint nothing less than everything I could muster.

I did not dare complain during the night, for fear a dislodged stone would fall on me. In the daytime I watched when I talked, I could jump to one side in time. I kept trying to figure out which of my words had the power to dislodge the rocks; it must have something to do with vibrations, wave-lengths.

In our city we are quite experimental. Even a private citizen like myself is infected with the spirit of experiment. I live off the income from my inheritance. My wife and I love gardening above everything. Our few friends are scattered throughout the city, we make a point of being strangers to our neighbors. Our rock garden, at the edge of a cliff overlooking a northern cove, is quite remarkable. I am sure it would win prizes and be much visited if we were interested in that sort of thing. But our friends respect our wish to keep our garden private, and our neighbors, whose gardens are severely arranged and have swept paths, do not notice the perfection of our succulents (which they think of as being no more than cliff plants anyway) nor do they see any order in the way our paths and stepping-stones adapt themselves to the terrain. My wife and I have little use for most of what our city gets excited about, we are inclined to scorn prizes and fashion, I had thought I was equally indifferent to the fervor for experimentation. Now, in this hole, I have learned better.

The second night, unable to sleep well because of the discomfort of the floor, I planned experiments to try the next day. I have never heard of anyone who was in a hole like mine. Perhaps these conditions are unique. There are plenty of holes into which our citizens have been known to have fallen; sometimes they were rescued, sometimes they died before they could be got out, often no doubt they just disappeared from sight as I have done. Perhaps no one else discovered how to dislodge boulders as I did. There might be something exceptional about my voice, though no one has ever commented on it. There certainly is nothing odd about my words. They are just ordinary words used with care. Still, though I am not slovenly in my use of words, neither am I a poet. I must not let this opportunity to experiment slip from me, even though, since I need all the physical strength I have to pile the rocks up, I must work fast before I give out. During the night I planned a series of speeches to try out.

I prayed. When our city was founded, many churches had been built, strong, handsome, stone structures. Our city had originally been built with walls, to withstand the assaults of pirates. To be sure, the pirates were suppressed two centuries ago, and the city grew far beyond the walls, which are now visited by tourists as museum pieces. But our churches, the best ones, which look like and once served as fortresses, have been kept in good repair, services are held in them, the choir schools still function at public expense. I knew many prayers, having been a boy soprano for a few years till my voice cracked. Neither the prayers I recollected nor the ones I made up worked to dislodge the stones.

I delivered the patriotic speeches memorized by every schoolchild— the salute to the flag, a constitution day address, the funeral oration which had been delivered by our first prime minister after the revolution had established parliamentary government, our oath of allegiance. None of them worked.

I gave an exact and full history of how I came to be where I was. I described my condition with scientific accuracy and offered every reasonable hypothesis about why I was doing what I was doing. Nothing happened.

I recited a poem, nursery rhymes, a folk tale, the prologue of our constitution. I counted to twenty in Latin, I recited as many of Euclid's axioms as I could recall. No result.

I recited a speech from a play I had acted in when I was in college. Actually I saved this till the last because the speech had become more than the character's words for me, it had come to say what I meant or at least I had come to mean what it said. The part was a small one. I was one of the lesser court gentlemen. At a crucial moment the king gives me a vital message, his throne depends on its delivery. Halfway to the nobleman to whom I am supposed to deliver it, I decide not to, and then the playwright gives me my only important speech, a soliloquy, the great speech of the play. I have no good political reason not to deliver the message, nothing but good will befall me if I do deliver it, I have never before done such a thing as I am now doing. The longer I try to account to myself and the audience for what I am doing, the stranger my action appears; I labor to find the right words, for my court language is insufficient. Twice in the history of our city this play, one of our classics, has been proscribed because of this speech, which cannot be cut out of the play, being its keystone. I recite it now in my hole. A boulder is dislodged all right, but it almost hits me. It is too large for me to lift to the top of the pile I have made. Worst, it comes from the mouth of the chimney above, enlarging it, so that now I must build up my pile even higher than before, in order to be able to brace myself in the chimney and work my way out.

I have to use our language in my own way, I have to speak for myself.

"I am in a hole, I want to get out. I don't know what I shall find when I make my way back into the city. I long to see my wife; if she is still alive and well, she will care for me while I recuperate; if she is injured, I will do what I can for her. These stones are heavy; after I put one up onto the pile, my muscles do not leave off trembling until I raise my voice to talk another rock down from the jumble about me and then hoist it into place; each time after such effort, the trembling penetrates into me deeper. I fear I will not have strength to work my way up the chimney once I have got myself into it. I want to cry, but I must save my strength for words. I do not know why I am here, I did nothing to deserve being thrown down here alone and abandoned."

So, the rocks fall.

What would happen if I did not pretend someone is listening to what I say? I know of course that no one hears my voice, but I speak as though I were being listened to. It must be that which gives my voice the right wave-length to dislodge the stones. It obviously is neither the words themselves nor their arrangement; my experiments have removed those possibilities. In the interests of exact knowledge I should complain without audience. I know well enough that I have no audience, not a sound from outside has reached me. But I cannot imagine doing anything so unreasonable as to complain without any audience at all, even though that is what I am in fact doing. Besides, suppose when I did that, all the rocks should fall in on me at once? If I had more strength I would take the risk, I would try to imagine myself as I am. Meanwhile, I had better get on with my complaining while I still have strength and time.

BERNARD MALAMUD

The Magic Barrel

Not long ago there lived in uptown New York, in a small almost meager room, though crowded with books, Leo Finkle, a rabbinical student in the Yeshivah University. Finkle, after six years of study, was to be ordained in June and had been advised by an acquaintance that he might find it easier to win himself a congregation if he were married. Since he had no present prospects of marriage, after two tormented days of turning it over in his mind, he called in Pinye Salzman, a marriage broker whose two-line advertisement he had read in the *Forward*.

The matchmaker appeared one night out of the dark fourth-floor hallway of the graystone rooming house where Finkle lived, grasping a black, strapped portfolio that had been worn thin with use. Salzman, who had been long in the business, was of slight but dignified build, wearing an old hat, and an overcoat too short and tight for him. He smelled frankly of fish, which he loved to eat, and although he was missing a few teeth, his presence was not displeasing, because of an amiable manner curiously contrasted with mournful eyes. His voice, his lips, his wisp of beard, his bony fingers were animated, but give him a moment of repose and his mild blue eyes revealed a depth of sadness, a characteristic that put Leo a little at ease although the situation, for him, was inherently tense.

He at once informed Salzman why he had asked him to come, explaining that his home was in Cleveland, and that but for his parents, who had married comparatively late in life, he was alone in the world. He had for six years devoted himself almost entirely to his studies, as a result of which, understandably, he had found himself without time for a social life and the company of young women. Therefore he thought it the better part of trial and error—of embarrassing fumbling— to call in an experienced person to advise him on these matters. He remarked in passing that the function of the marriage broker was ancient and honorable, highly approved in the Jewish community, because it made practical the necessary without hindering joy. Moreover, his own parents had been brought together by a matchmaker. They had made, if not a financially profitable marriage—since neither had possessed any worldly goods to speak of—at least a successful one in the sense of their everlasting devotion to each other. Salzman listened in embarrassed surprise, sensing a sort of apology. Later, however, he experienced a glow of pride in his work, an emotion that had left him years ago, and he heartily approved of Finkle.

The two went to their business. Leo had led Salzman to the only clear place in the room, a table near a window that overlooked the lamp-lit city. He seated himself at the matchmaker's side but facing him, attempting by an act of will to suppress the unpleasant tickle in his throat. Salzman eagerly unstrapped his portfolio and removed a loose rubber band from a thin packet of much-handled cards. As he flipped through them, a gesture and sound that physically hurt Leo, the student pretended not to see and gazed steadfastly out the window. Although it was still February, winter was on its last legs, signs of which he had for the first time in years begun to notice. He now observed the round white moon, moving high in the sky through a cloud menagerie, and watched with half-open mouth as it penetrated a huge hen, and dropped out of her like an egg laying itself. Salzman, though pretending through eyeglasses he had just slipped on, to be engaged in scanning the writing on the cards, stole occasional glances at the young man's distinguished face, noting with pleasure the long, severe scholar's nose, brown eyes heavy with learning, sensitive yet ascetic lips, and a certain, almost hollow quality of the dark cheeks. He gazed around at shelves upon shelves of books and let out a soft, contented sigh.

When Leo's eyes fell upon the cards, he counted six spread out in Salzman's hand.

"So few?" he asked in disappointment.

"You wouldn't believe me how much cards I got in my office," Salzman replied. "The drawers are already filled to the top, so I keep them now in a barrel, but is every girl good for a new rabbi?"

Leo blushed at this, regretting all he had revealed of himself in a curriculum vitae he had sent to Salzman. He had thought it best to acquaint him with his strict standards and specifications, but in having done so, felt he had told the marriage broker more than was absolutely necessary.

He hesitantly inquired, "Do you keep photographs of your clients on file?"

"First comes family, amount of dowry, also what kind promises," Salzman replied, unbuttoning his tight coat and settling himself in the chair. "After comes pictures, rabbi."

"Call me Mr. Finkle. I'm not yet a rabbi."

Salzman said he would, but instead called him doctor, which he changed to rabbi when Leo was not listening too attentively.

Salzman adjusted his horn-rimmed spectacles, gently cleared his throat and read in an eager voice the contents of the top card:

"Sophie P. Twenty four years. Widow one year. No children. Educated high school and two years college. Father promises eight thousand dollars. Has wonderful wholesale business. Also real estate. On the mother's side comes teachers, also one actor. Well known on Second Avenue."

Leo gazed up in surprise. "Did you say a widow?"

"A widow don't mean spoiled, rabbi. She lived with her husband maybe four months. He was a sick boy she made a mistake to marry him."

"Marrying a widow has never entered my mind."

"This is because you have no experience. A widow, especially if she is young and healthy like this girl, is a wonderful person to marry. She will be thankful to you the rest of her life. Believe me, if I was looking now for a bride, I would marry a widow."

Leo reflected, then shook his head.

Salzman hunched his shoulders in an almost imperceptible gesture of disappointment. He placed the card down on the wooden table and began to read another:

"Lily H. High school teacher. Regular. Not a substitute. Has savings and new Dodge car. Lived in Paris one year. Father is successful dentist thirty-five years. Interested in professional man. Well Americanized family. Wonderful opportunity."

"I knew her personally," said Salzman. "I wish you could see this girl. She is a doll. Also very intelligent. All day you could talk to her about books and theyater and what not. She also knows current events."

"I don't believe you mentioned her age?"

"Her age?" Salzman said, raising his brows. "Her age is thirty-two years."

Leo said after a while, "I'm afraid that seems a little too old."

Salzman let out a laugh. "So how old are you, rabbi?"

"Twenty-seven."

"So what is the difference, tell me, between twenty-seven and thirty-two? My own wife is seven years older than me. So what did I suffer? —Nothing. If Rothschild's a daughter wants to marry you, would you say on account her age, no?"

"Yes," Leo said dryly.

Salzman shook off the no in the yes. "Five years don't mean a thing. I give you my word that when you will live with her for one week you will forget her age. What does it mean five years—that she lived more and knows more than somebody who is younger? On this girl, God bless her, years are not wasted. Each one that it comes makes better the bargain."

"What subject does she teach in high school?"

"Languages. If you heard the way she speaks French, you will think it is music. I am in the business twenty-five years, and I recommend her with my whole heart. Believe me, I know what I'm talking, rabbi."

"What's on the next card?" Leo said abruptly.

Salzman reluctantly turned up the third card:

"Ruth K. Nineteen years. Honor student. Father offers thirteen thousand cash to the right bridegroom. He is a medical doctor. Stomach specialist with marvelous practice. Brother in law owns own garment business. Particular people."

Salzman looked as if he had read his trump card.

"Did you say nineteen?" Leo asked with interest.

"On the dot."

"Is she attractive?" He blushed. "Pretty?"

Salzman kissed his finger tips. "A little doll. On this I give you my word. Let me call the father tonight and you will see what means pretty."

But Leo was troubled. "You're sure she's that young?"

"This I am positive. The father will show you the birth certificate."

"Are you positive there isn't something wrong with her?" Leo insisted.

"Who says there is wrong?"

"I don't understand why an American girl her age should go to a marriage broker."

A smile spread over Salzman's face.

"So for the same reason you went, she comes."

Leo flushed. "I am pressed for time."

Salzman, realizing he had been tactless, quickly explained. "The father came, not her. He wants she should have the best, so he looks around himself. When we will locate the right boy he will introduce him and encourage. This makes a better marriage than if a young girl without experience takes for herself. I don't have to tell you this."

"But don't you think this young girl believes in love?" Leo spoke uneasily.

Salzman was about to guffaw but caught himself and said soberly, "Love comes with the right person, not before."

Leo parted dry lips but did not speak. Noticing that Salzman had snatched a glance at the next card, he cleverly asked, "How is her health?"

"Perfect," Salzman said, breathing with difficulty. "Of course, she is a little lame on her right foot from an auto accident that it happened to her when she was twelve years, but nobody notices on account she is so brilliant and also beautiful."

Leo got up heavily and went to the window. He felt curiously bitter and upbraided himself for having called in the marriage broker. Finally, he shook his head.

"Why not?" Salzman persisted, the pitch of his voice rising.

"Because I detest stomach specialists."

"So what do you care what is his business? After you marry her do you need him? Who says he must come every Friday night in your house?"

Ashamed of the way the talk was going, Leo dismissed Salzman, who went home with heavy, melancholy eyes.

Though he had felt only relief at the marriage broker's departure, Leo was in low spirits the next day. He explained it as arising from Salzman's failure to produce a suitable bride for him. He did not care for his type of clientele. But when Leo found himself hesitating whether to seek out another matchmaker, one more polished than Pinye, he wondered if it could be—his protestations to the contrary, and although he honored his father and mother—that he did not, in essence, care for the matchmaking institution? This thought he quickly put out of mind yet found himself still upset. All day he ran around in the woods—missed an important appointment, forgot to give out his laundry, walked out of a Broadway cafeteria without paying and had to run back with the ticket in his hand; had even not recognized his landlady in the street when she passed with a friend and courteously called out, "A good evening to you, Doctor Finkle." By nightfall, however, he had regained sufficient calm to sink his nose into a book and there found peace from his thoughts.

Almost at once there came a knock on the door. Before Leo could say enter, Salzman, commercial cupid, was standing in the room. His face was gray and meager, his expression hungry, and he looked as if he would expire on his feet. Yet the marriage broker managed, by some trick of the muscles, to display a broad smile.

"So good evening. I am invited?"

Leo nodded, disturbed to see him again, yet unwilling to ask the man to leave.

Beaming still, Salzman laid his portfolio on the table. "Rabbi, I got for you tonight good news."

"I've asked you not to call me rabbi. I'm still a student."

"Your worries are finished. I have for you a first-class bride."

"Leave me in peace concerning this subject." Leo pretended lack of interest.

"The world will dance at your wedding."

"Please, Mr. Salzman, no more."

"But first must come back my strength," Salzman said weakly. He fumbled with the portfolio straps and took out of the leather case an oily paper bag, from which he extracted a hard, seeded roll and a small, smoked white fish. With a quick motion of his hand he stripped the fish out of its skin and began ravenously to chew. "All day in a rush," he muttered.

Leo watched him eat.

"A sliced tomato you have maybe?" Salzman hesitantly inquired.

"No."

The marriage broker shut his eyes and ate. When he had finished he carefully cleaned up the crumbs and rolled up the remains of the fish, in the paper bag. His spectacled eyes roamed the room until he discovered, amid some piles of books, a one-burner gas stove. Lifting his hat he humbly asked, "A glass tea you got, rabbi?"

Conscience-stricken, Leo rose and brewed the tea. He served it with a chunk of lemon and two cubes of lump sugar, delighting Salzman.

After he had drunk his tea, Salzman's strength and good spirits were restored.

"So tell me, rabbi," he said amiably, "you considered some more the three clients I mentioned yesterday?"

"There was no need to consider."

"Why not?"

"None of them suits me."

"What then suits you?"

Leo let it pass because he could give only a confused answer.

Without waiting for a reply, Salzman asked, "You remember this girl I talked to you—the high school teacher?"

"Age thirty-two?"

But, surprisingly, Salzman's face lit in a smile. "Age twenty-nine."

Leo shot him a look. "Reduced from thirty-two?"

"A mistake," Salzman avowed. "I talked today with the dentist. He took me to his safety deposit box and showed me the birth certificate. She was twenty-nine years last August. They made her a party in the mountains where she went for her vacation. When her father spoke to me the first time I forgot to write the age and I told you thirty-two, but now I remember this was a different client, a widow."

"The same one you told me about? I thought she was twenty-four?"

"A different. Am I responsible that the world is filled with widows?"

"No, but I'm not interested in them, nor for that matter, in school teachers."

Salzman pulled his clasped hands to his breast. Looking at the ceiling he devoutly exclaimed, "Yiddishe kinder, what can I say to somebody that he is not interested in high school teachers? So what then you are interested?"

Leo flushed but controlled himself.

"In what else will you be interested," Salzman went on, "if you not interested in this fine girl that she speaks four languages and has personally in the bank ten thousand dollars? Also her father guarantees further twelve thousand. Also she has a new car, wonderful clothes, talks on all subjects, and she will give you a first-class home and children. How near do we come in our life to paradise?"

"If she's so wonderful, why wasn't she married ten years ago?"

"Why?" said Salzman with a heavy laugh. "—Why? Because she is *partikiler*. This is why. She wants the *best*."

Leo was silent, amused at how he had entangled himself. But Salzman had aroused his interest in Lily H., and he began seriously to consider calling on her. When the marriage broker observed how intently Leo's mind was at work on the facts he had supplied, he felt certain they would soon come to an agreement.

Late Saturday afternoon, conscious of Salzman, Leo Finkle walked with Lily Hirschorn along Riverside Drive. He walked briskly and erectly, wearing with distinction the black fedora he had that morning taken with trepidation out of the dusty hat box on his closet shelf, and the heavy black Saturday coat he had thoroughly whisked clean. Leo also owned a walking stick, a present from a distant relative, but quickly put temptation aside and did not use it. Lily, petite and not unpretty, had on something signifying the approach of spring. She was au courant, animatedly, with all sorts of subjects, and he weighed her words and found her surprisingly sound—score another for Salzman, whom he uneasily sensed to be somewhere around, hiding perhaps high in a tree along the street, flashing the lady signals with a pocket mirror; or perhaps a cloven-hoofed Pan, piping nuptial ditties as he danced his invisible way before them, strewing wild buds on the walk and purple grapes in their path, symbolizing fruit of a union, though there was of course still none.

Lily startled Leo by remarking, "I was thinking of Mr. Salzman, a curious figure, wouldn't you say?"

Not certain what to answer, he nodded.

She bravely went on, blushing, "I for one am grateful for his introducing us. Aren't you?"

He courteously replied, "I am."

"I mean," she said with a little laugh—and it was all in good taste, or at least gave the effect of being not in bad—"do you mind that we came together so?"

He was not displeased with her honesty, recognizing that she meant to set the relationship aright, and understanding that it took a certain amount of experience in life, and courage, to want to do it quite that way. One had to have some sort of past to make that kind of beginning.

He said that he did not mind. Salzman's function was traditional and honorable—valuable for what it might achieve, which, he pointed out, was frequently nothing.

Lily agreed with a sigh. They walked on for a while and she said after a long silence, again with a nervous laugh, "Would you mind if I asked you something a little bit personal? Frankly, I find the subject fascinating." Although Leo shrugged, she went on half embarrassedly, "How was it that you came to your calling? I mean was it a sudden passionate inspiration?"

Leo, after a time, slowly replied, "I was always interested in the Law."

"You saw revealed in it the presence of the Highest?"

He nodded and changed the subject. "I understand that you spent a little time in Paris, Miss Hirschorn?"

"Oh, did Mr. Salzman tell you, Rabbi Finkle?" Leo winced but she went on, "It was ages ago and almost forgotten. I remember I had to return for my sister's wedding."

And Lily would not be put off. "When," she asked in a trembly voice, "did you become enamored of God?"

He stared at her. Then it came to him that she was talking not about Leo Finkle, but of a total stranger, some mystical figure, perhaps even passionate prophet that Salzman had dreamed up for her—no relation to the living or dead. Leo trembled with rage and weakness. The trickster had obviously sold her a bill of goods, just as he had him, who'd expected to become acquainted with a young lady of twenty-nine, only to behold, the moment he laid eyes upon her strained and anxious face, a woman past thirty-five and aging rapidly. Only his self control had kept him this long in her presence.

"I am not," he said gravely, "a talented religious person," and in seeking words to go on, found himself possessed by shame and fear. "I think," he said in a strained manner, "that I came to God not because I loved Him, but because I did not."

This confession he spoke harshly because its unexpectedness shook him.

Lily wilted. Leo saw a profusion of loaves of bread go flying like ducks high over his head, not unlike the winged loaves by which he had counted himself to sleep last night. Mercifully, then, it snowed, which he would not put past Salzman's machinations.

He was infuriated with the marriage broker and swore he would throw him out of the room the minute he reappeared. But Salzman did not come that night, and when Leo's anger had subsided, an unaccountable despair grew in its place. At first he thought this was caused by his disappointment in Lily, but before long it became evident that he had involved himself with Salzman without a true knowledge of his own intent. He gradually realized—with an emptiness that seized him with six hands—that he had called in the broker to find him a bride because he was incapable of doing it himself. This terrifying insight he had derived as a result of his meeting and conversation with Lily Hirschorn. Her probing questions had somehow irritated him into revealing—to himself more than her—the true nature of his relationship to God, and from that it had come upon him, with shocking force, that apart from his parents, he had never loved anyone. Or perhaps it went the other way, that he did not love God so well as he might, because he had not loved man. It seemed to Leo that his whole life stood starkly revealed and he saw himself for the first time as he truly was—unloved and loveless. This bitter but somehow not fully unexpected revelation brought him to a point of panic, controlled only by extraordinary effort. He covered his face with his hands and cried.

The week that followed was the worst of his life. He did not eat and lost weight. His beard darkened and grew ragged. He stopped attending seminars and almost never opened a book. He seriously considered leaving the Yeshivah, although he was deeply troubled at the thought of the loss of all his years of study—saw them like pages torn from a book, strewn over the city—and at the devastating effect of this decision upon his parents. But he had lived without knowledge of himself, and never in the Five Books and all the Commentaries—mea culpa— had the truth been revealed to him. He did not know where to turn, and in all this desolating loneliness there was no *to whom*, although he often thought of Lily but not once could bring himself to go downstairs and make the call. He became touchy and irritable, especially with his landlady, who asked him all manner of personal questions; on the other hand, sensing his own disagreeableness, he waylaid her on the stairs and apologized abjectly, until mortified, she ran from him. Out of this, however, he drew the consolation that he was a Jew and that a Jew suffered. But gradually, as the long and terrible week drew to a close, he regained his composure and some idea of purpose in life: to go on as planned. Although he was imperfect, the ideal was not. As for his quest of a bride, the thought of continuing afflicted him with anxiety and heartburn, yet perhaps with this new knowledge of himself, he would be more successful than in the past. Perhaps love would now come to him and a bride to that love. And for this sanctified seeking who needed a Salzman?

The marriage broker, a skeleton with haunted eyes, returned that very night. He looked, withal, the picture of frustrated expectancy—as if he had steadfastly waited the week at Miss Lily Hirschorn's side for a telephone call that never came.

Casually coughing, Salzman came immediately to the point: "So how did you like her?"

Leo's anger rose and he could not refrain from chiding the matchmaker: "Why did you lie to me, Salzman?"

Salzman's pale face went dead white, the world had snowed on him.

"Did you not state that she was twenty-nine?" Leo insisted.

"I give you my word—"

"She was thirty-five, if a day. *At least* thirty-five."

"Of this don't be too sure. Her father told me—"

"Never mind. The worst of it was that you lied to her."

"How did I lie to her, tell me?"

"You told her things about me that weren't true. You made me out to be more, consequently less than I am. She had in mind a totally different person, a sort of semimystical Wonder Rabbi."

"All I said, you was a religious man."

"I can imagine."

Salzman sighed. "This is my weakness that I have," he confessed. "My wife says to me I shouldn't be a salesman, but when I have two fine people that they would be wonderful to be married, I am so happy that I talk too much." He smiled wanly. "This is why Salzman is a poor man."

Leo's anger left him. "Well, Salzman, I'm afraid that's all."

The marriage broker fastened hungry eyes on him.

"You don't want any more a bride?"

"I do," said Leo, "but I have decided to seek her in a different way. I am no longer interested in an arranged marriage. To be frank, I now admit the necessity of premarital love. That is, I want to be in love with the one I marry."

"Love?" said Salzman, astounded. After a moment he remarked, "For us, our love is our life, not for the ladies. In the ghetto they—"

"I know, I know," said Leo. "I've thought of it often. Love I have said to myself, should be a by-product of living and worship rather than its own end. Yet for myself I find it necessary to establish the level of my need and fulfill it."

Salzman shrugged but answered, "Listen, rabbi, if you want love, this I can find for you also. I have such beautiful clients that you will love them the minute your eyes will see them."

Leo smiled unhappily. "I'm afraid you don't understand."

But Salzman hastily unstrapped his portfolio and withdrew a manila packet from it.

"Pictures," he said, quickly laying the envelope on the table.

Leo called after him to take the pictures away, but as if on the wings of the wind, Salzman had disappeared.

March came. Leo had returned to his regular routine. Although he felt not quite himself yet—lacked energy—he was making plans for a more active social life. Of course it would cost something, but he was an expert in cutting corners; and when there were no corners left he would make circles rounder. All the while Salzman's pictures had lain on the table, gathering dust. Occasionally as Leo sat studying, or enjoying a cup of tea, his eyes fell on the manila envelope, but he never opened it.

The days went by and no social life to speak of developed with a member of the opposite sex—it was difficult, given the circumstances of his situation. One morning Leo toiled up the stairs to his room and stared out the window at the city. Although the day was bright his view of it was dark. For some time he watched the people in the street below hurrying along and then turned with a heavy heart to his little room. On the table was the packet. With a sudden relentless gesture he tore it open. For a half-hour he stood by the table in a state of excitement, examining the photographs of the ladies Salzman had included. Finally, with a deep sigh he put them down. There were six, of varying degrees of attractiveness, but look at them long enough and they all became Lily Hirschorn: all past their prime, all starved behind bright smiles, not a true personality in the lot. Life, despite their frantic yoohooings, had passed them by; they were pictures in a brief case that stank of fish. After a while, however, as Leo attempted to return the photographs into the envelope, he found in it another, a snapshot of the type taken by a machine for a quarter. He gazed at it a moment and let out a cry.

Her face deeply moved him. Why, he could at first not say. It gave him the impression of youth—spring flowers, yet age—a sense of having been used to the bone, wasted; this came from the eyes, which were hauntingly familiar, yet absolutely strange. He had a vivid impression that he had met her before, but try as he might he could not place her although he could almost recall her name, as if he had read it in her own handwriting. No, this couldn't be; he would have remembered her. It was not, he affirmed, that she had an extraordinary beauty—no, though her face was attractive enough; it was that *something* about her moved him. Feature for feature, even some of the ladies of the photographs could do better; but she leaped forth to his heart—had *lived*, or wanted to—more than just wanted, perhaps regretted how she had lived—had somehow deeply suffered: it could be seen in the depths of those reluctant eyes, and from the way the light enclosed and shone from her, and within her, opening realms of possibility: this was her own. Her he desired. His head ached and eyes narrowed with the intensity of his gazing, then as if an obscure fog had blown up in the mind, he experienced fear of her and was aware that he had received an impression, somehow, of evil. He shuddered, saying softly, it is thus with us all. Leo brewed some tea in a small pot and sat sipping it without sugar, to calm himself. But before he had finished drinking, again with excitement he examined the face and found it good: good for Leo Finkle. Only such a one could understand him and help him seek whatever he was seeking. She might, perhaps, love him. How she had happened to be among the discards in Salzman's barrel he could never guess, but he knew he must urgently go find her.

Leo rushed downstairs, grabbed up the Bronx telephone book, and searched for Salzman's home address. He was not listed, nor was his office. Neither was he in the Manhattan book. But Leo remembered having written down the address on a slip of paper after he had read Salzman's advertisement in the "personals" column of the *Forward*. He ran up to his room and tore through his papers, without luck. It was exasperating. Just when he needed the matchmaker he was nowhere to be found. Fortunately Leo remembered to look in his wallet. There on a card he found his name written and a Bronx address. No phone number was listed, the reason—Leo now recalled—he had originally communicated with Salzman by letter. He got on his coat, put a hat on over his skull cap and hurried to the subway station. All the way to the far end of the Bronx he sat on the edge of his seat. He was more than once tempted to take out the picture and see if the girl's face was as he remembered it, but he refrained, allowing the snapshot to remain in his inside coat pocket, content to have her so close. When the train pulled into the station he was waiting at the door and bolted out. He quickly located the street Salzman had advertised.

The building he sought was less than a block from the subway, but it was not an office building, nor even a loft, nor a store in which one could rent office space. It was a very old tenement house. Leo found Salzman's name in pencil on a soiled tag under the bell and climbed three dark flights to his apartment. When he knocked, the door was opened by a thin, asthmatic, gray-haired woman, in felt slippers.

"Yes?" she said, expecting nothing. She listened without listening. He could have sworn he had seen her, too, before but knew it was an illusion.

"Salzman—does he live here? Pinye Salzman," he said, "the match-maker?"

She stared at him a long minute. "Of course."

He felt embarrassed. "Is he in?"

"No." Her mouth, though left open, offered nothing more.

"The matter is urgent. Can you tell me where his office is?"

"In the air." She pointed upward.

"You mean he has no office?" Leo asked.

"In his socks."

He peered into the apartment. It was sunless and dingy, one large room divided by a half-open curtain, beyond which he could see a sagging metal bed. The near side of a room was crowded with rickety chairs, old bureaus, a three-legged table, racks of cooking utensils, and all the apparatus of a kitchen. But there was no sign of Salzman or his magic barrel, probably also a figment of the imagination. An odor of frying fish made Leo weak to the knees.

"Where is he?" he insisted. "I've got to see your husband."

At length she answered, "So who knows where he is? Every time he thinks a new thought he runs to a different place. Go home, he will find you."

"Tell him Leo Finkle."

She gave no sign she had heard.

He walked downstairs, depressed.

But Salzman, breathless, stood waiting at his door.

Leo was astounded and overjoyed. "How did you get here before me?"

"I rushed."

"Come inside."

They entered. Leo fixed tea, and a sardine sandwich for Salzman. As they were drinking he reached behind him for the packet of pictures and handed them to the marriage broker.

Salzman put down his glass and said expectantly, "You found somebody you like?"

"Not among these."

The marriage broker turned away.

"Here is the one I want." Leo held forth the snapshot.

Salzman slipped on his glasses and took the picture into his trembling hand. He turned ghastly and let out a groan.

"What's the matter?" cried Leo.

"Excuse me. Was an accident this picture. She isn't for you."

Salzman frantically shoved the manila packet into his portfolio. He thrust the snapshot into his pocket and fled down the stairs.

Leo, after momentary paralysis, gave chase and cornered the marriage broker in the vestibule. The landlady made hysterical outcries but neither of them listened.

"Give me back the picture, Salzman."

"No." The pain in his eyes was terrible.

"Tell me who she is then."

"This I can't tell you. Excuse me."

He made to depart, but Leo, forgetting himself, seized the matchmaker by his tight coat and shook him frenziedly.

"Please," sighed Salzman. "*Please.*"

Leo ashamedly let him go. "Tell me who she is," he begged. "It's very important for me to know."

"She is not for you. She is a wild one—wild, without shame. This is not a bride for a rabbi."

"What do you mean wild?"

"Like an animal. Like a dog. For her to be poor was a sin. This is why to me she is dead now."

"In God's name, what do you mean?"

"Her I can't introduce to you," Salzman cried.

"Why are you so excited?"

"Why, he asks," Salzman said, bursting into tears. "This is my baby, my Stella, she should burn in hell."

Leo hurried up to bed and hid under the covers. Under the covers he thought his life through. Although he soon fell asleep he could not sleep her out of his mind. He woke, beating his breast. Though he prayed to be rid of her, his prayers went unanswered. Through days of torment he endlessly struggled not to love her; fearing success, he escaped it. He then concluded to convert her to goodness, himself to God. The idea alternately nauseated and exalted him.

He perhaps did not know that he had come to a final decision until he encountered Salzman in a Broadway cafeteria. He was sitting alone at a rear table, sucking the bony remains of a fish. The marriage broker appeared haggard, and transparent to the point of vanishing.

Salzman looked up at first without recognizing him. Leo had grown a pointed beard and his eyes were weighted with wisdom.

"Salzman," he said, "love has at last come to my heart."

"Who can love from a picture?" mocked the marriage broker.

"It is not impossible."

"If you can love her, then you can love anybody. Let me show you some new clients that they just sent me their photographs. One is a little doll."

"Just her I want," Leo murmured.

"Don't be a fool, doctor. Don't bother with her."

"Put me in touch with her, Salzman," Leo said humbly. "Perhaps I can be of service."

Salzman had stopped eating and Leo understood with emotion that it was now arranged.

Leaving the cafeteria, he was, however, afflicted by a tormenting suspicion that Salzman had planned it all to happen this way.

Leo was informed by letter that she would meet him on a certain corner, and she was there one spring night, waiting under a street lamp. He appeared, carrying a small bouquet of violets and rosebuds. Stella stood by the lamp post, smoking. She wore white with red shoes, which fitted his expectations, although in a troubled moment he had imagined the dress red, and only the shoes white. She waited uneasily and shyly. From afar he saw that her eyes—clearly her father's —were filled with desperate innocence. He pictured, in her, his own redemption. Violins and lit candles revolved in the sky. Leo ran forward with flowers outthrust.

Around the corner, Salzman, leaning against a wall, chanted prayers for the dead.

FLANNERY O'CONNOR

The Comforts of Home

Thomas withdrew to the side of the window and with his head between the wall and the curtain he looked down on the driveway where the car had stopped. His mother and the little slut were getting out of it. His mother emerged slowly, stolid and awkward, and then the little slut's long slightly bowed legs slid out, the dress pulled above the knees. With a shriek of laughter she ran to meet the dog, who bounded, overjoyed, shaking with pleasure, to welcome her. Rage gathered throughout Thomas's large frame with a silent ominous intensity, like a mob assembling.

It was now up to him to pack a suitcase, go to the hotel, and stay there until the house should be cleared.

He did not know where a suitcase was, he disliked to pack, he needed his books, his typewriter was not portable, he was used to an electric blanket, he could not bear to eat in restaurants. His mother, with her daredevil charity, was about to wreck the peace of the house.

The back door slammed and the girl's laugh shot up from the kitchen, through the back hall, up the stairwell and into his room, making for him like a bolt of electricity. He jumped to the side and stood glaring about him. His words of the morning had been unequivocal: "If you bring that girl back into this house, I leave. You can choose—her or me."

She had made her choice. An intense pain gripped his throat. It was the first time in his thirty-five years . . . He felt a sudden burning moisture behind his eyes. Then he steadied himself, overcome by rage. On the contrary: she had not made any choice. She was counting on his attachment to his electric blanket. She would have to be shown.

The girl's laughter rang upward a second time and Thomas winced. He saw again her look of the night before. She had invaded his room. He had waked to find his door open and her in it. There was enough light from the hall to make her visible as she turned toward him. The face was like a comedienne's in a musical comedy—a pointed chin, wide apple cheeks and feline empty eyes. He had sprung out of his bed and snatched a straight chair and then he had backed her out the door, holding the chair in front of him like an animal trainer driving out a dangerous cat. He had driven her silently down the hall, pausing when he reached it to beat on his mother's door. The girl, with a gasp, turned and fled into the guest room.

In a moment his mother had opened her door and peered out apprehensively. Her face, greasy with whatever she put on it at night, was framed in pink rubber curlers. She looked down the hall where the girl had disappeared. Thomas stood before her, the chair still lifted in front of him as if he were about to quell another beast. "She tried to get in my room," he hissed, pushing in. "I woke up and she was trying to get in my room." He closed the door behind him and his voice rose in outrage. "I won't put up with this! I won't put up with it another day!"

His mother, backed by him to her bed, sat down on the edge of it. She had a heavy body on which sat a thin, mysteriously gaunt and incongruous head.

"I'm telling you for the last time," Thomas said, "I won't put up with this another day." There was an observable tendency in all of her actions. This was, with the best intentions in the world, to make a mockery of virtue, to pursue it with such a mindless intensity that everyone involved was made a fool of and virtue itself became ridiculous. "Not another day," he repeated.

His mother shook her head emphatically, her eyes still on the door.

Thomas put the chair on the floor in front of her and sat down on it. He leaned forward as if he were about to explain something to a defective child.

"That's just another way she's unfortunate," his mother said "So awful, so awful. She told me the name of it but I forget what it is but it's something she can't help. Something she was born with. Thomas," she said and put her hand to her jaw, "suppose it were you?"

Exasperation blocked his windpipe. "Can't I make you see," he croaked, "that if she can't help herself you can't help her?"

His mother's eyes, intimate but untouchable, were the blue of great distances after sunset. "Nimpermaniac," she murmured.

"Nymphomaniac," he said fiercely. "She doesn't need to supply you with any fancy names. She's a moral moron. That's all you need to know. Born without the moral faculty—like somebody else would be born without a kidney or a leg. Do you understand?"

"I keep thinking it might be you," she said, her hand still on her jaw. "If it were you, how do you think I'd feel if nobody took you in? What if you were a nimpermaniac and not a brilliant smart person and you did what you couldn't help and . . ."

Thomas felt a deep unbearable loathing for himself as if he were turning slowly into the girl.

"What did she have on?" she asked abruptly, her eyes narrowing.

"Nothing!" he roared. "Now will you get her out of here!"

"How can I turn her out in the cold?" she said. "This morning she was threatening to kill herself again."

"Send her back to jail," Thomas said.

"I would not send *you* back to jail, Thomas," she said.

He got up and snatched the chair and fled the room while he was still able to control himself.

Thomas loved his mother. He loved her because it was his nature to do so, but there were times when he could not endure her love for him. There were times when it became nothing but pure idiot mystery and he sensed about him forces, invisible currents entirely out of his control. She proceeded always from the tritest of considerations—it was the *nice thing to do*—into the most foolhardy engagements with the devil, whom, of course, she never recognized.

The devil for Thomas was only a manner of speaking, but it was a manner appropriate to the situations his mother got into. Had she been in any degree intellectual, he could have proved to her from early Christian history that no excess of virtue is justified, that a moderation of good produces likewise a moderation in evil, that if Antony of Egypt had stayed at home and attended to his sister, no devils would have plagued him.

Thomas was not cynical and so far from being opposed to virtue, he saw it as the principle of order and the only thing that makes life bearable. His own life was made bearable by the fruits of his mother's saner virtues—by the well-regulated house she kept and the excellent meals she served. But when virtue got out of hand with her, as now, a sense of devils grew upon him, and these were not mental quirks in himself or the old lady, they were denizens with personalities, present though not visible, who might any moment be expected to shriek or rattle a pot.

The girl had landed in the county jail a month ago on a bad check charge and his mother had seen her picture in the paper. At the breakfast table she had gazed at it for a long time and then had passed it over the coffee pot to him. "Imagine," she said, "only nineteen years old and in that filthy jail. And she doesn't look like a bad girl."

Thomas glanced at the picture. It showed the face of a shrewd ragamuffin. He observed that the average age for criminality was steadily lowering.

"She looks like a wholesome girl," his mother said.

"Wholesome people don't pass bad checks," Thomas said.

"You don't know what you'd do in a pinch."

"I wouldn't pass a bad check," Thomas said.

"I think," his mother said, "I'll take her a little box of candy."

If then and there he had put his foot down, nothing else would have happened. His father, had he been living, would have put his foot down at that point. Taking a box of candy was her favorite nice thing to do. When anyone within her social station moved to town, she called and took a box of candy; when any of her friend's children had babies or won a scholarship, she called and took a box of candy; when an old person broke his hip, she was at his bedside with a box of candy. He had been amused at the idea of her taking a box of candy to the jail.

He stood now in his room with the girl's laugh rocketing away in his head and cursed his amusement.

When his mother returned from the visit to the jail, she had burst into his study without knocking and had collapsed full-length on his couch, lifting her small swollen feet up on the arm of it. After a moment, she recovered herself enough to sit up and put a newspaper under them. Then she fell back again. "We don't know how the other half lives," she said.

Thomas knew that though her conversation moved from cliché to cliché there were real experiences behind them. He was less sorry for the girl's being in jail than for his mother having to see her there. He would have spared her all unpleasant sights. "Well," he said and put away his journal, "you had better forget it now. The girl has ample reason to be in jail."

"You can't imagine what all she's been through," she said, sitting up again, "listen." The poor girl, Star, had been brought up by a stepmother with three children of her own, one an almost grown boy who had taken advantage of her in such dreadful ways that she had been forced to run away and find her real mother. Once found, her real mother had sent her to various boarding schools to get rid of her. At each of these she had been forced to run away by the presence of perverts and sadists so monstrous that their acts defied description. Thomas could tell that his mother had not been spared the details that she was sparing him. Now and again when she spoke vaguely, her voice shook and he could tell that she was remembering some horror that had been put to her graphically. He had hoped that in a few days the memory of all this would wear off, but it did not. The next day she returned to the jail with Kleenex and cold-cream and a few days later, she announced that she had consulted a lawyer.

It was at these times that Thomas truly mourned the death of his father though he had not been able to endure him in life. The old man would have had none of this foolishness. Untouched by useless compassion, he would (behind her back) have pulled the necessary strings with his crony, the sheriff, and the girl would have been packed off to the state penitentiary to serve her time. He had always been engaged in some enraged action until one morning when (with an angry glance at his wife as if she alone were responsible) he had dropped dead at the breakfast table. Thomas had inherited his father's reason without his ruthlessness and his mother's love of good without her tendency to pursue it. His plan for all practical action was to wait and see what developed.

The lawyer found that the story of the repeated atrocities was for the most part untrue, but when he explained to her that the girl was a psychopathic personality, not insane enough for the asylum, not criminal enough for the jail, not stable enough for society, Thomas's mother was more deeply affected than ever. The girl readily admitted that her story was untrue on account of her being a congenital liar; she lied, she said, because she was insecure. She had passed through the hands of several psychiatrists who had put the finishing touches to her education. She knew there was no hope for her. In the presence of such an affliction as this, his mother seemed bowed down by some painful mystery that nothing would make endurable but a redoubling of effort. To his annoyance, she appeared to look on *him* with compassion, as if her hazy charity no longer made distinctions.

A few days later she burst in and said that the lawyer had got the girl paroled—to her.

Thomas rose from his Morris chair, dropping the review he had been reading. His large bland face contracted in anticipated pain. "You are not," he said, "going to bring that girl here!"

"No, no," she said, "calm yourself, Thomas." She had managed with difficulty to get the girl a job in a pet shop in town and a place to board with a crotchety old lady of her acquaintance. People were not kind. They did not put themselves in the place of someone like Star who had everything against her.

Thomas sat down again and retrieved his review. He seemed just to have escaped some danger which he did not care to make clear to himself. "Nobody can tell you anything," he said, "but in a few days that girl will have left town, having got what she could out of you. You'll never hear from her again."

Two nights later he came home and opened the parlor door and was speared by a shrill depthless laugh. His mother and the girl sat close to the fireplace where the gas logs were lit. The girl gave the immediate impression of being physically crooked. Her hair was cut like a dog's or an elf's and she was dressed in the latest fashion. She was training on him a long familiar sparkling stare that turned after a second into an intimate grin.

"Thomas!" his mother said, her voice firm with the injunction not to bolt, "this is Star you've heard so much about. Star is going to have supper with us."

The girl called herself Star Drake. The lawyer had found that her real name was Sarah Ham.

Thomas neither moved nor spoke but hung in the door in what seemed a savage perplexity. Finally he said, "How do you do, Sarah," in a tone of such loathing that he was shocked at the sound of it. He reddened, feeling it beneath him to show contempt for any creature so pathetic. He advanced into the room, determined at least on a decent politeness and sat down heavily in a straight chair.

"Thomas writes history," his mother said with a threatening look at him. "He's president of the local Historical Society this year."

The girl leaned forward and gave Thomas an even more pointed attention. "Fabulous!" she said in a throaty voice.

"Right now Thomas is writing about the first settlers in this county," his mother said.

"Fabulous!" the girl repeated.

Thomas by an effort of will managed to look if he were alone in the room.

"Say, you know who he looks like?" Star asked, her head on one side, taking him in at an angle.

"Oh some one very distinguished!" his mother said archly.

"This cop I saw in the movie I went to last night," Star said.

"Star," his mother said, "I think you ought to be careful about the kind of movies you go to. I think you ought to see only the best ones. I don't think crime stories would be good for you."

"Oh this was a crime-does-not-pay," Star said, "and I swear this cop looked exactly like him. They were always putting something over on the guy. He would look like he couldn't stand it a minute longer or he would blow up. He was a riot. And not bad looking," she added with an appreciative leer at Thomas.

"Star," his mother said, "I think it would be grand if you developed a taste for music."

Thomas sighed. His mother rattled on and the girl, paying no attention to her, let her eyes play over him. The quality of her look was such that it might have been her hands, resting now on his knees, now on his neck. Her eyes had a mocking glitter and he knew that she was well aware he could not stand the sight of her. He needed nothing to tell him he was in the presence of the very stuff of corruption, but blameless corruption because there was no responsible faculty behind it. He was looking at the most unendurable form of innocence. Absently he asked himself what the attitude of God was to this, meaning if possible to adopt it.

His mother's behavior throughout the meal was so idiotic that he could barely stand to look at her and since he could less stand to look at Sarah Ham, he fixed on the sideboard across the room a continuous gaze of disapproval and disgust. Every remark of the girl's his mother met as if it deserved serious attention. She advanced several plans for the wholesome use of Star's spare time. Sarah Ham paid no more attention to this advice than if it came from a parrot. Once when Thomas inadvertently looked in her direction, she winked. As soon as he swallowed the last spoonful of dessert, he rose and muttered, "I have to go, I have a meeting."

"Thomas," his mother said, "I want you to take Star home on your way. I don't want her riding in taxis by herself at night."

For a moment Thomas remained furiously silent. Then he turned and left the room. Presently he came back with a look of obscure determination on his face. The girl was ready, meekly waiting at the parlor door. She cast up at him a great look of admiration and confidence. Thomas did not offer his arm but she took it anyway and moved out of the house and down the steps, attached to what might have been a miraculously moving monument.

"Be good!" his mother called.

Sarah Ham snickered and poked him in the ribs.

While getting his coat he had decided that this would be his opportunity to tell the girl that unless she ceased to be a parasite on his mother, he would see to it, personally, that she was returned to jail. He would let her know that he understood what she was up to, that he was not an innocent and that there were certain things he would not put up with. At his desk, pen in hand, none was more articulate than Thomas. As soon as he found himself shut into the car with Sarah Ham, terror seized his tongue.

She curled her feet up under her and said, "Alone at last," and giggled.

Thomas swerved the car away from the house and drove fast toward the gate. Once on the highway, he shot forward as if he were being pursued.

"Jesus!" Sarah Ham said, swinging her feet off the seat, "where's the fire?"

Thomas did not answer. In a few seconds he could feel her edging closer. She stretched, eased nearer, and finally hung her hand limply over his shoulder. "Thomsee doesn't like me," she said, "but I think he's fabulously cute."

Thomas covered the three and half miles into town in a little over four minutes. The light at the first intersection was red but he ignored it. The old woman lived three blocks beyond. When the car screeched to a halt at the place, he jumped out and ran around to the girl's door and opened it. She did not move from the car and Thomas was obliged to wait. After a moment one leg emerged, then her small white crooked face appeared and stared up at him. There was something about the look of it that suggested blindness but it was the blindness of those who don't know that they cannot see. Thomas was curiously sickened. The empty eyes moved over him. "Nobody likes me," she said in a sullen tone. "What if you were me and I couldn't stand to ride you three miles?"

"My mother likes you," he muttered.

"Her!" the girl said. "She's just about seventy-five years behind the times!"

Breathlessly Thomas said, "If I find you bothering her again, I'll have you put back in jail." There was a dull force behind his voice though it came out barely above a whisper.

"You and who else?" she said and drew back in the car as if now she did not intend to get out at all. Thomas reached into it, blindly grasped the front of her coat, pulled her out by it and released her. Then he lunged back to the car and sped off. The other door was still hanging open and her laugh, bodiless but real, bounded up the street as if it were about to jump in the open side of the car and ride away with him. He reached over and slammed the door and then drove toward home, too angry to attend his meeting. He intended to make his mother well-aware of his displeasure. He intended to leave no doubt in her mind. The voice of his father rasped in his head.

Numbskull, the old man said, put your foot down now. Show her who's boss before she shows you.

But when Thomas reached home, his mother, wisely, had gone to bed.

The next morning he appeared at the breakfast table, his brow lowered and the thrust of his jaw indicating that he was in a dangerous humor. When he intended to be determined, Thomas began like a bull that, before charging, backs with his head lowered and paws the ground. "All right now listen," he began, yanking out his chair and sitting down, "I have something to say to you about that girl and I don't intend to say it but once." He drew breath. "She's nothing but a little slut. She makes fun of you behind your back. She means to get everything she can out of you and you are nothing to her."

His mother looked as if she too had spent a restless night. She did not dress in the morning but wore her bathrobe and a grey turban around her head, which gave her face a disconcerting omniscient look. He might have been breakfasting with a sibyl.

"You'll have to use canned cream this morning," she said, pouring his coffee. "I forgot the other."

"All right did you hear me?" Thomas growled.

"I'm not deaf," his mother said and put the pot back on the trivet. "I know I'm nothing but an old bag of wind to her."

"Then why do you persist in this foolhardy . . ."

"Thomas," she said, and put her hand to the side of her face, "it might be . . ."

"It is not me!" Thomas said, grasping the table leg at his knee.

She continued to hold her face, shaking her head slightly. "Think of all you have," she began. "All the comforts of home. And morals, Thomas. No bad inclinations, nothing bad you were born with."

Thomas began to breathe like some one who feels the onset of asthma. "You are not logical," he said in a limp voice. "*He* would have put his foot down."

The old lady stiffened. "You," she said, "are not like him."

Thomas opened his mouth silently.

"However," his mother said, in a tone of such subtle accusation that she might have been taking back the compliment, "I won't invite her back again since you're so dead set against her."

"I am not set against her," Thomas said. "I am set against your making a fool of yourself."

As soon as he left the table and closed the door of his study on himself, his father took up a squatting position in his mind. The old man had had the countryman' ability to converse squatting, though he was no countryman but had been born and brought up in the city and only moved to a smaller place later to exploit his talents. With steady skill he had made them think him one of them. In the midst of a conversation on the courthouse lawn, he would squat and his two or three companions would squat with him with no break in the surface of the talk. By gesture he had lived his lie; he had never deigned to tell one.

Let her run over you, he said. You ain't like me. Not enough to be a man.

Thomas began vigorously to read and presently the image faded. The girl had caused a disturbance in the depths of his being, somewhere out of the reach of his power of analysis. He felt as if he had seen a tornado pass a hundred yards away and had an intimation that it would turn again and head directly for him. He did not get his mind firmly on his work until midmorning.

Two nights later, his mother and he were sitting in the den after their supper, each reading a section of the evening paper, when the telephone began to ring with the brassy intensity of a fire alarm. Thomas reached for it. As soon as the receiver was in his hand, a shrill female voice screamed into the room, "Come get this girl! Come get her! Drunk! Drunk in my parlor and I won't have it! Lost her job and come back here drunk! I won't have it!"

His mother leapt up and snatched the receiver.

The ghost of Thomas's father rose before him. Call the sheriff, the old man prompted. "Call the sheriff," Thomas said in a loud voice. "Call the sheriff to go there and pick her up."

"We'll be right there," his mother was saying. "We'll come and get her right away. Tell her to get her things together."

"She ain't in no condition to get nothing together," the voice screamed. "You shouldn't have put something like her off on me! My house is respectable!"

"Tell her to call the sheriff," Thomas shouted.

His mother put the receiver down and looked at him. "I wouldn't turn a dog over to that man," she said.

Thomas sat in the chair with his arms folded and looked fixedly at the wall.

"Think of the poor girl, Thomas," his mother said, "with nothing. Nothing. And we have everything."

When they arrived, Sarah Ham was slumped spraddle-legged against the banister on the boarding house front-steps. Her tam was down on her forehead where the old woman had slammed it and her clothes were bulging out of her suitcase where the old woman had thrown them in. She was carrying on a drunken conversation with herself in a low personal tone. A streak of lipstick ran up one side of her face. She allowed herself to be guided by his mother to the car and put in the back seat without seeming to know who the rescuer was. "Nothing to talk to all day but a pack of goddamned parakeets," she said in a furious whisper.

Thomas, who had not got out of the car at all, or looked at her after the first revolted glance, said, "I'm telling you, once and for all, the place to take her is the jail."

His mother, sitting on the back seat, holding the girl's hand, did not answer.

"All right, take her to the hotel," he said.

"I cannot take a drunk girl to a hotel, Thomas," she said. "You know that."

"Then take her to a hospital."

"She doesn't need a jail or a hotel or a hospital," his mother said, "she needs a home."

"She does not need mine," Thomas said.

"Only for tonight, Thomas," the old lady sighed. "Only for tonight."

Since then eight days had passed. The little slut was established in the guest room. Every day his mother set out to find her a job and a place to board, and failed, for the old woman had broadcast a warning. Thomas kept to his room or the den. His home was to him home, workshop, church, as personal as the shell of a turtle and as necessary. He could not believe that it could be violated in this way. His flushed face had a constant look of stunned outrage.

As soon as the girl was up in the morning, her voice throbbed out in a blues song that would rise and waver, then plunge low with insinuations of passion about to be satisfied and Thomas, at his desk, would lunge up and begin frantically stuffing his ears with Kleenex. Each time he started from one room to another, one floor to another, she would be certain to appear. Each time he was half way up or down the stairs, she would either meet him and pass, cringing coyly, or go up or down behind him, breathing small tragic spearmint-flavored sighs. She appeared to adore Thomas's repugnance to her and to draw it out of him every chance she got as if it added delectably to her martyrdom.

The old man—small, wasp-like, in his yellowed panama hat, his seersucker suit, his pink carefully-soiled shirt, his small string tie— appeared to have taken up his station in Thomas's mind and from there, usually squatting, he shot out the same rasping suggestion every time the boy paused from his forced studies. Put your foot down. Go to see the sheriff.

The sheriff was another edition of Thomas's father except that he wore a checkered shirt and a Texas type hat and was ten years younger. He was as easily dishonest, and he had genuinely admired the old man. Thomas, like his mother, would have gone far out of his way to avoid his glassy blue gaze. He kept hoping for another solution, for a miracle.

With Sarah Ham in the house, meals were unbearable.

"Tomsee doesn't like me," she said the third or fourth night at the supper table and cast her pouting gaze across at the large rigid figure of Thomas, whose face was set with the look of a man trapped by insufferable odors. "He doesn't want me here. Nobody wants me anywhere."

"Thomas's name is Thomas," his mother interrupted. "Not Tomsee."

"I made Tomsee up," she said. "I think it's cute. He hates me."

"Thomas does not hate you," his mother said. "We are not the kind of people who hate," she added, as if this were an imperfection that had been bred out of them generations ago.

"Oh, I know when I'm not wanted," Sarah Ham continued. "They didn't even want me in jail. If I killed myself I wonder would God want me?"

"Try it and see," Thomas muttered.

The girl screamed with laughter. Then she stopped abruptly, her face puckered and she began to shake. "The best thing to do," she said, her teeth clattering, "is to kill myself. Then I'll be out of everybody's way. I'll go to hell and be out of God's way. And even the devil won't want me. He'll kick me out of hell, not even in hell . . ." she wailed.

Thomas rose, picked up his plate and knife and fork and carried them to the den to finish his supper. After that, he had not eaten another meal at the table but had had his mother serve him at his desk. At these meals, the old man was intensely present to him. He appeared to be tipping backwards in his chair, his thumbs beneath his galluses, while he said such things as, She never ran me away from my own table.

A few nights later, Sarah Ham slashed her wrists with a paring knife and had hysterics. From the den where he was closeted after supper, Thomas heard a shriek, then a series of screams, then his mother's scurrying footsteps through the house. He did not move. His first instant of hope that the girl had cut her throat faded as he realized she could not have done it and continue to scream the way she was doing.

He returned to his journal and presently the screams subsided. In a moment his mother burst in with his coat and hat. "We have to take her to the hospital," she said. "She tried to do away with herself. I have a tourniquet on her arm. Oh Lord, Thomas," she said, "imagine being so low you'd do a thing like that!"

Thomas rose woodenly and put on his hat and coat. "We will take her to the hospital," he said, "and we will leave her there."

"And drive her to despair again?" the old lady cried. "Thomas!"

Standing in the center of his room now, realizing that he had reached the point where action was inevitable, that he must pack, that he must leave, that he must go, Thomas remained immovable.

His fury was directed not at the little slut but at his mother. Even though the doctor had found that she had barely damaged herself and had raised the girl's wrath by laughing at the tourniquet and putting only a streak of iodine on the cut, his mother could not get over the incident. Some new weight of sorrow seemed to have been thrown across her shoulders, and not only Thomas, but Sarah Ham was infuriated by this, for it appeared to be a general sorrow that would have found another object no matter what good fortune came to either of them. The experience of Sarah Ham had plunged the old lady into mourning for the world.

The morning after the attempted suicide, she had gone through the house and collected all the knives and scissors and locked them in a drawer. She emptied a bottle of rat poison down the toilet and took up the roach tablets from the kitchen floor. Then she came to Thomas's study and said in a whisper, "Where is that gun of his? I want you to lock it up."

"The gun is in my drawer," Thomas roared, "and I will not lock it up. If she shoots herself, so much the better!"

"Thomas," his mother said, "she'll hear you!"

"Let her hear me!" Thomas yelled. "Don't you know she has no intention of killing herself? Don't you know her kind never kill themselves? Don't you . . ."

His mother slipped out the door and closed it to silence him and Sarah Ham's laugh, quite close in the hall, came rattling into his room. "Tomsee'll find out. I'll kill myself and then he'll be sorry he wasn't nice to me. I'll use his own lil gun, his own lil ol' pearl-handled revollervuh!" she shouted and let out a loud tormented-sounding laugh in imitation of a movie monster.

Thomas ground his teeth. He pulled out his desk drawer and felt for the pistol. It was an inheritance from the old man, whose opinion it had been that every house should contain a loaded gun. He had discharged two bullets one night into the side of a prowler, but Thomas had never shot anything. He had no fear that the girl would use the gun on herself and he closed the drawer. Her kind clung tenaciously to life and were able to wrest some histrionic advantage from every moment.

Several ideas for getting rid of her had entered his head but each of these had been suggestions whose moral tone indicated that they had come from a mind akin to his father's, and Thomas had rejected them. He could not get the girl locked up again until she did something illegal. The old man would have been able with no qualms at all to get her drunk and send her out on the highway in his car, meanwhile notifying the highway patrol of her presence on the road, but Thomas considered this below his moral stature. Suggestions continued to come to him, each more outrageous than the last.

He had not the vaguest hope that the girl would get the gun and shoot herself, but that afternoon when he looked in the drawer, the gun was gone. His study locked from the inside, not the out. He cared nothing about the gun, but the thought of Sarah Ham's hands sliding among his papers infuriated him. Now even his study was contaminated. The only place left untouched by her was his bedroom.

That night she entered it.

In the morning at breakfast, he did not eat and did not sit down. He stood behind his chair and delivered his ultimatum while his mother sipped her coffee as if she were both alone in the room and in great pain. "I have stood this," he said, "for as long as I am able. Since I see plainly that you care nothing about me, about my peace or comfort or working conditions, I am about to take the only step open to me. I will give you one more day. If you bring that girl back into this house this afternoon, I leave. You can choose—her or me." He had had more to say but at that point his voice cracked and he left.

At ten o'clock his mother and Sarah Ham left the house.

At four he heard the car wheels on the gravel and rushed to the window. As the car stopped, the dog stood up, alert, shaking.

He seemed unable to take the first step that would set him walking to the closet in the hall to look for the suitcase. He was like a man handed a knife and told to operate on himself if he wished to live. His huge hands clenched helplessly. His expression was a turmoil of indecision and outrage. His pale blue eyes seemed to sweat in his broiling face. He closed them for a moment and on the back of his lids, his father's image leered at him. Idiot! the old man hissed, idiot! The criminal slut stold your gun! See the sheriff! See the sheriff!

It was a moment before Thomas opened his eyes. He seemed newly stunned. He stood where he was for at least three minutes, then he turned slowly like a large vessel reversing its direction and faced the door. He stood there a moment longer, then he left, his face set to see the ordeal through.

He did not know where he would find the sheriff. The man made his own rules and kept his own hours. Thomas stopped first at the jail where his office was, but he was not in it. He went to the courthouse and was told by a clerk that the sheriff had gone to the barber-shop across the street. "Yonder's the deppity," the clerk said and pointed out the window to the large figure of a man in a checkered shirt, who was leaning against the side of a police car, looking into space.

"It has to be the sheriff," Thomas said and left for the barber-shop. As little as he wanted anything to do with the sheriff, he realized that the man was at least intelligent and not simply a mound of sweating flesh.

The barber said the sheriff had just left. Thomas started back to the courthouse and as he stepped on to the sidewalk from the street, he saw a lean, slightly stooped figure gesticulating angrily at the deputy.

Thomas approached with an aggressiveness brought on by nervous agitation. He stopped abruptly three feet away and said in an over-loud voice, "Can I have a word with you?" without adding the sheriff's name, which was Farebrother.

Farebrother turned his sharp creased face just enough to take Thomas in, and the deputy did likewise, but neither spoke. The sheriff removed a very small piece of cigaret from his lip and dropped it at his feet. "I told you what to do," he said to the deputy. Then he moved off with a slight nod that indicated Thomas could follow him if he wanted to see him. The deputy slunk around the front of the police car and got inside.

Farebrother, with Thomas following, headed across the courthouse square and stopped beneath a tree that shaded a quarter of the front lawn. He waited, leaning slightly forward, and lit another cigaret.

Thomas began to blurt out his business. As he had not had time to prepare his words, he was barely coherent. By repeating the same thing over several times, he managed at length to get out what he wanted to say. When he finished, the sheriff was still leaning slightly forward, at an angle to him, his eyes on nothing in particular. He remained that way without speaking.

Thomas began again, slower and in a lamer voice, and Farebrother let him continue for some time before he said, "We had her oncet." He then allowed himself a slow, creased, all-knowing, quarter smile.

"I had nothing to do with that," Thomas said. "That was my mother."

Farebrother squatted.

"She was trying to help the girl," Thomas said. "She didn't know she couldn't be helped."

"Bit off more than she could chew, I reckon," the voice below him mused.

"She has nothing to do with this," Thomas said. "She doesn't know I'm here. The girl is dangerous with that gun."

"*He,*" the sheriff said, "never let nothing grow under his feet. Particularly nothing a woman planted."

"She might kill somebody with that gun," Thomas said weakly, looking down at the round top of the Texas type hat.

There was a long time of silence.

"Where's she got it?" Farebrother asked.

"I don't know. She sleeps in the guest room. It must be in there, in her suitcase probably," Thomas said.

Farebrother lapsed into silence again.

"You could come search the guest room," Thomas said in a strained voice. "I can go home and leave the latch off the front door and you can come in quietly and go upstairs and search her room."

Farebrother turned his head so that his eyes looked boldly at Thomas's knees. "You seem to know how it ought to be done," he said. "Want to swap jobs?"

Thomas said nothing because he could not think of anything to say, but he waited doggedly. Farbrother removed the cigaret butt from his lips and dropped it on the grass. Beyond him on the courthouse porch a group of loiterers who had been leaning at the left of the door moved over to the right where a patch of sunlight had settled. From one of the upper window's a crumpled piece of paper blew out and drifted down.

"I'll come along about six," Farebrother said. "Leave the latch off the door and keep out of my way—yourself and them two women too."

Thomas let out a rasping sound of relief meant to be "Thanks," and struck off across the grass like some one released. The phrase, "them two women," stuck like a burr in his brain—the subtlety of the insult to his mother hurting him more than any of Farebrother's references to his own incompetence. As he got into his car, his face suddenly flushed. Had he delivered his mother over to the sheriff—to be a butt for the man's tongue? Was he betraying her to get rid of the little slut? He saw at once that this was not the case. He was doing what he was doing for her own good, to rid her of a parasite that would ruin their peace. He started his car and drove quickly home but once he had turned in the driveway, he decided it would be better to park some distance from the house and go quietly in by the back door. He parked on the grass and on the grass walked in a circle toward the rear of the house. The sky was lined with mustard-colored streaks. The dog was asleep on the back dormat. At the approach of his master's step, he opened one yellow eye, took him in, and closed it again.

Thomas let himself into the kitchen. It was empty and the house was quiet enough for him to be aware of the loud ticking of the kitchen clock. It was a quarter to six. He tiptoed hurriedly through the hall to the front door and took the latch off it. Then he stood for a moment listening. From behind the closed parlor door, he heard his mother snoring softly and presumed that she had gone to sleep while reading. On the other side of the hall, not three feet from his study, the little slut's black coat and red pocketbook were slung on a chair. He heard water running upstairs and decided she was taking a bath.

He went into his study and sat down at his desk to wait, noting with distaste that every few moments a tremor ran through him. He sat for a minute or two doing nothing. Then he picked up a pen and began to draw squares on the back of an envelope that lay before him. He looked at his watch. It was eleven minutes to six. After a moment he idly drew the center drawer of the desk out over his lap. For a moment he stared at the gun without recognition. Then he gave a yelp and leaped up. She had put it back!

Idiot! his father hissed, idiot! Go plant it in her pocketbook. Don't just stand there. Go plant it in her pocketbook!

Thomas stood staring at the drawer.

Moron! the old man fumed. Quick while there's time! Go plant it in her pocketbook.

Thomas did not move.

Imbecile! his father cried.

Thomas picked up the gun.

Make haste, the old man ordered.

Thomas started forward, holding the gun away from him. He opened the door and looked at the chair. The black coat and red pocketbook were lying on it almost within reach.

Hurry up, you fool, his father said.

From behind the parlor door the almost inaudible snores of his mother rose and fell. They seemed to mark an order of time that had nothing to do with the instants left to Thomas. There was no other sound.

Quick, you imbecile, before she wakes up, the old man said.

The snores stopped and Thomas heard the sofa springs groan. He grabbed the red pocketbook. It had a skin-like feel to his touch and as it opened, he caught an unmistakable odor of the girl. Wincing, he thrust in the gun and then drew back. His face burned an ugly dull red.

"What is Tomsee putting in my purse?" she called and her pleased laugh bounced down the staircase. Thomas whirled.

She was at the top of the stair, coming down in the manner of a fashion model, one bare leg and then the other thrusting out the front of her kimona in a definite rhythm. "Tomsee is being naughty," she said in a throaty voice. She reached the bottom and cast a possessive leer at Thomas whose face was now more grey than red. She reached out, pulled the bag open with her finger and peered at the gun.

His mother opened the parlor door and looked out.

"Tomsee put his pistol in my bag!" the girl shrieked.

"Ridiculous," his mother said, yawning. "What would Thomas want to put his pistol in your bag for?"

Thomas stood slightly hunched, his hands hanging helplessly at the wrists as if he had just pulled them up out of a pool of blood.

"I don't know what for," the girl said, "but he sure did it," and she proceeded to walk around Thomas, her hands on her hips, her neck thrust forward and her intimate grin fixed on him fiercely. All at once her expression seemed to open as the purse had opened when Thomas touched it. She stood with her head cocked on one side in an attitude of disbelief. "Oh boy," she said slowly, "is he a case."

At that instant Thomas damned not only the girl but the entire order of the universe that made her possible.

"Thomas wouldn't put a gun in your bag," his mother said. "Thomas is a gentleman."

The girl made a chortling noise. "You can see it in there," she said and pointed to the open purse.

You *found* it in her bag, you dimwit! the old man hissed.

"I found it in her bag!" Thomas shouted. "The dirty criminal slut stole my gun!"

His mother gasped at the sound of the other presence in his voice. The old lady's sybil-like face turned pale.

"Found it my eye!" Sarah Ham shrieked and started for the pocketbook, but Thomas, as if his arm were guided by his father, caught it first and snatched the gun. The girl in a frenzy lunged at Thomas's throat and would actually have caught him around the neck had not his mother thrown herself forward to protect her.

Fire! the old man yelled.

Thomas fired. The blast was like a sound meant to bring an end to evil in the world. Thomas heard it as a sound that would shatter the laughter of sluts until all shrieks were stilled and nothing was left to disturb the peace of perfect order.

The echo died away in waves. Before the last one had faded, Farebrother opened the door and put his head inside the hall. His nose wrinkled. His expression for some few seconds was that of a man unwilling to admit surprise. His eyes were clear as glass, reflecting the scene. The old lady lay on the floor between the girl and Thomas.

The sheriff's brain worked instantly like a calculating machine. He saw the facts as if they were already in print: the fellow had intended all along to kill his mother and pin it on the girl. But Farebrother had been too quick for him. They were not yet aware of his head in the door. As he scrutinized the scene, further insights were flashed to him. Over her body, the killer and the slut were about to collapse into each other's arms. The sheriff knew a nasty bit when he saw it. He was accustomed to enter upon scenes that were not as bad as he had hoped to find them, but this one met his expectations.

Johnny Panic and the Bible of Dreams

Every day from nine to five I sit at my desk facing the door of the office and type up other people's dreams. Not just dreams. That wouldn't be practical enough for my bosses. I type up also people's daytime complaints: trouble with mother, trouble with father, trouble with the bottle, the bed, the headache that bangs home and blacks out the sweet world for no known reason. Nobody comes to our office unless they have troubles. Troubles that can't be pinpointed by Wassermanns or Wechsler-Bellevues alone.

Maybe a mouse gets to thinking pretty early on how the whole world is run by these enormous feet. Well, from where I sit I figure the world is run by one thing and this one thing only. Panic with a dog-face, devil-face, hag-face, whore-face, panic in capital letters with no face at all—it's the same Johnny Panic, awake or sleep.

When people ask me where I work, I tell them I'm assistant to the secretary in one of the outpatient departments of the Clinics Building of the City Hospital. This sounds so be-all, end-all they seldom get around to asking me more than what I do, and what I do is mainly type up records. On my own hook though, and completely under cover, I am pursuing a vocation that would set these doctors on their

ears. In the privacy of my one-room apartment I call myself secretary
to none other than Johnny Panic himself.

Dream by dream I am educating myself to become that rare character, rarer, in truth, than any member of the Psychoanalytic Institute:
a dream connoisseur. Not a dream-stopper, a dream-explainer, an ex-
ploiter of dreams for the crass practical ends of health and happiness,
but an unsordid collector of dreams for themselves alone. A lover of
dreams for Johnny Panic's sake, the Maker of them all.

There isn't a dream I've typed up in our record books that I don't
know by heart. There isn't a dream I haven't copied out at home into
Johnny Panic's Bible of Dreams.

This is my real calling.

Some nights I take the elevator up to the roof of my apartment
building. Some nights, about 3 A.M. Over the trees at the far side of the
Common the United Fund torch flare flattens and recovers under
some witchy invisible push, and here and there in the hunks of stone
and brick I see a light. Most of all, though, I feel the city sleeping.
Sleeping from the river on the west to the ocean on the east, like some
rootless island rockabying itself on nothing at all.

I can be tight and nervy as the top string on a violin, and yet by the
time the sky begins to blue I'm ready for sleep. It's the thought of all
those dreamers and what they're dreaming wears me down till I sleep
the sleep of fever. Monday to Friday what do I do but type up those
same dreams. Sure, I don't touch a fraction of them the city over, but
page by page, dream by dream, my Intake books fatten and weigh down
the bookshelves of the cabinet in the narrow passage running parallel
to the main hall, off which passage the doors to all the doctors' little
interviewing cubicles open.

I've got a funny habit of identifying the people who come in by
their dreams. As far as I'm concerned, the dreams single them out more
than any Christian name. This one guy, for example, who works for a
ball-bearing company in town, dreams every night how he's lying on
his back with a grain of sand on his chest. Bit by bit this grain of sand
grows bigger and bigger till it's big as a fair-sized house and he can't
draw breath. Another fellow I know of has had a certain dream ever
since they gave him ether and cut out his tonsils and adenoids when
he was a kid. In this dream he's caught in the rollers of a cotton mill,
fighting for his life. Oh, he's not alone, although he thinks he is. A lot
of people these days dream they're being run over or eaten by machines.
They're the cagey ones who won't go on the subway or the elevators.
Coming back from my lunch hour in the hospital cafeteria I often pass

them, puffing up the unswept stone stairs to our office on the fourth floor. I wonder, now and then, what dreams people had before ball bearings and cotton mills were invented.

I've got a dream of my own. My one dream. A dream of dreams.

In this dream there's a great half-transparent lake stretching away in every direction, too big for me to see the shores of it, if there are any shores, and I'm hanging over it looking down from the glass belly of some helicopter. At the bottom of the lake—so deep I can only guess at the dark masses moving and heaving—are the real dragons. The ones that were around before men started living in caves and cooking meat over fires and figuring out the wheel and the alphabet. Enormous isn't the word for them; they've got more wrinkles than Johnny Panic himself. Dream about these long enough, and your feet and hands shrivel away when you look at them too closely; the sun shrinks to the size of an orange, only chillier, and you've been living in Roxbury since the last Ice Age. No place for you but a room padded soft as the first room you knew of, where you can dream and float, float and dream, till at last you actually are back among those great originals and there's no point in any dreams at all.

It's into this lake people's minds run at night, brooks and gutter-trickles to one borderless common reservoir. It bears no resemblance to those pure sparkling blue sources of drinking water the suburbs guard more jealously than the Hope diamond in the middle of pinewoods and barbed fences.

It's the sewage of the ages, transparence aside.

Now the water in this lake naturally stinks and smokes from what dreams have been left sogging around in it over the centuries. When you think how much room one night of dream props would take up for one person in one city, and that city a mere pinprick on a map of the world, and when you start multiplying this space by the population of the world, and that space by the number of nights there have been since the apes took to chipping axes out of stone and losing their hair, you have some idea what I mean. I'm not the mathematical type: my head starts splitting when I get only as far as the number of dreams going on during one night in the state of Massachusetts.

By this time, I already see the surface of the lake swarming with snakes, dead bodies puffed as blowfish, human embryos bobbing around in laboratory bottles like so many unfinished messages from the great I Am. I see whole storehouses of hardware: knives, paper cutters, pistons and cogs and nutcrackers; the shiny fronts of cars looming up, glass-eyed and evil-toothed. Then there's the spider-man and the web-footed man from Mars, and the simple, lugubrious vision of a human face turning aside forever, in spite of rings and vows, to the last lover of all.

One of the most frequent shapes in this large stew is so common-place it seems silly to mention it. It's a grain of dirt. The water is thick with these grains. They seep in among everything else and revolve under some queer power of their own, opaque, ubiquitous. Call the water what you will, Lake Nightmare, Bog of Madness, it's here the sleeping people lie and toss together among the props of their worst dreams, one great brotherhood, though each of them, waking, thinks himself singular, utterly apart.

This is my dream. You won't find it written up in any casebook.

Now the routine in our office is very different from the routine in Skin Clinic, for example, or in Tumor. The other clinics have strong similarities to each other; none are like ours. In our clinic, treatment doesn't get prescribed. It is invisible. It goes right on in those little cubicles, each with its desk, its two chairs, its window, and its door with the opaque glass rectangle set in the wood. There is a certain spiritual purity about this kind of doctoring. I can't help feeling the special privilege of my position as assistant secretary in the Adult Psychiatric Clinic. My sense of pride is borne out by the rude invasions of other clinics into our cubicles on certain days of the week for lack of space elsewhere: our building is a very old one, and the facilities have not expanded with the expanding needs of the time. On these days of over-lap the contrast between us and the other clinics is marked.

On Tuesdays and Thursdays, for instance, we have lumbar punctures in one of our offices in the morning. If the practical nurse chances to leave the door of the cubicle open, as she usually does, I can glimpse the end of the white cot and the dirty yellow-soled bare feet of the patient sticking out from under the sheet. In spite of my distaste at this sight, I can't keep my eyes away from the bare feet, and I find myself glancing back from my typing every few minutes to see if they are still there, if they have changed their position at all. You can under-stand what a distraction this is in the middle of my work. I often have to reread what I have typed several times, under the pretense of careful proofreading, in order to memorize the dreams I have copied down from the doctor's voice over the audograph.

Nerve Clinic next door, which tends to the grosser, more unimagi-native end of our business, also disturbs us in the mornings. We use their offices for therapy in the afternoon, as they are only a morning clinic, but to have their people crying, or singing, or chattering loudly in Italian or Chinese, as they often do, without break for four hours at a stretch every morning is distracting to say the least. The patients down there are often referred to us if their troubles have no ostensible basis in the body.

In spite of such interruptions by other clinics, my own work is advancing at a great rate. By now I am far beyond copying only what comes after the patient's saying: "I have this dream, Doctor." I am at the point of re-creating dreams that are not even written down at all. Dreams that shadow themselves forth in the vaguest way, but are themselves hid, like a statue under red velvet before the grand unveiling.

To illustrate. This woman came in with her tongue swollen and stuck out so far she had to leave a party she was giving for twenty friends of her French-Canadian mother-in-law and be rushed to our emergency ward. She thought she didn't want her tongue to stick out, and to tell the truth, it was an exceedingly embarrassing affair for her, but she hated that French-Canadian mother-in-law worse than pigs, and her tongue was true to her opinion, even if the rest of her wasn't. Now she didn't lay claim to any dreams. I have only the bare facts above to begin with, yet behind them I detect the bulge and promise of a dream. So I set myself to uprooting this dream from its comfortable purchase under her tongue.

Whatever the dream I unearth, by work, taxing work, and even by a kind of prayer, I am sure to find a thumbprint in the corner, a bodiless midair Cheshire cat grin, which shows the whole work to be gotten up by the genius of Johnny Panic, and him alone. He's sly, he's subtle, he's sudden as thunder, but he gives himself away only too often. He simply can't resist melodrama. Melodrama of the oldest, most obvious variety.

I remember one guy, a stocky fellow in a gold studded black leather jacket, running straight into us from a boxing match at Mechanics Hall, Johnny Panic hot at his heels. This guy, good Catholic though he was, young and upright and all, had one mean fear of death. He was actually scared blue he'd go to hell. He was a pieceworker at a fluorescent light plant. I remember this detail because I thought it funny he should work there, him being so afraid of the dark as it turned out. Johnny Panic injects a poetic element in this business you don't often find elsewhere. And for that he has my eternal gratitude.

I also remember quite clearly the scenario of the dream I had worked out for this guy: a Gothic interior in some monastery cellar, going on and on as far as you could see, one of those endless perspectives between two mirrors, and the pillars and walls were made of nothing but human skulls and bones, and in every niche there was a body laid out, and it was the Hall of Time, with the bodies in the foreground still warm, discoloring and starting to rot in the middle distance, and the bones emerging, clean as a whistle, in a kind of white futuristic glow at the end of the line. As I recall, I had the whole scene lighted, for the sake of accuracy, not with candles, but with the ice-bright fluorescence that makes the skin look green and all the pink and red flushes dead black-purple.

You ask, how do I know this was the dream of the guy in the black leather jacket. I don't know. I only believe this was his dream, and I work at belief with more energy and tears and entreaties than I work at re-creating the dream itself.

My office, of course, has its limitations. The lady with her tongue stuck out, the guy from Mechanics Hall—these are our wildest ones. The people who have really gone floating down toward the bottom of that boggy lake come in only once, and are then referred to a place more permanent than our office, which receives the public from nine to five, five days a week only. Even those people who are barely able to walk about the streets and keep working, who aren't yet halfway down in the lake, get sent to the outpatient department at another hospital specializing in severer cases. Or they may stay a month or so in our own observation ward in the central hospital, which I've never seen.

I've seen the secretary of that ward, though. Something about her merely smoking and drinking her coffee in the cafeteria at the ten o'clock break put me off so I never went to sit next to her again. She has a funny name I don't ever quite remember correctly, something really odd, like Miss Milleravage. One of those names that seem more like a pun mixing up Milltown and Ravage than anything in the city phone directory. But not so odd a name, after all, if you've ever read through the phone directory, with its Hyman Diddlebockers and Sasparilla Greenleafs. I read through the phone book, once, never mind when, and it satisfied a deep need in me to realize how many people aren't called Smith.

Anyhow, this Miss Milleravage is a large woman, not fat, but all sturdy muscle and tall on top of it. She wears a gray suit over her hard bulk that reminds me vaguely of some kind of uniform, without the details of cut having anything strikingly military about them. Her face, hefty as a bullock's, is covered with a remarkable number of tiny maculae, as if she'd been lying under water for some time and little algae had latched onto her skin, smutching it over with tobacco-browns and greens. These moles are noticeable mainly because the skin around them is so pallid. I sometimes wonder if Miss Milleravage has ever seen the wholesome light of day. I wouldn't be a bit surprised if she'd been brought up from the cradle with the sole benefit of artificial lighting.

Byrna, the secretary in Alcoholic Clinic just across the hall from us, introduced me to Miss Milleravage with the gambit that I'd "been in England too."

Miss Milleravage, it turned out, had spent the best years of her life in London hospitals.

"Had a friend," she boomed in her queer, doggish basso, not favoring me with a direct look, "a nurse at St. Bart's. Tried to get in touch with her after the war, but the head of the nurses had changed, everybody'd changed, nobody'd heard of her. She must've gone down with the old head nurse, rubbish and all, in the bombings." She followed this with a large grin.

Now I've seen medical students cutting up cadavers, four stiffs to a classroom about as recognizably human as Moby Dick, and the students playing catch with the dead men's livers. I've heard guys joke about sewing a woman up wrong after a delivery at the charity ward of the Lying-In. But I wouldn't want to see what Miss Milleravage would write off as the biggest laugh of all time. No thanks and then some. You could scratch her eyes with a pin and swear you'd struck solid quartz.

My boss has a sense of humor too, only it's gentle. Generous as Santa on Christmas Eve.

I work for a middle-aged lady named Miss Taylor who is the head secretary of the clinic and has been since the clinic started thirty-three years ago—the year of my birth, oddly enough. Miss Taylor knows every doctor, every patient, every outmoded appointment slip, referral slip, and billing procedure the hospital has ever used or thought of using. She plans to stick with the clinic until she's farmed out in the green pastures of social security checks. A woman more dedicated to her work I never saw. She's the same way about statistics as I am about dreams: if the building caught fire she would throw every last one of those books of statistics to the firemen below at the serious risk of her own skin.

I get along extremely well with Miss Taylor. The one thing I never let her catch me doing is reading the old record books. I have actually very little time for this. Our office is busier than the stock exchange with the staff of twenty-five doctors in and out, medical students in training, patients, patients' relatives, and visiting officials from other clinics referring patients to us, so even when I'm covering the office alone, during Miss Taylor's coffee break and lunch hour, I seldom get to dash down more than a note or two.

This kind of catch-as-catch-can is nerve-racking, to say the least. A lot of the best dreamers are in the old books, the dreamers that come in to us only once or twice for evaluation before they're sent elsewhere. For copying out these dreams I need time, a lot of time. My circumstances are hardly ideal for the unhurried pursuit of my art. There is, of course, a certain derring-do in working under such hazards, but I long for the rich leizure of the true connoisseur who indulges his nostrils above the brandy snifter for an hour before his tongue reaches out for the first taste.

I find myself all too often lately imagining what a relief it would be to bring a briefcase into work, big enough to hold one of those thick, blue, cloth-bound record books full of dreams. At Miss Taylor's lunchtime, in the lull before the doctors and students crowd in to take their afternoon patients, I could simply slip one of the books, dated ten or fifteen years back, into my briefcase, and leave the briefcase under my desk till five o'clock struck. Of course, odd-looking bundles are inspected by the doorman of the Clinics Building, and the hospital has its own staff of flatfeet to check up on the multiple varieties of thievery that go on, but for heaven's sake, I'm not thinking of making off with typewriters or heroin. I'd only borrow the book overnight and slip it back on the shelf first thing the next day before anybody else came in. Still, being caught taking a book out of the hospital would probably mean losing my job and all my source material with it.

This idea of mulling over a record book in the privacy and comfort of my own apartment, even if I have to stay up night after night for this purpose, attracts me so much I become more and more impatient with my usual method of snatching minutes to look up dreams in Miss Taylor's half hours out of the office.

The trouble is, I can never tell exactly when Miss Taylor will come back to the office. She is so conscientious about her job she'd be likely to cut her half hour at lunch short and her twenty minutes at coffee shorter if it weren't for her lame left leg. The distinct sound of this lame leg in the corridor warns me of her approach in time for me to whip the record book I'm reading into my drawer out of sight and pretend to be putting down the final flourishes on a phone message, or some such alibi. The only catch, as far as my nerves are concerned, is that Amputee Clinic is around the corner from us in the opposite direction from Nerve Clinic, and I've gotten really jumpy due to a lot of false alarms where I've mistaken some pegleg's hitching step for the step of Miss Taylor herself returning early to the office.

On the blackest days when I've scarcely time to squeeze one dream out of the old books and my copy work is nothing but weepy college sophomores who can't get a lead in *Camino Real*, I feel Johnny Panic turn his back, stony as Everest, higher than Orion, and the motto of the great Bible of Dreams, "Perfect fear casteth out all else," is ash and lemon water on my lips. I'm a wormy hermit in a country of prize pigs so corn-happy they can't see the slaughterhouse at the end of the track. I'm Jeremiah vision-bitten in the Land of Cockaigne.

What's worse: day by day I see these psyche-doctors studying to win Johnny Panic's converts from him by hook, crook, and talk, talk, talk. These deep-eyed, bush-bearded dream-collectors who preceded me in history, and their contemporary inheritors with their white jackets and knotty-pine-paneled offices and leather couches, practiced and still practice their dream-gathering for worldly ends: health and money, money and health. To be a true member of Johnny Panic's congregation one must forget the dreamer and remember the dream: the dreamer is merely a flimsy vehicle for the great Dream-Maker himself. This they will not do. Johnny Panic is gold in the bowels, and they try to root him out by spiritual stomach pumps.

Take what happened to Harry Bilbo. Mr. Bilbo came into our office with the hand of Johnny Panic heavy as a lead coffin on his shoulder. He had an interesting notion about the filth in this world. I figured him for a prominent part in Johnny Panic's Bible of Dreams, Third Book of Fear, Chapter Nine on Dirt, Disease, and General Decay. A friend of Harry's blew a trumpet in the Boy Scout band when they were kids. Harry Bilbo'd also blown on this friend's trumpet. Years later the friend got cancer and died. Then, one day not so long ago, a cancer doctor came into Harry's house, sat down in a chair, passed the top of the morning with Harry's mother, and on leaving, shook her hand and opened the door for himself. Suddenly Harry Bilbo wouldn't blow trumpets or sit down on chairs or shake hands if all the cardinals of Rome took to blessing him twenty four hours around the clock for fear of catching cancer. His mother had to go turning the TV knob and water faucets on and off and opening doors for him. Pretty soon Harry stopped going to work because of the spit and dog droppings in the street. First that stuff gets on your shoes, and then when you take your shoes off it gets on your hands, and then at dinner it's a quick trip into your mouth, and not a hundred Hail Mary's can keep you from the chain reaction. The last straw was, Harry quit weight lifting at the public gym when he saw this cripple exercising with the dumbbells. You can never tell what germs cripples carry behind their ears and under their fingernails. Day and night Harry Bilbo lived in holy worship of Johnny Panic, devout as any priest among censers and sacraments. He had a beauty all his own.

Well, these white-coated tinkers managed, the lot of them, to talk Harry into turning on the TV himself, and the water faucets, and to opening closet doors, front doors, bar doors. Before they were through with him, he was sitting down on movie-house chairs, and benches all over the Public Garden, and weight lifting every day of the week at the gym in spite of the fact another cripple took to using the rowing machine. At the end of his treatment he came in to shake hands with the clinic director. In Harry Bilbo's own words, he was "a changed man." The pure Panic-light had left his face; he went out of the office doomed to the crass fate these doctors call health and happiness.

About the time of Harry Bilbo's cure a new idea starts nudging at the bottom of my brain. I find it as hard to ignore as those bare feet sticking out of the lumbar puncture room. If I don't want to risk carrying a record book out of the hospital in case I get discovered and fired and have to end my research forever, I can really speed up work by staying in the Clinics Building overnight. I am nowhere near exhausting the clinic's resources, and the piddling amount of cases I am able to read in Miss Taylor's brief absences during the day are nothing to what I could get through in a few nights of steady copying. I need to accelerate my work if only to counteract those doctors.

Before I know it I am putting on my coat at five and saying goodnight to Miss Taylor, who usually stays a few minutes overtime to clear up the day's statistics, and sneaking around the corner into the ladies' room. It is empty. I slip into the patient's john, lock the door from the inside, and wait. For all I know, one of the clinic cleaning ladies may try to knock the door down, thinking some patient's passed out on the seat. My fingers are crossed. About twenty minutes later the door of the lavatory opens and someone limps over the threshold like a chicken favoring a bad leg. It is Miss Taylor, I can tell by the resigned sigh as she meets the jaundiced eye of the lavatory mirror. I hear the click-cluck of various touch-up equipment on the bowl, water sloshing, the scritch of a comb in frizzed hair, and then the door is closing with a slow-hinged wheeze behind her.

I am lucky. When I come out of the ladies' room at six o'clock the corridor lights are off and the fourth floor hall is empty as church on Monday. I have my own key to our office; I come in first every morning, so that's no trouble. The typewriters are folded back into the desks, the locks are on the dial phones, all's right with the world.

Outside the window the last of the winter light is fading. Yet I do not forget myself and turn on the overhead bulb. I don't want to be spotted by any hawk-eyed doctor or janitor in the hospital buildings across the little courtyard. The cabinet with the record books is in the windowless passage opening onto the doctor's cubicles, which have windows overlooking the courtyard. I make sure the doors to all the cubicles are shut. Then I switch on the passage light, a sallow twenty-five-watt affair blackening at the top. Better than an altarful of candles to me at this point, though. I didn't think to bring a sandwich. There is an apple in my desk drawer left over from lunch, so I reserve that for whatever pangs I may feel about one o'clock in the morning, and get out my pocket notebook. At home every evening it is my habit to tear out the notebook pages I've written on at the office during the day and pile them up to be copied in my manuscript. In this way I cover my tracks so no one idly picking up my notebook at the office could ever guess the type or scope of my work.

I begin systematically by opening the oldest book on the bottom shelf. The once blue cover is no-color now, the pages are thumbed and blurry carbons, but I'm humming from foot to topknot: this dream book was spanking new the day I was born. When I really get organized I'll have hot soup in a thermos for the dead of winter nights, turkey pies, and chocolate eclairs. I'll bring hair curlers and four changes of blouse to work in my biggest handbag Monday mornings so no one will notice me going downhill in looks and start suspecting unhappy love affairs or pink affiliations or my working on dream books in the clinic four nights a week.

Eleven hours later. I am down to apple core and seeds and in the month of May, nineteen thirty-four, with a private nurse who has just opened a laundry bag in her patient's closet and found five severed heads in it, including her mother's.

A chill air touches the nape of my neck. From where I am sitting cross-legged on the floor in front of the cabinet, the record book heavy on my lap, I notice out of the corner of my eye that the door of the cubicle beside me is letting in a little crack of blue light. Not only along the floor, but up the side of the door too. This is odd since I made sure from the first that all the doors were shut tight. The crack of blue light is widening and my eyes are fastened to two motionless shoes in the doorway, toes pointing toward me.

They are brown leather shoes of a foreign make, with thick elevator soles. Above the shoes are black silk socks through which shows a pallor of flesh. I get as far as the gray pinstripe trouser cuffs.

"*Tch, tch,*" chides an infinitely gentle voice from the cloudy regions above my head. "Such an uncomfortable position! Your legs must be asleep by now. Let me help you up. The sun will be rising shortly."

Two hands slip under my arms from behind, and I am raised, wobbly as an unset custard, to my feet, which I cannot feel because my legs are, in fact, asleep. The record book slumps to the floor, pages splayed.

"Stand still a minute." The clinic director's voice fans the lobe of my right ear. "Then the circulation will receive."

The blood in my not-there legs starts pinging under a million sewing machine needles, and a vision of the clinic director acid-etches itself on my brain. I don't even need to look around: the fat potbelly buttoned into his gray pinstripe waistcoat, woodchuck teeth yellow and buck, every-color eyes behind the thick-lensed glasses quick as minnows.

I clutch my notebook. The last floating timber of the *Titanic*.

What does he know, what does he know?

Everything.

"I know where there is a nice hot bowl of chicken noodle soup." His voice rustles, dust under the bed, mice in the straw. His hand welds onto my left upper arm in fatherly love. The record book of all the dreams going on in the city of my birth at my first yawp in this world's air he nudges under the bookcase with a polished toe.

We meet nobody in the dawn-dark hall. Nobody on the chill stone stair down to the basement corridors where Jerry the Record Room boy cracked his head skipping steps one night on a rush errand.

I begin to double-quickstep so he won't think it's me he's hustling. "You can't fire me," I say calmly. "I quit."

The clinic director's laugh wheezes up from his accordion-pleated bottom gut. "We mustn't lose you so soon." His whisper snakes off down the whitewashed basement passages, echoing among the elbow pipes, the wheelchairs and stretchers beached for the night along the steam-stained walls. "Why, we need you more than you know."

We wind and double, and my legs keep time with his until we come, somewhere in those barren rat tunnels, to an all-night elevator run by a one-armed Negro. We get on and the door grinds shut like the door on a cattle car and we go up and up. It is a freight elevator, crude and clanky, a far cry from the plush one in the Clinics Building.

We get off at an indeterminate floor. The clinic director leads me down a bare corridor lit at intervals by socketed bulbs in little wire cages on the ceiling. Locked doors set with screened windows line the hall on either hand. I plan to part company with the clinic director at the first red exit sign, but on our journey there are none. I am in alien territory, coat on the hanger in the office, handbag and money in my top desk drawer, notebook in my hand, and only Johnny Panic to warm me against the Ice Age outside.

Ahead a light gathers, brightens. The clinic director, puffing slightly at the walk, brisk and long, to which he is obviously unaccustomed, propels me around a bend and into a square, brilliantly lit room.

"Here she is."

"The little witch!"

Miss Milleravage hoists her tonnage up from behind the steel desk facing the door.

The walls and the ceiling of the room are riveted metal battleship plates. There are no windows.

From small, barred cells lining the sides and back of the room I see Johnny Panic's top priests staring out at me, arms swaddled behind their backs in the white ward nightshirts, eyes redder than coals and hungry-hot.

They welcome me with queer croaks and grunts as if their tongues were locked in their jaws. They have no doubt heard of my work by way of Johnny Panic's grapevine and want to know how his apostles thrive in the world.

I lift my hands to reassure them, holding up my notebook, my voice loud as Johnny Panic's organ with all stops out.

"Peace! I bring to you . . ."

The Book.

"None of that old stuff, sweetie," Miss Milleravage is dancing out at me from behind her desk like a trick elephant.

The clinic director closes the door to the room.

The minute Miss Milleravage moves I notice what her hulk has been hiding from view behind the desk—a white cot high as a man's waist with a single sheet stretched over the mattress, spotless and drumskin tight. At the head of the cot is a table on which sits a metal box covered with dials and gauges. The box seems to be eyeing me, copperhead-ugly, from its coil of electric wires, the latest model in Johnny-Panic-Killers.

I get ready to dodge to one side. When Miss Milleravage grabs, her fat hand comes away a fist full of nothing. She starts for me again, her smile heavy as dogdays in August.

"None of that. None of that. I'll have that little black book."

Fast as I run around the high white cot, Miss Milleravage is so fast you'd think she wore roller skates. She grabs and gets. Against her great bulk I beat my fists, and against her whopping milkless breasts, until her hands on my wrists are iron hoops and her breath hushabys me with a love-stink fouler than Undertaker's Basement.

"My baby, my own baby's come back to me . . ."

"She," the clinic director says, sad and stern, "has been making time with Johnny Panic again."

"Naughty naughty."

The white cot is ready. With a terrible gentleness Miss Milleravage takes the watch from my wrist, the rings from my fingers, the hairpins from my hair. She begins to undress me. When I am bare, I am anointed on the temples and robed in sheets virginal as the first snow. Then, from the four corners of the room and from the door behind me come five false priests in white surgical gowns and masks whose one lifework is to unseat Johnny Panic from his own throne. They extend me full-length on my back on the cot. The crown of wire is placed on my head, the water of forgetfulness on my tongue. The masked priests move to their posts and take hold: one of my left leg, one of my right, one of my right arm, one of my left. One behind my head at the metal box where I can't see.

From their cramped niches along the wall, the votaries raise their voices in protest. They begin the devotional chant:

> The only thing to love is Fear itself.
> Love of Fear is the beginning of wisdom.
> The only thing to love is Fear itself.
> May Fear and Fear and Fear be everywhere.

There is no time for Miss Milleravage or the clinic director or the priests to muzzle them.

The signal is given.

The machine betrays them.

At the moment when I think I am most lost the face of Johnny Panic appears in a nimbus of arc lights on the ceiling overhead. I am shaken like a leaf in the teeth of glory. His beard is lightning. Lightning is in his eye. His Word charges and illumes the universe.

The air crackles with the blue-tonged, lightning-haloed angels.

His love is the twenty-story leap, the rope at the throat, the knife at the heart.

He forgets not his own.

HENRY ROTH

Final Dwarf

> "...*the final dwarf of you*
> *That is woven and woven and waiting to be*
> *worn* ..."   —WALLACE STEVENS

He was so pleased with the reading glasses he had ordered through the catalogue and he was so ingenuous in his enthusiasm that the woman behind the counter, the Sears mail-order clerk, asked his permission to try them on. She was middle-aged too, or past middle age, like himself, and wore bifocals, as he did. He tendered them to her, and she put them on, but apparently they didn't procure the same results for her that they did for him. She looked down at the invoice in her hand with a rather bewildered expression and handed the glasses back.

"Not strong enough?" Kestrel asked sympathetically.

"I don't know what they are." She took refuge behind her own bifocals as if she had been disturbed by what she had seen. "But they're not for me, that's for sure."

"I was told by an optician some time ago that my eyes were still fairly young according to my age. So I got the weaker ones: forty to forty-five age group instead of my own, fifty-five to sixty."

She no longer seemed to be listening and had begun totting up the price of the glasses, the shipping charge, and the sales tax. "That's four twenty-one, please."

He smiled, placed a five-dollar bill on the counter, and while she made change, he slipped the glasses into their case and pocketed them. At least fifteen bucks to the good, he thought triumphantly; that's how much more the unholy alliance of opticians and the American Optical Society would have soaked him. True, the lenses weren't prescription lenses and did nothing to correct his astigmatism. But that was a minor matter compared with the boon the glasses would be when he hunted up a word in a dictionary or read a carpenter's scale. He received his change, thanked the clerk, and folding the invoice, walked briskly through the center aisle of the store toward the doorway. Sears retail store, compact with merchandise and glistening under its many fluorescents, was always an interesting place to Kestrel, especially the hardware department, with its array of highly polished tools. But he had no time to stop and browse today; his father was waiting for him in the car.

The street he came out on was Water Street, the former commercial center of town. For many years Water Street had tried to keep abreast of the times by fusing new chromium trim onto old brick facades. With the advent of the shopping plaza, the street seemed to have given up and become dormant, as if waiting for a rebirth. His car was on Haymarket Street, the next street west. He crossed with the WALK of the traffic light and made his way up the inclined sidewalk that led sharply around the corner. Haymarket Street served as a kind of ancillary to Water Street. It provided extra room for parking meters, ventilating ducts, and traffic circulation.

"Where to, Pop?" He opened the car door and slipped in behind the wheel. "My errand's all done. What are yours?" It was always necessary to shield Pop from the idea that the trip to town was being made on his behalf. Otherwise he would balk at going, and then sulk.

His father continued to bow over his homemade cane. "I would like to go to the First National. First to the First National in the plaza. I need a little meat, a can tuna, a couple oranges. Then I want to go to the A & P and buy coffee." Pop always adopted a whimsical, placating drawl when he wanted a favor.

"Why the A & P?" Kestrel sensed an old ruse. "Why not the First National coffee?"

"I like A & P coffee better. I like better Eight O'Clock coffee. It ain't so strong."

"Oh, yes." Eight O'Clock coffee was a cent cheaper than any other brand in town. The usual guile was at work. "I think you'd better shop in one place, Pop. No sense running to two places just to buy a

pound of coffee." Kestrel hoped that the gravel that had entered his
voice was lost in the starting of the motor. "You get better trades at
the A & P anyway."

"OK. You want A & P? So A & P."

Kestrel fastened his seat belt. The old boy would have him run all
over town for a couple of cents. To save *him* a couple of cents, blind
to the expense of running the car. As Norma said, Pop certainly had
a knack of bringing out the worst in people. Kestrel smirked and
steered right to cross the railroad tracks. Just a few days ago, before
Pop arrived for the summer, she had proposed a scheme of levying a
fifty-cent toll on everyone who accompanied them to town and then
suspending the rule for everyone except Pop. And this coming from
Norma, the most generous of women . . .

Behind them the bank and the abandoned theater, behind them the
bowling alley and the car wash, they climbed Winslow Hill to the
traffic light on the terrace and then drove on past the porticos and
the fanlights, the prim round windows of the fine homes of another
age, to the rear entrance of the A & P parking lot.

"OK, Pop?" Kestrel undid his seat belt and got out of the car on
one side as his father got out, more slowly, on the other. "Norma
didn't want anything special. Cigarettes. But I've got plenty of time.
So shop for everything you need." He preceded the old man to the
glass door and held it open. Pop hobbled in on arthritic legs. "You
know where the car is. I'll be around somewhere."

"Yeh. Yeh." The old man dismmissed him with a curt wave of the
hand. "I'll find you." He hobbled over to the telescoped shopping carts
in front of the brightly arranged aisles, separated one, and trundled
it inside.

Kestrel debated with himself for a moment. It was just barely possible that Grant's in the shopping plaza across the avenue had the kind
of lock he was looking for, a freezer lock. He hadn't thought of it
while he was in Sears. On the impulse, he hurried to the edge of the
A & P blacktop and crossed the highway to the immensity of the
plaza parking area opposite. The First National where Pop had wanted
to shop lay directly ahead, to the left of Grant's and Kestrel realized
he could as easily have stopped there as not. But it was the principle
of the thing, he argued with himself. He resented being gulled, being
cajoled into doing his father a service for the wrong reason, for
spurious reasons. It came back to what Norma said: Pop brought out
the worst in people.

Grant's had no freezer locks. They had bicycle locks with in-
ordinately long hasps, but no freezer locks. Leaving the emporium, he
hurried back toward the avenue, meanwhile trying to descry the car

from a distance. Was his father already in it and observing his son's breach of faith? No, he had beaten the old boy to it. He waited impatiently at the curb for an opening in the flux of traffic, crossed in haste, and panting slightly with exertion, leaned against his car. "Oh, the cigarettes!" He started toward the A & P and reached the door just as his father emerged with a bag of groceries on his arm.

Kestrel hesitated. "Want a hand, Pop?"

"I don't need it." The old man elbowed the extended hand to one side. "Here." He pressed a batch of trading stamps into the empty palm.

"Why do you give me these?"

"I don't want them. You save them."

"I don't save them."

"Your wife saves them."

"OK." Kestrel followed his father to the car. "Now where?" They both got in.

"Maybe I could get a few day-old cookies down at Arlene's. I like a few cookies in the house."

"I suppose so." They had been on Water Street once, Kestrel was about to remind his father, but checked the impulse under a fleeting yet complex illumination of how the old man continually led away from any objection. Who could object to a few cookies in the house? "OK. Arlene's."

"We don't have to go if you ain't got time. If you're in a hurry to get home—"

"Oh, I'm in no hurry," Kestrel said resolutely. "No hurry at all. What else?"

"Onion sets," Pop took out his shopping list. "Onion sets at Russel's Hardware Store. One pound." He read the words as if the list shielded him from responsibility. "And that's all."

"Onion sets at Russel's." Kestrel started the motor.

"They had hamburg." The sign in the A & P window caught Pop's eye. "I didn't see that."

"That's the come-on for today. Do you want any?"

"That ain't bad. Forty-nine cents a pound. I could have used a little hamburg."

"I can still stop." Kestrel made a token thrust at the brake pedal.

"No, Too late. If I had more time to look around—" Pop sat back in regret.

"Who said you didn't have time?"

"You don't have to say. I can tell."

Kestrel took a firmer grip on the steering wheel.

"Instead I paid thirty-three cents a pound for chicken wings. Thirty-three cents," the old man intoned. "Nineteen cents a pound, twenty-one cents a pound, most twenty-five cents a pound they charge in New York. Here in your state where they raise chickens, thirty-three cents a pound!"

"Pop," Kestrel grated. "Your seat belt."

The old man felt behind him for the buckle and pushed it out of the way.

They drove back to the center of town. Arlene's was at the south end of Water Street. Kestrel spied an empty parking place, but it seemed too tight. He chose to drive on. "Best I can do, Pop," he said apologetically, and parked the car beside a twelve-minute meter in front of the post office.

"I saw back there a nice place near Arlene's."

"Too many cars behind me. I didn't want to hold up traffic."

"For them you got consideration," Pop muttered. "But for me—" He got out of the car and hobbled in the direction of Arlene's. There seemed to be a special emphasis about the way he hobbled, as though he were trying to impress the pain he felt on his son.

Oh, hell, Kestrel thought as he waited. He never could do anything to please his father. Ever since childhood it had been that way. Still, he had to get over it. It was ridiculous to bear a grudge against the old guy. There was nothing left of him. A little old dwarf in a baggy pair of pants. *The final dwarf.* Kestrel smiled.

The car door opened.

"That was snappy, Pop!" said Kestrel.

His father slid into the seat with a self-satisfied look, shut the door, and picked up his cane.

"What about the cookies?" Kestrel asked. His father seemed to be flaunting the fact that he had made no purchase.

"Another time," said Pop airily.

"Why? Didn't they have day-old cookies?"

"They had. They had."

"Were they too high?"

"No, they was the regular half price."

"Then for Pete's sake why didn't you get some?"

"There was only one girl behind the counter and maybe ten customers."

"Oh, please! I come down here for you to buy cookies, and now you come back empty-handed." Kestrel was sure the old man was retaliating for the way his son had parked the car.

"*Noo, nischt gefehrlich.* I got yet a few cookies in the house."

"Wait a minute." Kestrel was loathe to start the engine. "That isn't the point. You wanted to come down here to buy cookies. I brought you down. Now you tell me you've got a few in the house. Why don't you buy some while you have a chance? You're down here."

"I don't need them. You would have to wait a for-sure fifteen minutes."

"I don't care. I waited this long."

"I don't need them!" his father snapped. "Meantime the money is by me, no?"

"Well, for Christ sake!" Kestrel started the motor. "That's a fine trick. The whole trip down here is for nothing!"

"So you'll be home a few minutes later to your wife. She won't miss you." His voice reeked with contempt.

You son of a bitch! thought Kestrel. There it was again, the same mockery that had rankled so in childhood, in boyhood, in youth, disabling mockery against which there was no remedy and no redress. Furiously Kestrel steered into the near lane of traffic. Penney's clothing store passed on one side like a standard of his wrath, and Woolworth's across the street like another. And so did McClellan's and Sears and the pawnshop. He made a right turn at the traffic light, crossed the low bridge over the river, and climbed the opposite hill. He had almost reached their destination before he could force himself to say, "Now you want onion sets."

"Yeh, if he's got," said his father.

Kestrel stopped the car. The hardware store was across the street. He shut off the ignition and waited. His father made no move to go. "Well?" Kestrel asked.

"There's so much traffic," said his father.

"Do you want me to go?" Compassion now made headway against his anger. "I suppose I can get across the street faster than you can."

"Go if you want to go. I'll pay you later."

Kestrel got out of the car. "Onion sets, right?"

"One pound, not more. You hear?"

Kestrel's lip curled. With his back turned to his father, he could safely sneer. As if he would deliberately buy more than a pound.

They were on their way home now. Kestrel had bought the onion sets—and the freezer lock too, even though he had taken a longer time to shop than his father had anticipated. When he came out of the store, Pop was sitting half-turned around in his seat with a frown on his face, gazing fixedly in his direction. Fine, Kestrel had thought with a certain nervous malice as he quickened his step toward the car, it's your turn now. And he had made some remark about how few clerks there were in all the stores on a Tuesday.

"Oh, sure," was his father's neutral reply.

Town slipped past at a leisurely twenty-five miles an hour: shade tree and utility pole, service station and abandoned cemetery.

"This time I got my supply of matzohs for the summer. I brought five pounds from New York."

"Five pounds! All that way on a bus?" Kestrel felt a little indulgent after his own retaliation. "You must really like them."

"Oh, for a matzoli I'm crazy," said his father. "I eat matzohs not only on Passover."

"That's evident."

"With a matzoh you got a bite or you got a meal," Pop continued sententiously. "It's crisp, good, or you can dunk it in coffee. There's matzoh-brei, matzoh kugel, mutzoh pancakes. You can crumble it. Dip in it. It's better than cracker meal. A lot cheaper too, believe me, especially if you go down to the East Side to get the broken ones."

"Marvelous. Can you wipe up gravy with a matzoh?"

"Of course you can wipe up gravy. You forgot already. You wet the matzoh before you sit down to eat, and it becomes soft like bread."

"The stuff's universal," Kestrel twitted. "Khrushchev should have known better than to ban them."

"Oh, that dog!" said Pop.

The Gulf station was passing, with its used-car lot in front and its desolate auto graveyard in the rear. "You know, Pop—" Kestrel began, and then stopped. He had been on the point of remarking that matzohs could be bought in the chain stores in town, but they would be more expensive. "Oh, well—"

"What?" his father asked.

"Nothing."

They drove on in silence. Some of the newly constructed houses slipped by, the cute little boxes, as Norma called them, gray and brown and red, that had begun to line the highway.

Pop fingered the onion sets in the bag, picked out a withered one, and let it fall back significantly. He still hadn't paid for them. "Noo, there was a big fuss here over this Kennedy?" He put the bag to one side.

"This Kennedy?" Kestrel was startled. "Which Kennedy?"

"Bobby Kennedy. About John Kennedy I'm not talking."

"Of course. Everyone was shocked, just as with John Kennedy. Why?"

His father leaned on his cane and smiled. "I'm only sorry the other one wasn't shot too before he became President."

Kestrel's face furrowed as he glanced into the rearview mirror. For a moment it seemed to him that the old man's tone of voice was almost solicitous, as though he wished John Kennedy had been spared the trials of the presidency. He turned to look at his father, still smiling ambiguously. "What do you mean, Pop?"

"I mean both of them should have been shot before they became President. We would all be better off."

"Why? I don't get you. I was no admirer of the Kennedys but—"

"Why?" The new sign advertising the Grand View Motel 6 Mi. vanished on the right among second-growth trees. "The Niggehs!" Pop said vehemently. Where the sheep had once ranged, the juniper-studded field on the left reeled about the corrugated-iron sheep cote in the distance. "The Niggehs, that's why."

"The Niggers?" Kestrel repeated stunned.

"Yeh, the Niggehs! What they made such a good friend from the Niggehs. You're such a good friend from the Niggehs? There!"

"What's that got to do with it?"

"Good for them!"

"But that's got nothing to do with it!" Kestrel's voice sharpened. "That wasn't why they were shot."

"No. But that's why I'm glad they was shot."

Whew, Kestrel whistled silently to himself; you goddamned venomous little worm!

"You know, you can't talk to a Niggeh no more since the Kennedys?" his father demanded. "Not to a man, not to a women, not to a child. Even a child'll tell you: go to hell, you old white fool."

"I see. I wish you'd put your seat belt on, Pop." Kestrel tapped the buckle of his own.

"I don't like it."

"You'd like going through the windshield less."

"I don't wear that kind. I told you. When you get them so they go around the shoulder, then I'll wear them. They press me here." He rubbed his abdomen.

You damned idiot: Kestrel stared straight ahead.

"The Kennedys," said his father. "There's where the mugging and the robbing started. Only Kennedys. *Noo*, sure, they know a President is their friend. So, whatever they do, he'll say: Nebich! It's a pity! So they rape," he slapped his hands together, "so they rob, so they mug, so they loot. That poor Jewish man what they hit him in the face with a bottle last week in the subway—a plain Jewish working man—the Kennedys is the cause of all that!"

The side road where they lived was only a short distance away, and peering deeply into the rearview mirror, Kestrel saw himself forbidding and ominous against the empty highway. Was the old man baiting him this last time in retaliation for having been made to wait, or were his own thoughts about his father of such force that they communicated? He could almost believe it. "Nobody is the cause," said Kestrel. "Nobody in particular. All of us."

"All of us? Go! You and the other *philosophes*. I had something to do with that Niggeh what he mugged me in the elevator and took away my watch and two hundred and eight dollars? And put me in the hospital? And who knows, gave me this arthritis? You should have seen that detective how he beat his fist on the wall when he seen my face. And the others what they get mugged and beat up—and raped. *They* the cause of it? With you *philosophes* you can't talk."

"OK."

"Come live in New York a few months, you'll see. Let's see how you'll be a *philosophe*."

"OK." Kestrel braked the car gently, made his left turn into the side road with a minimum of swerve.

Pop glanced at the crowds of white cockerels behind the screen in the big doorways of the three-story broiler plant on the corner. "You should see them in the waiters' union, how they push us away when there's a good job—in the Waldorf or where. The best is for them. Old waiters like me, white waiters—throw them out and make jobs for *them*. They come first!"

Oh, shit. Kestrel pressed his foot down on the accelerator.

"Everything all at once," Pop continued. "More, more! Colleges and schools and beaches and motels. Regular princes make from them. And yesterday they was eating each other."

The stretch of road they were approaching had been cut through ledge—straightened out—leaving a few run-down buildings stranded in the bend on the left. On the right was the ledge. On top of it, in the gloom of overhanging trees, he had once seen two pretty deer, a buck and a doe, poised for flight, and the memory of the sight always drew his gaze to the spot thereafter. Two inches to the right, he thought, two inches that way with the steering wheel, and it would all be over with the old fool. Just two inches *now;* he'd go through the windshield like a maul, he'd slam that rusty granite. And who would know? Instinctively Kestrel shied away from the rough shoulder of the road. "Don't you think that's enough of politics, Pop?"

"Sure. On another's behind it's good to smack, like they say. Here in the country you don't see a *schwartzer* face for I don't know. A mile. How will it be if they moved next door?"

"Oh, please!"

"Yeh," his father nodded. "You'll be just like me in a few years. Just wait. All I'm saying you'll say."

A truck came over the brow of the hill. Top-heavy and loaded with logs, it picked up momentum as it rolled downhill toward them, lurched at the road's shoulder. And once again Kestrel heard himself urge: two inches on this wheel, a glancing blow, and the brakes. He skirted the other vehicle, glimpsed its driver, Reynolds, owner of a nearby lumber mill. "That was Reynolds," he said to Pop.

Pop rejected the overture with a slighting gesture. "You'll be just like me. Wait. I seen already *philosophes* like you. Your cousin Louis Cantor when he lived was a *philosophe*, a socialist. Every time he came to the house he brought the socialist *Call*. So what happened in the end? He laughed from it. 'What a fool I was,' he used to say."

The top of Turner's Hill was open on the left, open and sloping downward over sunlit boulders toward the woodland and the river valley. Almost inviting it seemed, inviting for a hideous spin and a rending of metal. Who would survive? Kestrel held the car grimly to the center of the road.

"And that's what you'll say," said Pop.

"You think so?"

"I know it."

"All right. Then let's drop it. I'm driving a car."

"Ah, if there only was a Verwoerd here like in South Africa," Pop lamented. "A Verwoerd. He should be like a bulldozer for those brutes. Even a Wallace. A Wallace I would vote for."

Kestrel could fee his jaw tremble. Christ, if the old fool didn't stop —They still had two miles to go. "That's enough!"

Pop hitched a scornful shoulder, crossed his legs over his cane. "So what did you get at Sears?"

"At Sears? Oh. Reading glasses."

"Reading glasses? At Sears?"

"Yes, they have them. I've been getting my bifocals chipped working around the place."

"How much did they cost?"

Brusquely Kestrel pulled the case out of his pocket, handed it to his father. "Here. You tell me."

The old man took the spectacles out of their sheath, appraised them, and adjusted them on his nose. "Oy!" He recoiled.

"What's the matter?"

"You're going right into the stone wall." Pop pulled the glasses off.

"I am?"

"Into a stone wall. I mean they look like it. Pheh! Only from Sears you can buy glasses like this." He slipped them into the case, handed the case to his son.

Kestrel sighed. He felt shriveled. He removed a hand from the wheel, replaced the glasses in his pocket.

"Boy, you gave me some scare!" The old man groped beside him for the seat-belt buckles.

JOHN UPDIKE

Under the Microscope

It was not his kind of pond; the water tasted slightly acid. He was a
Cyclops, the commonest of copepods, and this crowd seemed exotically
cladoceran—stylish water-fleas with transparent carapaces, all shimmer and bubbles and twitch. His hostess, a magnificent Daphnia fully
an eighth of an inch tall, her heart and cephalic ganglion visibly
pulsing, welcomed him with a lavish gesture of her ciliate, branching
antennae; for a moment he feared she would eat him. Instead she
offered him a plate of living desmids. They were bright green in color
and shaped like crescents, hourglasses, omens. "Who do you know
here?" Her sizable voice loomed above the din. "Everybody knows
you, of course. They've read your books." His books, taken all together, with generous margins, would easily have fitted on the period
that ends this sentence.

The Cyclops modestly grimaced, answered "No one," and turned to
a young speciman of water-mite, probably *Hydrachna geographica*,
still bearing ruddy traces of the larval stage. "Have you been here
long?" he asked, meaning less the party than the pond.

"Long enough." Her answer came as swiftly as a reflex. "I go back
to the surface now and then; we breathe air, you know."

"Oh I know. I envy you." He noticed she had only six legs. She was newly hatched, then. Between her eyes, arranged in two pairs, he counted a fifth, in the middle, and wondered if in her he might find his own central single optic amplified and confirmed. His antennules yearned to touch her red spots; he wanted to ask her, *What do you see?* Young as she was, partially formed, she appeared, alerted by his abrupt confession of envy, ready to respond to any question, however presuming.

But at that moment a monstrous fairy shrimp, an inch in length and extravagantly tinted blue, green, and bronze, swam by on its back, and the water shuddered. Furious, the Cyclops asked the water-mite, "Who invites *them?* They're not even in our scale."

She shrugged permissively, showing that indeed she had been here long enough. "They're entomostracans," she said, "just like Daphnia. They amuse her."

"They're going to eat her up," the Cyclops predicted.

Though she laughed, her fifth eye gazed steadily into his wide long one. "But isn't that what we all want? Subconsciously, of course."

"Of course."

An elegant, melancholy flatworm was passing *hors d'œuvres*. The Cyclops took some diatoms, cracked their delicate shells of silica, and ate them. They were golden brown. Growing hungrier, he pushed through to the serving table and had a Volvox in algae dip. A shrill little rotifer, his head cilia whirling, his three-toothed mastax chattering, leaped up before him, saying, with the mixture of put-on and pleading characteristic of this pond, "I wead all your wunnaful books, and I have a wittle bag of pomes I wote myself, and I would wove it, *wove* it if you would wead them and wecommend them to a big bad pubwisher!" At a loss for a civil answer, the Cyclops considered the rotifer silently, then ate him. He tasted slightly acid.

The party was thickening. A host of protozoans drifted in on a raft of sphagnum moss: a trumpet-shaped Stentor, apparently famous, interlocked with a lanky, bleached Spirostomum; a claque of paramœcia, swishing back and forth tickling the crustacea on the backs of their knees; an old Voticella, a plantlike animalcule as dreary, the Cyclops thought, as the batch of puffs rooted to the flap of last year's *succès d'estime*. The kitchen was crammed with ostracods and flagellates engaged in mutually consuming conversation, and over in a corner, beneath an African mask, a great brown hydra, the real thing, attached by its sticky foot to the hissing steam radiator, rhythmically swung its tentacles here and there until one of them touched, in the circle of admirers, something appetizing; then the poison sacs exploded, the other tentacles contracted, and the prey was stuffed into the hydra's swollen coelenteron, which gluttony had stretched to a transparency that veiled the preceding meals like polyethylene film protecting a rack of dry-cleaned suits. Hairy with bacteria, a Simocephalus was munching a rapt nematode. The fairy shrimps, having multiplied, their crimson tails glowing with hæmoglobin, came cruising in from the empty bedrooms. The party was thinning.

Suddenly fearful, fearing he had lost her forever, the Cyclops searched for the water-mite, and found her miserably crouching in a corner, quite drunk, her seventh and eighth legs almost sprouted. "What do you see?" he now dared ask.

"Too much," she answered swiftly. "Everything. Oh, it's horrible, horrible."

Out of mercy as much as appetite, he ate her. She felt nervous and prickly inside him. Hurriedly—the rooms were almost depleted, it was late—he sought his hostess. She was by the doorway, her antennae frazzled from waving goodbye, but still magnificent, Daphnia, her carapace a liquid shimmer of psychedelic pastel. "Don't go," she commanded, expanding, "I have a *mini*scule favor to ask. Now that my children, all thirteen billion of them, thank God, are off at school, I've taken a part-time editing job, and my first real break is this manuscript I'd be *so* grateful to have you read and comment on, whatever comes into your head, I admit it's a little long, maybe you can skim the part where Napoleon invades Russia, but it's the first *eff*ort by a perfectly delightful midge larva I know you'd enjoy meeting—"

"I'd adore to, but I can't," he said, explaining, "my eye. I can't afford to strain it, I have only this one. . ." He trailed off, he felt, feebly. He was beginning to feel permeable, acidic.

"You poor dear," Daphnia solemnly pronounced, and ate him.

And the next instant, a fairy shrimp, oaring by inverted, casually gathered her into the trough between his eleven pairs of undulating gill-feet and passed her toward his brazen mouth. Her scream, much tinier than the dot on this "i," was unobserved.